Last Dance at the

Rothesay Pavilion

To   Kathleen .
With by lst wshes,

[signature] Duffy

MYRA DUFFY

New Generation Publishing

Last Dance at the Rothesay Pavilion

An Alison Cameron Mystery

MYRA DUFFY

www.myraduffy.co.uk

http://myraduffy-awriterslot.blogspot.com

Cover design by Mandy Sinclair
www.mandysinclair.com

The Isle of Bute

The Isle of Bute lies in Scotland's Firth of Clyde, off the west coast of Scotland, a short journey from the city of Glasgow.

It has been occupied for over five thousand years but rose to prominence in Victorian days when its proximity to a major city made it a favoured spot for the wealthy to build summer houses and the not so wealthy to enjoy the delights of the seaside in the many rooms available for rent during the holiday season.

Bute is the ancestral home of the Stuart kings of Scotland and the 800 year old Rothesay castle (now ruined) was built by a hereditary High Steward of Scotland, from which the name is derived.

Today the island is a haven from the hustle and bustle of city life with quiet beaches, woodland walks and an abundance of wildlife, including seals.

For more information about Bute:
www.visitbute.com

For Joan Weeple, a friend for all seasons.

PROLOGUE

'Ladies and Gentlemen, please take your partners for the last waltz.'

Jacky, the Master of Ceremonies, wrested the mike from its stand with a flourish born of long experience and strolled to the front of the stage, before turning to the orchestra to give the signal for the music to start. There was a hum of excitement as the dancers, gathered chattering in little knots around the room, began to move on to the floor, swaying in time to the haunting notes of 'Now We Say Goodbye.'

The glitter ball suspended from the pleated folds of cream material draping the ceiling of the Rothesay Pavilion made little sparkles of coloured light on the polished wooden floor and dappled the dancers as they glided round.

The music died away in an arpeggio of mournful notes, followed by a burst of rapturous applause. Jacky lifted his hand for silence. 'Ladies and gentlemen, I don't need to tell you this is a very important occasion - the last dance at the Rothesay Pavilion. No, don't look so unhappy - it's only the last dance for a little while.' This remark addressed to an elderly lady on his right who looked close to tears. 'The renovations begin in the next few weeks.'

He acknowledged a little whoop from a smartly dressed couple in the far corner before continuing, 'And when this building opens again the transformation will amaze you, that much I can promise. If you've seen the plans in the foyer you'll have a good idea of what I mean.'

He moved back, replaced the microphone on its stand and added, 'Now it's time to say goodnight, goodbye and thank you for being such a wonderful crowd.'

As the dancers slowly left the hall, laughing and gossiping, the lights dimmed little by little until the hall was in complete darkness.

Jacky tugged at his collar. He would miss this place, not only because of the loss of income. Nowhere else he worked gave him quite the same feeling of excitement as this Art Deco building that was the Rothesay Pavilion. But there was much to look forward to: once the renovation was finished, the building would be restored to its former glory. In no time at all he'd be back here once again, hosting the grand opening.

But that was before they found the skeleton.

ONE

It had been a mad idea, quite mad. But there was no going back now.

As the ferry MV Bute from Weymss Bay swung round into the calm waters of Rothesay Bay to dock at the pier, I went out on deck to catch a first glimpse of the Rothesay Pavilion, sitting on the far side of the town. Would the commission I'd secured to write a history of this building be the opportunity for a new career?

I thought back to the conversations I'd had with Simon, my husband, before making the final decision.

'Alison, you know you've wanted to do something different for a long time.'

'Yes, but I've been teaching for years.'

'Only part-time,' he pointed out, not unreasonably. 'You've turned down a couple of offers of a full-time post. That says to me you're ready for a change.'

He was right. I didn't need persuading, I needed reassurance.

'And,' he went on, 'you've been successful in getting this contract to write the history of the Rothesay Pavilion. Seems like fate.'

So I'd given in my resignation, had the obligatory farewell party to lots of good wishes and calls of 'We'll miss you,' by colleagues and left Strathelder High for the last time. I even shed a tear, but not for long.

We were still too far off to see the plaque announcing the date of 1938 when this square set, grey stone building had been completed, but its bay windows, angular lines and twin balconies below a flat roof gave the clues to its design era. It was one of the last of its kind to be completed before the outbreak of the Second World War.

I drove off the ferry, busy with cars and foot passengers and joined the traffic heading for Rothesay, the main town on the island, carefully avoiding the people thronging the streets, milling around, strolling from shop to shop. It was the start of the summer school holidays in Scotland and already many families were taking advantage of this spell of good weather for a trip to the island of Bute, conveniently situated close to Glasgow. The shaky economy would encourage lots of people to holiday close to home this year.

The boats still anchored in the Marina swayed gently to and fro in the light breeze, jostling together and there was a smell of summer in the air, the tang of salt water and seaweed. Overhead young seagulls screamed and squawked as they swooped and dived in the warm currents of air, seeking titbits from those visitors happily lunching on fish and chips.

The only set of traffic lights on the island was at green and within a few minutes I'd found a space in one of the bays immediately outside the Pavilion front entrance. All my confidence again disappeared, my hands trembling as I ran through the opening speech I'd prepared for my first meeting with my contact, Gerry Nutall. I had to sit for a few minutes, breathing deeply, trying to gather my thoughts. Was I the right person to take on this task? Perhaps people on the island would have preferred someone local?

Stop it, I scolded myself. This wouldn't help. I'd won the contract fair and square and after all, though not born on Bute, I knew the place well. Very well. Besides, the project included the appointment of a research assistant - and Tara McKenna was someone who lived on the island.

I pulled down the driving mirror and ran a comb through my hair. It had been a sensible decision to have it cut very short. Not only would it be easy to manage, but any grey hairs coming through over the next few weeks would be less noticeable. I slicked on some lipstick, but in the bright sunlight it only made me look washed out, so I hastily licked it off before leaving the car and striding purposefully towards the main entrance at the side of the building.

Even at first sight, there was no doubt the building was in serious need of a makeover. The paint was peeling from the metal window frames, the fabric of the building pitted and cracking. The Atlantic weather, winter storms and driving rain had taken their toll on the once splendid edifice. The task of returning it to its former glory wouldn't be easy, but what a striking venue it would be once restored.

I pushed open the door and went in through the curve of the foyer, its marble floor chequered in an Art Deco pattern of green, black and blue and headed for the main entrance hall before I could change my mind.

The place seemed deserted, deathly quiet, even a little forlorn. The pictures had been stripped from the walls, the giant ferns in stone tubs which usually adorned the comers and the stairway had been removed, the carpets lifted, showing the original parquet patterned floor underneath. The place had a hushed and expectant air, waiting for the work to begin, but there was a faint smell of coffee in the air, so someone must be around.

Last time I had been here had been for the thirty years' reunion with my former classmates from college and the place had rung to the sounds of laughter and chat. Now even the ghosts made no sound.

As I was considering my next move, the door on the right, the main office, suddenly opened and a portly man middle-aged man came out.

He looked startled. 'Thought I heard something,' he said, stroking his carefully groomed moustache. I couldn't help but stare at it because it looked odd, almost as if he had glued it on. It was a curious shade of dark brown while his sparse hair was steel grey.

I moved forward. 'I'm Alison Cameron,' I said, holding out my hand.

He grasped my hand with both of his and pumped it up and down vigorously, making me wince slightly. 'I'm Ewan Flisch,' he said, with only the trace of a smile. He obviously had no idea who I was. Not a good start.

'I've come to meet Gerry Nutall,' I said. 'We're going to discuss my project to write a history of the Pavilion.'

He frowned. 'Gerry didn't say you were coming today.'

'Is there a problem? I made the appointment a couple of weeks ago.'

'Not at all.' He drew himself up to his full height of five and a half feet. 'But I'm in charge of the initial part of the Pavilion renovation project. Gerry is only my deputy. I'm the one you should deal with.'

Oh, oh. There was some history here between the two men. Not something I wanted to be involved in.

Ewan Flisch was determined to make his position clear. 'I was the successful applicant for this job and I make the decisions,' adding in a low voice, 'though Gerry would like to.'

'I'm more than happy to work with you, Mr Flisch,' I said, putting on what I hoped was a winsome smile. If he was as touchy as he appeared I didn't want to make the mistake of calling him by his first name.

He seemed to relent a little, now he'd made it clear he was the person in charge.

'Sorry, sorry, what am I thinking of?' he muttered. 'Come through.'

He walked carefully backwards into the office saying, 'Call me Ewan, there's no need to stand on ceremony,' and I followed him in, but he seemed restless and instead of sitting down in the large swivel chair behind the carved mahogany desk strewn with papers in jumbled heaps, he paced up and down, forcing me to squash into the corner.

Before I could utter another word he said, 'Access to the Pavilion will soon be limited, so it's as well you've come now. The workmen are due to move in next week. At least that's what they say will happen, but I'm not so sure. And I have to move out of here and find some other office accommodation. I've responsibility for the place while the organisation of the renovations goes ahead....'

Several times I opened my mouth to speak, trying to find a gap in the conversation. Unless I could interrupt this flow, I'd be unlikely to get answers to my many questions. So much for my prepared speech about my plans for the book on the history of the Pavilion. My enthusiasm was rapidly waning.

He sat down abruptly. 'I'll help you as much as I can, but I'm sure there will be plenty of people on the island better able than I am to give you stories about the place in its glory days.'

This was the moment to jump in with my first request. 'Can I start here, have a look around, to get a feel of the building?'

'Everything's a bit of a jumble at the moment, but of course you must have a good look around,' he said, waving his hand expansively, sending a tray of papers flying. He frowned. 'Do you mean today?'

'Not necessarily,' I said. 'I've yet to meet up with my assistant, Tara and it would be better if we were both here. Would tomorrow suit? And,' hesitating how to say this, not wanting to upset him, 'perhaps we could go round on our own?'

He stood up again, scrabbled around on the floor and gathered the papers up to put them back on the desk, evidently not too concerned about order. He sat down with a thump on his chair, suddenly overcome it would seem, by politeness. 'Please have a seat.'

I looked round, but the only other chair in the room was a tiny dining style chair. Still, better than nothing.

'Mmm,' he said, leaning forward. 'I have to do a bit of clearing up here. The Pavilion manager has been recruited to a new Tourism Bute project and I'm the person on the island responsible for everything meantime. And I mean everything.' He obviously still had some concerns I didn't fully appreciate his status. He stroked his luxuriant moustache again. 'Health and Safety issues - I'm sure you'll understand. There have been a few problems already - bits of concrete falling off. One only narrowly missed me last week. Gave me a real fright, I can tell you.'

'Sorry to hear that, but I assure you I'll be very careful.'

He fiddled with a paperclip on his desk. 'There are other problems you know nothing about,' he said. 'Decisions may have to be made soon. The renovation may not all go according to plan.'

I ignored this remark, judging it was his way of boosting his status yet again.

'I'm sure everyone will be very helpful,' I said, 'but I do have permission to see the building itself.' I scrabbled in my bag and came up with the letter from Argyll and Bute Council.

He took it from me and scrutinised it carefully. 'I see,' he said at last.

'I don't want to take up too much of your time,' I said. 'If you're not available when Tara and I come back perhaps we could liaise with Gerry Nutall?'

He paused for a moment, then frowned. 'Only in extreme circumstances. I don't want him to think that he can make any of the decisions.'

This was all becoming wearisome, this insistence on how important he was. I would have to tread very carefully here, but I also had a job to do. 'Would it be possible to meet Gerry while I'm here today?'

'No,' he said, gazing around as though Gerry might be lurking in a corner somewhere. 'I've given him some tasks to do, though he should be back soon.'

'That sounds perfectly fine,' I said, standing up. 'I'll come along tomorrow morning.' Best to meet firmness with firmness.

If he was upset by my sharpness, he gave no sign. He gazed at me for a moment as though unsure what to say. 'As long as you don't hold me responsible for anything that happens.'

I laughed. 'Of course not.' After all, what could possibly go wrong?

TWO

A few wisps of clouds drifted across the sun as I came out of the Pavilion, my mind a jumble of thoughts. I perched on the little wall at the front of the building, lifting up my face to catch the sun's rays, going over all Ewan had said, trying to create some kind of order. I clutched the set of plans he had reluctantly given to me saying, 'These are expensive to produce, so please take care of them.' On close inspection, they proved to be no more than a photocopy. I wasn't sure how well I'd be able to work with him. He seemed more than a little haphazard in his approach to life in general and work in particular.

That was for later. I sat in the sunshine, leafed quickly through the pages, made some notes and came up with lots of questions. It would be better to have some answers before going off to meet Tara, but back inside the Pavilion, Ewan was nowhere to be seen.

As I gazed around the empty hallway, a tall, thin woman, identified by her badge as 'Doris: Catering Manager,' came down the stairs.

'You must be Alison,' she said coming towards me. 'If you're looking for Ewan, you've just missed him: he's gone over to a meeting in the Moat Centre. Can I help?'

As I had been sitting on the wall at the front of the building I could only guess he'd used another exit. Surely he wasn't trying to avoid me? I dismissed this thought as ungracious as I said, 'Is Gerry Nutall about?'

'Mmm...that's a different story.'

That was interesting. 'Is there a problem?'

She leaned closer as though afraid of being overheard, though there was no one in sight. 'Gerry

10

isn't too happy about the arrangements. He doesn't get on too well with Ewan.'

Great, I thought, exactly as I'd suspected and something I didn't need. To end up involved in a clash of project managers.

I moved away. 'There's nothing urgent,' I said. 'Any questions can wait till tomorrow.'

But now she'd started on the story, she was determined to finish it. 'Gerry should've got the job, if you want my opinion. He's the one who knows the place well.' She sniffed. 'Ewan isn't from the island, you know.'

Neither am I, was the thought that went through my head, but aloud I said, 'I must go. I'm due to meet someone in about twenty minutes.'

In a flurry of goodbyes and thanks I turned and left hurriedly, aware she was standing looking after me. Well, it was no concern of mine, this spat between the members of the project team at the Pavilion: I'd have to get on with both of them as best I could.

My meeting was with Tara McKenna, the research assistant who would be working with me. I knew very little about her, except that she had been one of the many who had replied to the advert in *The Buteman*, the local paper. As the main post had gone to someone outside the island, it was only proper that the research job should go to a local. Or was it no more than a coincidence? Whatever the reason, it was good to be working with someone whose local knowledge would be a great asset, help fill in any gaps.

I drove out through Ardbeg and Port Bannatyne to take the road to Ettrick Bay. Everywhere there were signs of summer activity: families down on the beaches exploring whatever the tide had brought in, the little bay at Port Bannatyne crowded with boats, their rigging clinking in the slight breeze that stirred the water.

11

In a late night phone call, Tara and I had agreed to meet in the Ettrick Bay tearoom. Or rather, I had suggested the venue and was looking forward to a piping hot cup of coffee and a home baked scone.

I tried to focus on the task ahead, the need to outline my plans for the project to Tara, but my mind kept drifting back to the Pavilion and the worry that Ewan Flisch might try to obstruct our work, though why he might do this wasn't immediately clear.

At the Post Office cum general store in Port Bannatyne where I stopped off to buy a morning paper, the little zinc tables and chairs outside were already full, screened off by a colourful windbreak and it looked as if the cafe was in for an extremely busy day. Some of the customers were on holiday, judging by their outfits of jeans and T-shirts, but inside a couple of regulars had their heads bent over their laptops, taking advantage of the wi fi connection. How the modern world had infiltrated even this sleepy part of the island.

A few minutes spent in chat, catching up on the latest gossip and it was off through the village to Ettrick Bay. There was a car parked outside the lodge at Kames Castle, a couple busy unloading suitcases, no doubt in anticipation of a relaxing holiday.

In the boatyard at the end of the village, boats crowded behind the walls, awaiting their owners. It might be the school holidays here in Scotland but in other parts of Britain people were still hard at work and it would be some weeks before all the boats were re-painted, re-varnished and out on the waters of the Kyles of Bute.

At the graveyard next to the old ruined church of Croc An Rath a funeral was taking place, the age of the dead person evident from the few mourners gathered round the newly dug grave. In this part of the world a long life was not unusual.

And then as I rounded the corner into Ettrick Bay, I felt that sudden pleasure, a tingle in the veins, of returning to a well-loved place. Along the curve of the sands a few families were already enjoying the start of summer. One dad was holding on to his son's kite, trying to make it fly, but there wasn't enough wind, even here, to make it rise more than a few feet from the ground. Mum sat on a large checked blanket on the rock at the roadside, shouting encouragement. Whether it was to the boy or to the dad I couldn't tell at this distance. Their selected spot on the sands was clearly defined by a collection of children's buckets, spades and an overlarge picnic basket.

Down where the water lapped the beach in a froth of surf, a group of giggling girls, jeans rolled up, hopped up and down at the edge, daring each other to take the first step into the water, cold even at this time of year.

I pushed open the door of the long low building that was the Ettrick Bay tearoom to be met by the aroma of fresh coffee and sizzling bacon as another 'All Day' breakfast was prepared.

'How will I recognise you?' I'd asked Tara at the end of our last phone call.

'I won't be difficult to identify,' she'd said with a chuckle, leaving me feeling very intrigued, but in spite of my prompting she would say no more.

The café was even busier than usual. The tables and banquettes ranged along the windows were always the first to be taken, but even the tables and chairs in the middle of the room were almost all occupied. The tearoom had been refurbished in cheerful shades of blue and cream since my last visit and there was still a smell of new flooring underlying the aroma of food. It took me a moment to scan all the faces in front of me. A coach party had evidently arrived earlier and they were easy to pick out by the way they crowded together

13

in the far side of the tearoom, silver heads bent to the goodies in front of them, the noise of chat and laughter rising and falling.

Near the door, a couple of families squashed in, children moving restlessly at the tables, jumping up and down to admonitions from harassed parents.

And then, with a sudden feeling of alarm, I spotted her in the far corner. She'd been right about being easy to recognise, especially among these very traditionally-dressed customers. Her shock of spiky pink hair and wealth of jewellery, including several earrings in each ear, would make her stand out in any crowd.

She sat gazing out through the large window overlooking the beach, fiddling with her phone, in front of her an empty glass containing the dregs of a strawberry milk shake.

I walked briskly over and sat down in the chair opposite. 'Tara?' I said.

She turned to look at me a huge smile lit up her thin face, her over-plucked eyebrows giving her a slightly surprised look.

'Yes. You must be Alison?'

I nodded. 'Good to see you.'

'And good to meet you, Alison,' she said. Her voice was light, melodic. I had this sudden impression we would get on well, very well, in spite of her odd appearance. To be truthful I was relieved, more than anything, thinking about how much work there was to do.

The waitress came bustling over, notepad poised to take the order. 'This is Ginny,' said Tara, with a wave of her hand, smiling at her. 'She works here during the school holidays.' My hunch had been correct. Having Tara as a research assistant would be having someone who knew a lot about the island...and the people.

Ginny nodded her head and removed the pen from behind her ear. She looked young, very young indeed with her blonde hair tied back in a ponytail and a face devoid of make up, but she promised efficiency. 'What can I get you?'

Tara quickly opted for another milk shake. 'I'll have chocolate this time,' and after some deliberation I settled for white coffee and a scone with butter and jam. 'The Bute air makes you so hungry, 'I said, 'and it's been a long time since breakfast.' Though why I needed to justify myself to Tara I'd no idea. Guilt probably. Six weeks of sampling the Bute fare and there might be more problems with my weight than usual. Still, one treat wouldn't hurt. And I could eat less tomorrow.

There was an awkward pause as Ginny hurried to the kitchen with our order and then Tara said, 'Tell me a bit about yourself, Alison.'

Surprised by the suddenness of this question, it took me a moment or two to answer. 'I was a teacher,' I began and went on to give her a potted history of my career.

She nodded from time to time, smiling encouragingly, though I was aware my story must have been incredibly boring.

When I paused for breath, she said, 'You mentioned your husband would be away on business for the six weeks you're on the island?'

'Mmm, yes. It's all worked out very well indeed, to be honest. By the time he comes back I hope to have enough information to spend the rest of the time writing up the research at home in Glasgow.' Then I added hastily, 'That's why I'm looking forward to working with you, someone who knows the island well.'

'There's no one else with you? You've come here on your own?'

15

A strange question, but I replied almost without thinking. 'No - my son Alastair teaches at a university in Canada, my elder daughter Maura lives in London and Deborah, the youngest is in Italy at the moment on a course.' One of the many courses Deborah had been on in the past few years, I reflected, with little to show for it in the way of paid work. Still, mustn't complain. Two out of three isn't bad. Though where Deborah had inherited her artistic temperament from I couldn't imagine.

This was all becoming a bit too personal. Tara had said nothing about herself. All I knew was what she had put on her application for the post of research assistant. I tried to recall exactly what that was.

The waitress returned with our order and it was a few moments before we resumed our conversation as Tara sipped her milk shake while I made short work of my freshly-baked scone.

It didn't appear she was going to volunteer any information so, 'What about you, Tara? I gather you're from the island?' I said.

She put her cup down and stared at me. 'Whatever gave you that idea?'

'Why, your application of course.'

She hesitated for a moment, but only for a moment. She blushed a little and a wary look came into her eyes. 'Well, yes, I suppose I can claim that.'

What was I to make of this comment? You're either born on the island and are a true 'Brandane' or you're not. There are no half measures.

'I'm glad about that,' I went on, determined not to let this thread of our conversation slip. 'Because that's exactly what's needed for this project: someone who knows the island and the people on it well.'

There was another silence. 'You have been employed on other projects like this - projects where

you had to interview people?' I searched my memory.
'You worked on a newspaper for a while?'

'Not...exactly. I did have some work experience...' her voice tailed off.

By now she was looking into her glass, avoiding my gaze. I'd have to look again at her application, but I was sure that her qualifications in this field had been one of the deciding factors in appointing her. Why had Tara claimed to have experience on a newspaper? And was she a genuine Brandane? Surely it had all been checked out? Or had she exaggerated her qualifications as a way of giving her the edge over other competitors for the job? If she had lied about that, what else might she have lied about? Yet another problem to deal with.

THREE

Deciding what to do about accommodation during my stay on the island had cost me many sleepless nights. Six weeks in a hotel would be too expensive, yet most of the flats to rent required a long lease and though there would be several trips back to the mainland and our house in Glasgow while writing up the research, these would be deliberately short.

Then I had a stroke of luck. One of the teachers at Strathelder High had a friend who owned a holiday flat out at Kilchattan Bay. She was anxious to let it for the summer as she and her husband were off to Australia for a niece's wedding, to be combined with the trip of a lifetime for their Silver Wedding celebrations. It was too good an opportunity to miss: I lost no time in contacting her, we discussed terms and the deal was sealed. I didn't bother to enquire too closely about the accommodation - whatever it was would be sufficient for me over the summer.

Kilchattan Bay is on the far side of the island, a single street of solid houses, cottages and flats overlooking the curve of the bay, nipped off at one end by the Kingarth Hotel and on the other side by the entrance to the West Island Way. Originally a centre for fishing, where the island crops of potatoes were landed, it eventually became the destination for a steamer service from Weymss Bay, Fairlie and Millport.

Now it's a popular spot for holidaymakers and those who live on the island, but prefer a location quieter than the hustle and bustle of Rothesay.

The 'flat' turned out to be a tiny terraced cottage, in the middle of a row of the original fishermen's cottages on the main street, overlooking the bay, an ideal spot

18

for my purposes. The green algae that streaked the whitewash showed the effects of the previous winter storms and the paint on the bright red door was peeling a little, but that didn't concern me. It seemed perfect: big enough for one, or two at a pinch. Not that I anticipated any visitors. I'd made it very clear to everyone I was here to work.

Opposite the cottages, across the only road, one of the many memorial benches that dot the island sat at the edge of the path down to the beach and I looked forward to early morning walks along the shore. Across the water the twin beacons on the tiny island of Little Cumbrae were a reminder of the hazards the fishermen who lived here once faced, but the only boats to be seen now were those being sailed for pleasure.

I parked the car outside and after a few false starts managed to turn the key in the lock to find myself straight into a cosy, low-ceilinged living room with a tiny kitchen, fashioned from what had once been a bed recess. The narrow wooden staircase at the side led to a tiny landing with a small cupboard and a bedroom tucked into the eaves on either side, each with a huge skylight. The little shower room was squashed in between them. More than ample for my needs over the summer. The kitchen door led out into a minute garden, rising at the bottom into a steeply wooded hillside, as did all the houses in this row.

As I looked round, I didn't see myself being able to do much entertaining here, but that wasn't my intention. This would be six weeks of hard work and in a way, though I'm gregarious, I was looking forward to the solitude. This was the start of a new career and I had to make a success of it, make a good impression with this first commission.

In a cottage this size it didn't take me much time to organise my few belongings and after a trip to the local store cum Post Office to stock up on bread and milk and a few other essentials that I could squash into the microscopic fridge, I set about arranging my workspace.

There was a fold down table in the living room overlooking the bay, but fearing the view might prove to be far too distracting, I moved it to the corner of the room and set the only lamp at an angle to give me some good light. I unpacked my laptop, stacked paper into the printer and positioned a notepad and a pen beside me for jottings. Then I sat back. Now what? My mind had gone blank.

This would never do. I typed 'A History of the Pavilion, Rothesay, Isle of Bute 1938 - present day' but on the screen it looked less than enthralling as a title. I played around with some alternatives, but none of them seemed adequate. I sat back with a sigh. Perhaps more coffee would help? But even after another large cup, I was no further forward.

By now it was growing late and the sun was beginning to set in a haze of pink and purple over the waters of the bay. Would a walk along the shore help to clear my mind? Or perhaps I was hungry? I suddenly realised I hadn't eaten since my coffee and scone at the Ettrick Bay tearoom. The village shop would be closed by now and there was nothing substantial enough in the fridge to make a meal. There was no alternative but to head for the Kingarth Hotel at the far end of the village unless I wanted to make another trip into Rothesay. I decided on the Kingarth, being in no mood for cooking.

As I closed down the computer, still with an almost blank first page, the enormity of this project struck me yet again. What on earth had possessed me to give up the job I knew to take up this entirely new way of earning a living? And if I couldn't even think of a title, how would I manage the rest of this book?

With a sinking heart, I locked up the little cottage to walk along the road to the Kingarth. Surely everything would be better in the morning. But as I walked the short distance to the hotel, I kept thinking about Tara and our conversation at the Ettrick Bay tearoom. If she had exaggerated her qualifications, she might not be as helpful for the project as I'd thought.

I'd have to check her out; ask to have another look at her application form. Was there some other reason she wanted to be involved in this project, a reason that caused her to lie?

FOUR

The restaurant at the Kingarth hotel was unexpectedly quiet for a Thursday night in summer, almost deserted, though the bar was lively enough. A glance at my watch told me I'd only made it in time for last orders for meals.

I crossed through the corner bar, past customers perched on high stools, to the restaurant where high backed bench style seating, reminding me of old church pews, sat solidly beside rough hewn tables, enhancing the rustic air of what was the oldest coaching inn on the island.

The specials menu was scrawled on the blackboard beside the main door, but at this time of night many of them would be 'off'. Trouble was, they all looked tempting and I was hungry. I finally settled on the Bute lamb with all the trimmings from one of the local farms, hoping the generosity of portions here might deter me from the more than tempting desserts. After choosing the seat facing the bar, I settled down with the book on Bute I'd brought with me. I was unlikely to know anyone here and wasn't in the mood for chat with strangers at the moment.

When the waitress departed with my order (fortunately the lamb was still available) I resumed reading, scarcely registering those around me until a loud guffaw from the far end of the bar roused me. I peered round the side of the settle and caught sight of a couple with their backs towards me, perched on stools at the bar.

Suddenly the man gave a another loud laugh as he bent his head to catch the words of his companion, a woman whose blonde hair and short skirt made her look much younger than he was, with his grey streaked hair and beard.

When she stood up, giving me a clearer view, I saw my first impressions were wrong. Laughter lines round her mouth and her eyes had settled into permanent wrinkles and there was more than a hint of grey at the roots of her hair.

I dropped my book, making a loud thud on the wooden floor and they both glanced briefly in my direction, before resuming their conversation.

It was a strange feeling, being on my own, even with a book for company. Another waitress returned for the rest of my order, and this one seemed determined to engage me in conversation. Perhaps she felt sorry for me all on my own, or was merely curious. She had no doubt heard through the local gossip I was staying at one of the cottages in the village.

'Just visiting, are you?' She said this loudly as she took my order, a sign she was slightly deaf.

As I hadn't spoken to a soul since my meeting earlier in the morning with Tara, I was torn between telling her the full story of my reason for being on the island and that city-style desire for privacy. 'You could say that,' I replied, raising my voice to accommodate her.

She persisted with more questions as she laid down the cutlery in front of me. 'And are you planning on staying long?'

'About six weeks, I expect.'

'What did you say?' As I repeated my reply a smile of understanding crossed her face. 'Ah, are you the woman who's writing the history of the Pavilion? I've read about you in *The Buteman*. It all sounds very exciting.'

'Yes, that's me. I hope to finish most of the research this summer and then spend the winter writing it up in good time for publication next year when the Pavilion re-opens.' I was aware I was almost shouting, that the loudness of my voice would carry across the room, but didn't want to be rude.

Out of the corner of my eye I caught a glimpse of the bearded man raising his head and looking in my direction. There was a lot of interest on the island about the future of the Pavilion after so many years of fighting for funding to undertake the restoration. The idea of having to give a regular update on my progress didn't appeal one little bit. I'd had some experience of that kind of thing and it was a sure fire way not to get any work done.

'There's a lot to do,' I said, 'a lot of research, but fortunately I'll have some expert help with that.'

The waitress seemed to have forgotten there might be other customers waiting as she continued, gently tapping my dessert spoon on the table, 'And you'll be going right back through all the history of the Pavilion? It was a really popular venue, still is and it'll be missed while it's closed.' The scent of the spicy apple crumble I'd selected drifted towards me, but until the waitress released the spoon, it was impossible to make a start on it.

'That's the idea. Lots happened here in the early days, especially during the last war.'

A disembodied voice from the direction of the kitchen summoned her back to her tasks. 'I'll have to go,' she said, as though I'd been detaining her.

As I savoured the cooling spicy apple crumble at last, I noticed the bearded man say something to his companion. She nodded, looked in my direction and then he went out, banging the door loudly behind him. From my secluded seat it was impossible to see his face, but I had the distinct impression that for some reason he was very angry. I scraped my spoon round the dish to get the last crumbs, telling myself their quarrel was none of my business, nothing to so with me.

The waitress bustled over with my coffee, but said no more. A group of late diners, clad in hiking gear, had entered in a flurry of discarded jackets and loud laughter, requesting food. I turned my attention to the fragrant cup of coffee now sitting before me. While it was the only possible way to end an excellent meal, it would mean I'd find it hard to sleep. No matter, there was plenty to keep me occupied. Perhaps inspiration would seize me later in the quiet of the night. I might even manage to write a killer opening chapter.

I paid my bill at the bar and left the Kingarth. The blonde woman was still seated at the bar, continuing to nurse the same drink by the looks of it. None of my business, really, but I couldn't help wondering, concocting a little drama round the relationship of the blonde woman and the bearded man.

Outside the air was cool, a shock to the system after the cosy ambience of the hotel and darkness had closed in, that complete darkness that only exists in the countryside. Where we live in Glasgow there's always the loom of the city to obscure the sky, even on the starriest of nights, but here the inky blackness of a clouded sky lent an eerie appearance to the trees, creaking ominously in the little breeze that had sprung up across the water, almost drowning out the rhythmic whoosh of the waves on the shore.

I made for the welcoming street lights of the village at a brisk pace, past the empty Kingarth stables where the For Sale sign swayed in the wind, along by the fields of slumbering cattle.

The row of cottages was at the very edge of the village, only a short walk alongside the shore, but in the darkness I had to pick my way carefully. Next time I would bring a torch. Once or twice I almost stumbled and began to walk more slowly. An accident here would not be a good idea.

I stopped to recover my balance, suddenly aware of a slight noise behind me. When I looked round there was nothing to be seen except some horses in the field beside the road, standing in silence, quietly asleep.

My heart began to beat faster as I quickened my pace; all the while telling myself not to be stupid, it was my imagination, that any slight noise would be magnified in this stillness.

I stopped at the edge of the village, scrabbling through my bag to have my key ready to open the door, listening intently. Nothing, except the swish of the waves, the hooting of a distant owl. Reassured, I set off again towards the cottage.

Suddenly there was a loud cough, seemingly right behind me. I whirled round, but there was no sign of anyone in the darkness. I quickened my pace. Only a few more yards and I'd be safe.

On reaching the cottage my courage completely failed me and I ran towards the front door. Emboldened to investigate from this safe position, I looked back.

There it was again, that faint noise, a light crunching sound. I screwed up my eyes, seeming to glimpse an outline in the shadows down by the old boatshed on the shore. The sliver of a moon suddenly disappeared behind thick clouds and I peered into the gloom, tried to get a better view, but all was peaceful.

Anxious to be inside with the door firmly shut and bolted, I fumbled with the keys, but in my haste dropped them and had to scramble about on the ground for a few moments to locate them, my pulse quickening with every movement. Next time I went out at night, as well as taking a torch, I'd remember to leave the front light on.

I pushed open the door, then slammed it, careless that the noise might disturb the residents of the other cottages in this little row. I stood absolutely still for a moment, leaning against the door, waiting for the rapid beating of my heart to subside. This was ridiculous. If there had been anyone and not a mere figment of my imagination, it was surely some other villager making their way back home or someone out for an evening stroll. There were lots of holidaymakers in the village at this time of year.

Even so, I couldn't resist peeping out of the window, pulling the heavy curtain aside a mere fraction in the still darkened room.

For a moment it appeared the road was deserted, but suddenly there was a break in the clouds and the moon sailed into view. As my eyes became accustomed to the shimmering light I was sure there was someone standing down by the shore, next to the boatshed.

The moon again disappeared from sight, leaving the shore in darkness. I was about to turn away, but suddenly there was a spark of light. It wasn't my imagination this time. Someone was lurking there, had lit up a cigarette, the flame from the match briefly illuminating his face.

For a moment I was perplexed, puzzled. I recognised this man. I'd seen him somewhere very recently. Of course. It was the bearded man from the bar at the Kingarth.

That was it. I must have heard him following me back to the village. What was he doing here outside the cottage? Was he watching me? And if so, why?

FIVE

I slept badly that night, very badly, tossing and turning, watching the hours creep slowly past on the illuminated dial of the alarm clock beside the bed. Twice I crept downstairs in the dark to peer out from behind the curtain at the front window but there was no sign of the bearded man.

On the second occasion, I picked up the book about Bute. If I couldn't sleep, I could try to use the time profitably. After re-reading the same page several times, I abandoned it and went back upstairs to bed, to drift off to sleep as dawn was breaking, dreaming of the bearded man.

People say the difference between the city and the country is that at night in the country there is no noise. That's not true: it's only that the sounds are different. I was aware of the water swishing rhythmically against the shore, the wind rustling in the trees behind the cottage, the restless mooing of cattle and as morning approached, the sound of birds wakening to a new day. And I must have fallen into a really deep sleep because suddenly it was after eight o'clock and I was due at the Pavilion at nine. Try as I might to recall the details of my dreams they escaped me, leaving only a lingering sense of unease.

I leapt out of bed and straight into the shower, setting it to 'cool' to try to jolt myself into wakefulness. By eight thirty I was down in the little kitchen, brewing some strong coffee. Hopefully there would be something to eat at the Pavilion. On Bute there isn't the same urgency about time, but it wouldn't be a good idea to turn up late and flustered. Very unprofessional.

My mobile rang as I was unlocking the car door. 'Hello,' I said absentmindedly, watching a haze drift across the water of the bay, bringing the promise of another day of fine weather and heat.

Down on the sands, several people were already out walking, throwing sticks for their frisking dogs. When the weather is as changeable as it is in the West, you learn to take advantage of every single minute of good weather. Needless to say there was no sign of the bearded man and in the light of day all my fears of the previous night seemed melodramatic, ridiculous.

The call was from my friend Susie, phoning from California where she's currently on an exchange visit at an American High school. 'Hi,' I said in delight, 'how are you?'

'Fine - I've got the time right, haven't I? I'm not phoning you in the middle of the night?'

'No, no, you're okay. Though I am heading off to the Pavilion in a few minutes.'

Much as I like my friend Susie, she doesn't use one word when she could use several. 'Is there some special reason you're phoning me?'

'I couldn't believe it when I got your e-mail.'

Oh,oh. Was I in trouble?

'I still don't understand why you did it, Alison.'

I started to reply, then paused. A phone call wasn't the place to discuss this.

'I thought you liked teaching,' she went on, 'liked working with young people.'

'I did, I did,' I replied lamely, 'but it was time for something different.'

'I suppose it's too late to change your mind now. I'll hear all about it when I come back next week.'

That took me by surprise. 'You're coming back next week?' After a 'short' secondment at an American High School, stretching to two years, I'd some doubts about Susie's desire to return to her teaching job in Scotland.

'Of course,' she said as though it was the most natural thing in the world. 'Anyway, the Head says she can't keep my job open if I decide to stay in America any longer. So I'm coming back for a while to let them know my final decision. That's only fair.'

'That's good news.' Susie returning to Strathelder High was something I found hard to imagine, so taken did she seem with life in California.

'Yes, indeed. Got my ticket all booked.'

'This is very sudden.' I was astonished. What had prompted this unexpected return?

'Mmm...long story, but I'll tell you when I see you. Any chance you could pick me up at the airport? I thought I'd come over to Bute for a few days.'

I hesitated. How could I refuse my friend, someone I'd known since college? Yet it would mean a trip of at least a morning off the island. 'Fine,' I replied, hoping she didn't notice the hesitation in my voice, 'e-mail me details of your flight and I'll come over to meet you.'

Well, I thought, Susie would be company for a few days and although it would be a bit of a squeeze in the tiny cottage, it would be great to see her again. And, if I was honest, it would be useful to have someone else staying in the cottage. I wasn't quite as good at living on my own as I thought I'd be.

But as I drove out of Kilchattan Bay, I scolded myself again for allowing my imagination to make me so fearful of that bearded man. He'd probably been doing no more than taking a late stroll home and making the most of the long summer nights. I tried to forget all about him and concentrate on the task ahead.

This morning we were due to have a full tour of the Pavilion, an exploration of all its nooks and crannies before the builders moved in. Hopefully Ewan, disorganised though he was, would have remembered our nine o'clock appointment.

I had other concerns. If Tara and I wanted to do some further research in the building, would we be allowed in once the workmen started? It would be difficult to manage everything in this one visit, but we might have to make the best of it.

I didn't do my usual stop off in Guildford Square to buy a morning paper, but headed straight for the Pavilion, conscious nine o'clock was approaching fast.

Outside the building a large van blocked most of the parking spaces, leaving me no option but to drive round to the side of the building to find a space on the hill. This road was busy with parents dropping children off at the Appletree Nursery and the noise of toddlers at play in the garden drifted down.

Inside the Pavilion the reason for the large van parked outside soon became evident. All was hustle and bustle, workmen coming and going, clanging and banging in a determined fashion. Surely they hadn't started the renovations already?

Annoyed at this unexpected turn of events, I headed straight for the office and knocked loudly on the door, but it wasn't Ewan who answered. It was someone I didn't recognise.

'I'm looking for Ewan,' I said, trying not to betray my irritation.

'I'm Gerry Nutall,' the man said. 'I'm afraid he's not turned up yet.' He looked flustered, his face red, little beads of sweat glistening on his brow. He adjusted his glasses as he spoke.

'Ah, so you're Gerry. We've spoken on the phone.' I introduced myself. 'Ewan and I had an appointment for nine o'clock,' I said.

He shrugged as he smoothed his hand over his bald head. 'Sorry about that. Could you come back later?'

31

I wasn't to be put off. 'Surely you're in charge if Ewan isn't here?' I didn't mention Ewan's reluctance to delegate.

He avoided my gaze. 'I suppose so...' He hitched up his trousers which were slowly falling below his large paunch.

'I'm working to a tight deadline. All I want to do is have a good look around the Pavilion. You know all about the book I've been commissioned to write. Ewan told me it would be at least next week before the work started.'

'Yes, but the builders had a cancellation and decided they would start right away with organising everything, though the actual work won't start for a couple of days yet.' He sounded peevish.

'But what about my access to the building? I really do need to get some feel for the place,' I said, aware the pitch of my voice was gradually rising.

He shrugged. 'I'm not sure how I can help you,' he said and his tone made me very doubtful about the outcome. 'The builders turned up this morning out of the blue and we don't want to lose any time.'

I stood my ground. I had to get this commission started, explore the building, before access was a problem. 'We had an agreement. I was to have the opportunity to see everything in the building before the renovations started and then at the various stages of development.'

'Has this to go?' said one of the builders, a tall, skinny but very muscular man asked, lifting with ease a large table from one of the little rooms at the side of the main hallway.

'Yes, yes,' said Gerry, obviously distracted. So that was it. He had also been taken by surprise and didn't quite know what to do. Probably he was worried about Ewan's reaction, if he started making decisions without permission. Well, I did know what to do. I pulled out my notebook. Decision made, whether or not it suited Gerry. 'I'm going to start at the top of the building,' I said, 'and work my way down. Will you be available for any questions?' I tried to imagine myself in front of a class of recalcitrant fourth year boys and put on my sternest look.

'Of course, of course, that should be fine,' he said, but I could tell his mind wasn't on my problem, but on the builders who were now moving with startling efficiency. At this rate they'd have the whole place stripped out in no time.

As I turned to go upstairs, he grabbed one of the builders who was going past and said, 'You can do this floor and the top one today, but the rest will have to wait.'

'You're the boss.' The builder shrugged and went to join his mates, whistling loudly.

'I won't be long.' I turned to hurry up the broad marble stairs before he could change his mind and call me back, but then heard a shout.

'Alison, I'm here,' said Tara as she came rushing towards me. 'Sorry I'm a bit late.'

'No matter.' In truth I was pleased to see her, beginning to regret I'd been quite so forceful. Gerry was looking after me in some dismay. 'Same goes for you, Alison. Best if you keep to these two floors.'

'But I have to see it all,' I said. 'I gather even the basements are used here?'

'Yes,' said Gerry, 'but there's nothing of interest down there.'

Gerry would take some time to finish with the builders. The problem of the basements could be sorted out later. 'I think we should start with the main room,' I said to Tara, looking at the plans of the building Ewan had given me.

33

Tara whipped out a recorder from the large bag she had slung over her shoulder. Today her hair was a bright shade of red, gelled to be even spikier and she was wearing a long flowing top in black and red.

As we moved off together, Gerry grabbed my arm. 'There's no way you can go round on your own. Far too dangerous. I'll come with you. Just give me a minute to sort this out.' He rushed off to talk to the builders.

'Let's do as he says. We'll wait through here,' I said, making for the foyer where a table and chairs had been set up.

'We can talk about how we want to start this before we set off,' I said and we spread the plans and what information we had out in front of us as we tried to determine what might be included in the opening chapter. Tara was fortunately much more inspired than I'd been and within a short time we had the bones of the draft outline of the introduction.

'I think that's more than enough for now. We can always change things round later.' I said. There was still no sign of Gerry who had now disappeared somewhere with the builders. 'Let's see if we can rustle up a cup of coffee...and hopefully Ewan will have arrived.' For whatever reason I had the distinct impression Gerry didn't want us here.

Tara rummaged again in her capacious bag. 'I prefer to drink herbal tea,' she said, 'unless there's none available, but don't worry. I always carry a supply with me. You could try one if you want?'

I politely declined - a good strong cup of coffee was what I was after. Tara went through to the staffroom to find hot water to brew up her concoction, and I went in search of Gerry to find out what the system was for making coffee.

34

As I made for the office, I heard Gerry's voice as he came down the main stairs. He sounded much calmer: perhaps he'd managed to get the builders under control.

'Alison,' he said as he came towards me, 'This is Rufus Beale. He's in charge of the building works, he owns the firm that won the contract for this first stage of the renovations.' He gestured to the man behind him.

I smiled, ready to greet the new arrival, but the smile froze on my face as the newcomer stepped out from behind Gerry. Rufus Beale was none other than the bearded man I'd seen last night on the shore at Kilchattan Bay.

SIX

Rufus gave no sign of recognition as he came towards me, wiping his hands on his stained overalls. 'Pleased to meet you,' he said, betraying by not a flicker that he was the man I suspected of following me home from the Kingarth Hotel.

Now face to face with him, I was more convinced than ever that he had been the watcher, the man on the seashore. I tried to smile, but somehow my facial muscles refused to work as instructed and I was aware of grimacing instead.

Unable to stop myself, I blurted out, 'Haven't I seen you somewhere before?'

'I don't think so,' he said smoothly, betraying not the slightest hint of anxiety. He turned to Gerry. 'I'd better be getting on. I've a couple of meetings this morning - one with the architect - and I've a lot of details to clear up before the work can properly begin.' He turned on his heel, leaving me gazing after him, wondering yet again if I'd made an awful mistake. Surely if he was the person I'd seen last night he'd only been out for a late night stroll?

'When will you be back?' Gerry called after him. 'We need to talk.'

Rufus stopped at the door through to the foyer and waved. 'I'll be back here within the hour and I'll pick up that stuff from your office. I'll leave Harry with you. He can fill you in.' He gestured to the tall builder I'd seen moving the table earlier.

'What stuff is that?' I asked, realising immediately how rude that must have sounded.

Gerry narrowed his eyes. For a moment he appeared to ignore my question then he said hurriedly, 'Oh, just some papers about the permit for the work to start. You know what bureaucracy is like. If Ewan doesn't appear soon, I'll have to decide what to do.'

Somehow I thought that would please him, making an important decision in the absence of his boss, though I didn't understand why Rufus should be so involved.

Here at least was common ground, something I could sympathise with. 'Don't I just know about red tape,' I sighed, glad to have left all that behind me when I'd resigned from Strathelder High. Whatever rules I had to comply with in the writing of this history of the Pavilion, I wouldn't have to fill in endless forms. At least I hoped this would be the case, that someone else would deal with any paperwork.

'So are we ready to start?' I said. 'I gather there are two main floors and a couple of basements?'

'There's nothing much down in the basements,' he said hurriedly. 'A waste of your time.'

'I'd like to be the judge of that,' I said. 'Isn't the main basement used by at least one club? So there must be something of interest.'

Harry broke in. 'If she doesn't see it now, she won't see it once we get started. It'll be far too dangerous. I can take her down if you like.'

There was a moment's silence as we stood and looked at one another, then Gerry said with great reluctance. 'If you really must see it, I have to come with you.'

This was unfortunate as I'd the feeling Gerry would be anxious to rush us through, while what we had planned was a leisurely tour of the building, making notes and taking photos as we went.

We'd have to go along with him meantime. Once Ewan Flisch returned I could speak to him, ask for permission to go round on our own. 'I'll collect Tara,' I said and crossed to the kitchen where she was leaning against the little work surface, evidently enjoying her cup of herbal tea.

'Ready?' I said.

'Gosh, have you finished your coffee already?' She put her half finished cup down on the work surface. 'I thought I'd a good fifteen minutes.'

I didn't reply, didn't say that the sight of Rufus had put all thoughts of coffee out of my head. No doubt I'd be regretting that later, but there was no time now as we set off to begin our inspection of the building with Gerry.

'We'll start at the top,' he said, but as we reached the bottom of the main staircase the phone in his office rang. He hesitated, as thought trying to decide whether or not to answer it. 'I'll pick that up later,' he said. 'This shouldn't take too long,' bustling ahead of us so that we had to break into a trot to keep up.

'Whatever you think best,' I said, resigned to this guided tour.

He bounded off in front of us.

'He seems to be in training for a marathon,' muttered Tara who seemed even more out of breath than I was as we climbed the stairs.

He led us into the main hall, pointing out the original Art Deco lights, the elegant columns supporting the roof, the once beautiful wooden floor. 'This draped ceiling can be retracted,' he said and moved over to the corner where he pulled a couple of levers to show us exactly what he meant. At his touch the cream drapery glided from the middle to the sides of the room, revealing a ceiling that seemed to stretch up to infinity, so high was it.

'This is one of the main areas for renovation,' he said. 'You can see the central panel was covered over at one time, probably in the seventies. Underneath that monstrosity there's a huge glass panel that lets in lots of light.'

We moved towards the door. He pointed to a long flimsy partitioned area against the wall. 'And this café/bar area was added on - another awful decision.' Contrary to my expectations, it was very useful having him with us, highlighting features we might have missed, even with a set of plans.

We expressed suitable amazement as he ushered us out to the balconies overlooking the bay. 'The top balcony was designed to be used for open air dancing - not that there are many opportunities for that with the weather we have.' He turned to see if we appreciated his joke and we dutifully smiled.

I peered over the edge: it was a long way down, but it was a peaceful scene far below. The ferry was approaching Rothesay, turning towards the harbour as it came in. Strange that something so huge could look so graceful and could so deftly avoid the numerous boats of all shapes and sizes cluttering the water. One sailing boat, obviously a visitor to Bute, judging by its name - *The Folkestone Girl* - only just managed to avoid a collision, but the CalMac captain was a man of long experience, well used to avoiding disasters such as these.

Most of the yachts usually berthed in Rothesay marina would be out on the Firth. There were more large boats than ever using the calm waters around Bute, but here and there were still old fashioned wooden boats, some lovingly restored, some in need of attention. It was good to see the bay so busy again. At one time the place would have been crammed with steamers bringing holidaymakers down to the pleasant coastal resort of Rothesay, but the temptations of warmer countries had seduced many away until recently.

Tara broke into my musings, tugging at my sleeve. 'We have to move on, Alison.'

I reluctantly left the balcony and the pleasant sea breezes to follow them. I wanted to include as much technical information about the building as possible, knowing that would interest a lot of people who had visited the Pavilion, but had no knowledge of its inner workings. This wasn't my area of expertise, but Gerry would be able to fill me in and answer our many questions.

We made our way back downstairs, pausing only as Gerry drew our attention to the handrails. 'Have a good look at the original photos - the handrails will also be restored. You can use those photos in your book.'

By now I was more than ready for that postponed cup of coffee. 'If you really want to go down to the basement for a quick look, let's stop for a breather,' said Gerry.

'Good idea,' I replied.

The coffee was unexpectedly good, hot and strong and afterwards I felt much revived and ready to continue. Tara waved aside an offer of another cup of herbal tea. Perhaps there was a limit as to how much she could drink.

As we came to the end of our tour of the ground floor Gerry said, frowning and looking at his watch, 'Perhaps you've seen enough? There is really very little else of interest.'

So that was it: he hoped by taking us on this extensive tour of the Pavilion, we'd be less interested in the basement.

This only made me more determined than ever. 'If we don't see this place now we might not have another chance. Surely it won't take long.'

Gerry seemed to hesitate for a moment then he shrugged, put the cups to one side and we followed him meekly to the far corner beside the wooden, oblong shaped ticket office. Where was he going?

He pulled a large key from the bunch that seemed to accompany him everywhere and led us through to what was called the lesser hall. He inserted it into a keyhole almost invisible in a smooth wooden panel. 'This leads to the basement. Truth to tell, I haven't been down here for a long time. There's no need because a number of years ago the systems were updated so that everything could be controlled from up here in the office.'

He glanced at us. 'I hope you're not wearing your best clothes,' he said, 'because it's bound to be very dusty down here.'

Tara and I shook our heads. We were both sensibly clad, having anticipated there might be some disused corners in the building.

'Okay,' he said, 'follow me and watch your feet on the stairs. Keep right behind me. We may not be able to see everything. If it becomes too dangerous, we'll have to turn back.'

We followed him down the stairs, grimy and cobwebby, into the basement, through the gloomy area with pipes running along the wall. Down here there seemed to be a series of interconnected rooms with no doors, the pillars essential to support the building designating one room from the other. The ceilings were low and we had to stoop down to get through. 'The rifle club meets here,' he said, 'but the rest of the place isn't used. No point in going any further.'

'Since we've come all this way, we might as well see it all.'

'There's nothing to see,' he protested. 'A waste of time.'

'Even so.' I refused to budge and he sighed, 'Oh, come on then, but it will only be a very quick look.'

41

We followed him through to the next section of the basement, brushing off the dust of many years as we went.

'Almost at the end now,' he said, as we turned a corner and went down another set of stairs. 'Be very careful. No one has been down here in a very long time. I don't think I've ever seen this part of the building. This is where the old boilers are located. When they put in the new heating system they left this place untouched.'

I didn't see a description of these dusty recesses taking up much space in our history of the Pavilion and my mind began to wander. Gerry was right: there was nothing of interest here.

'Perhaps we could skip this bit of the tour,' said Tara, brushing away yet another cobweb and shuddering.

'Good idea,' said Gerry, seizing on her words. 'Let's go back upstairs. I don't want you tripping and falling here.'

'Now we're here we might as well see everything.' The more he tried to dissuade us, the more determined I became, though in truth I was no more keen on this dusty, uninteresting part of the building than Tara.

He opened another door and flicked the switch on the wall but no light came on. 'The bulb must have gone. Not surprising after so many years with no one coming down here. It's probably the original light bulb. Well, that's it, I'm afraid.' He turned to usher us out.

I wasn't prepared to give up quite so easily. 'I have a torch with me.'

He waved it away. 'I have one of my own, thanks,' adding, 'You'd better wait here till I make sure it's safe.'

Tara and I hung back, preferring to stay where we were, neither of us particularly keen to venture down into the darkness of this part of the basement. We watched in silence as Gerry fumbled his way through, finally disappearing into the gloom, the torchlight making very little impression on the enveloping darkness.

We waited impatiently for a few moments, anxious to be above ground as soon as possible, but there was a sudden shout, then another, then all went quiet. We looked at each other. Had Gerry had an accident? We listened, straining our ears for some further sound. But there was none.

'Come on,' I said, 'we'll have to make our way down, find out what's happened to Gerry.'

Tara hung back. 'Can't we wait a few more minutes?' she said. 'See if he comes back?' She shivered.

'No, what if he's fallen, been injured? Even a few minutes would make a difference. You wait here if you want, but I'm going to find out where he is.'

I started to move down the stairs, but Tara grabbed my arm. 'I don't want to be left here all alone,' she whimpered.

'Then let's go. We can't come to much harm if we stay together.' We moved forward very slowly, clinging together, flashing the torch as we gingerly edged down one step in front of another till we were almost at the foot of the staircase.

Gerry was standing on the bottom step, clutching his leg.

'Are you okay?'

'I stumbled, that's all. I'll be fine. There's nothing here,' he said gruffly. 'It's just as I thought - old rubbish that hasn't been touched in years.' He continued to block our view. 'Let's leave it.'

Tara was looking past him, down into the far corner. 'What's that?' she said, grabbing the torch from me. She shone it over what appeared to be a bundle of rags.

'What's wrong?' I said, unable to make out anything in the gloom.

Gerry spun round to face what Tara had seen and then spun back, shining the torch directly into my face, momentarily dazzling me. I put up my hand to shield my eyes as he moved down and into the basement, directing the beam this time into the far corner.

Tara shrank back towards the stairs. 'What is it?' she whispered.

'Looks like some rags, a bundle of clothes,' I said. 'Is there a problem, Gerry?'

He made no reply, but moved down closer and stared at the heap in front of him. He didn't seem to be too badly hurt, which was more than you could say for the person lying in a twisted heap in front of him, the features only just visible by the dim, wavering light of the torch.

'What's going on?' I said. 'Has something happened?'

Gerry whirled round to look at me with a strange expression on his face, as though he wasn't really seeing me. 'I'll have to call the police,' he stuttered. 'I didn't want you to see this.'

'What is it?' called Tara from her position of safety beside the stairs, but she made no move towards us.

'Looks like someone has had an accident,' I said quickly, with no idea about what had really happened.

'Do you know him?' Tara said, now inching her way forward to join us. I craned my neck to get a better look.

At last Gerry seemed to remember we were still there and he faced us, though it was hard to read his expression. 'Know him, of course I know him.'

As Gerry swung the torch round again to illuminate the person lying in front of us I also realised who it was. Whatever he was doing here, there was no doubt it was Ewan Flisch and he wasn't just hurt - he was dead.

SEVEN

For a moment no one spoke, and then we all started at once.

'We need to get the police now,' I said, as Gerry muttered, 'This is very odd,' and Tara cried, 'We can't leave the poor man here.'

We all turned, bumping in to one another as we rushed for the stairs. No one spoke until we were back up in the hallway, though Gerry muttered under his breath from time to time.

We waited in the office as Gerry made his call to the police station and all the while my mind was working overtime. Why had Gerry not wanted us to go down into that part of the basement? Was it really because he thought it would be too dangerous? He offered coffee, but somehow I didn't feel in the mood.

'But why would he be there? What could have happened to him? Tara voiced my thoughts.

'He must have slipped and banged his head, got concussed badly.' Gerry seemed to be lost in a world of his own. 'There was no reason for him to be in the basement. It must have been an accident.'

The police car arrived within minutes and much to my relief, Gerry elected to take them down to see the body. After that there was a whirl of activity as one of the doctors who act as police surgeons arrived, much surprised at this turn of events. 'It's not often this happens,' he said looking at us, as though we had some information we weren't revealing. Perhaps he recognised me from a previous occasion and I sat with my head bowed, trying to keep a low profile.

We waited in the office in an uncomfortable silence: there didn't seem to be anything to say. The minutes dragged on, each one seeming like an hour, but at last one of the officers came to take our statements.

The constable who interviewed us was young and fresh- faced, eager to do a thorough job, no doubt. 'Are you one of the people who found the body?' he said, producing his notebook.

'Yes.' I stood up, though I wasn't sure why.

'You are?'

'Alison Cameron.'

'And you live on Bute? I don't recognise you.'

'No,' I shook my head and explained in as few words as possible why I was on the island and how I had come to be down in the disused basement.

'But I don't understand why you had to explore the basement,' he said. 'I thought you were doing a history of the place. Who would be interested in the basement?' It seemed everyone on the island had heard about my commission.

Exactly what Gerry had thought, I was about to say, then realised how ridiculous that would sound. 'I was trying to be thorough,' I said. 'Trying to get a feel for the whole place. I'd no idea someone could have had an accident down there.' I shuddered at the memory of Ewan's body, crumpled into the corner at the foot of the stairs.

'We'll have to interview each of you separately later but for the moment I have to advise you not to leave the island without letting us know.' He snapped his notebook shut as one of the other policemen came into the room.

This one, older and greyer and obviously much more experienced, whispered something in the younger policeman's ear, making him turn bright red.

He turned to speak to us again. 'I'm afraid the news isn't good,' he said. 'Please make sure we can reach you easily. We'll have to interview you all again.'

47

What was going on? From the mutterings and the looks in our direction, I could only guess that whatever had happened to Ewan Flisch, it had been no accident.

Gerry said nothing, but stared at the floor, avoiding my gaze.

The policeman wasn't the only one with questions.

EIGHT

I was so looking forward to seeing Susie again. Phone calls (brief) and e-mails (intermittent) weren't the same as a face to face gossip. What's more, she'd agreed to stay for several days with me on Bute before heading back to the mainland. But for now, having duly informed the police I'd be off the island for a while, I had to meet her at Glasgow airport.

I'd rushed up the motorway, taking a few chances in overtaking other drivers who appeared less pressed for time than I was, determined not to be late. All for nothing, of course, because the flight was delayed, though fortunately not for long. And all the way to the airport, my thoughts kept drifting back to Ewan Flisch. No matter which way I looked at it, the episode was very strange. Did Gerry really think the basement would be of no interest to us, or was there another reason? I thought about what Ewan had said, how he and Gerry didn't agree about the project. Was that anything to do with what was happening? Surely Gerry wouldn't have been so desperate for the job he would have been involved in Ewan's death?

No matter, it was now in the hands of the police and the C.I.D. had come over from the mainland to investigate the circumstances. We'd hear soon enough. I only hoped it had been an accident. There was no denying it had been very dark in that basement and there'd been no sign of a torch with Ewan's body. But until the police had completed their work, any explanation was possible.

I tried to dismiss these gloomy thoughts and once inside the terminal, appraised of the delay to Susie's flight, wandered round the busy airport shops, marvelling at the variety on offer. Did they actually

49

make a profit? I wondered, watching the queues at the tills. Perhaps long delayed flights persuaded people to pass the time buying stuff they didn't need. There were a couple of harassed businessmen wandering round, easily identified by their smart suits and laptop bags, probably seeking inspiration for last minute gifts.

Susie's flight from Los Angeles had been delayed and I hoped she hadn't missed the London connection. With a sense of eager anticipation I hurried to wait among a pressing throng of relatives and friends at the arrivals gate, hoping she'd be here.

The first passengers came sauntering up the ramp towards the exit; many optimistically dressed for a summer in Scotland in shorts and T shirts, although a few of the more aware at least sported a coat or a jumper over their arm.

There was no sign of Susie among the crush of arrivals. Surely she hadn't missed the plane? Knowing how scatty she could be, it wouldn't have surprised me at all.

'Hellooo,' a voice beside me said and there she was - a completely unrecognisable Susie.

'Good gracious, Susie, is it you?'

'Why, who else would it be,' she grinned, hugging me and casually bumping me with a very heavy in-flight bag as she tried to control a trolley crammed with luggage.

I took a step back and held her at arm's length. 'I don't think I'd have recognised you.'

'Oh, come on, Alison. Of course you would.'

But she had changed. For one thing her dark hair was now blonde, straight instead of curly and she had shed a lot of weight. This svelte person in front of me bore little resemblance to the bouncy, plump Susie I had known, though she still sported the long dangly earrings she favoured and a gaudily patterned top in a brilliant shade of pink.

'Quite a surprise, then?' She gave a twirl, now almost knocking over the man behind her with her heavy bag. He moved away quickly, muttering to himself, but Susie appeared not to notice. 'You can see how life out in California agrees with me.'

'I can't dispute that,' I said and together we began to push the trolley towards the exit.

'I'd have hired a bigger car had I known you were bringing the entire contents of your wardrobe,' I said, thinking about the lack of space at the cottage.

She gave me a grin. 'Let's not exaggerate, Alison.'

We made our way slowly to the car park, pausing every now and again to rearrange some item of luggage that threatened to slide off.

'So,' she said as we settled in the car, our seats pushed forward to the limit to accommodate the various pieces of luggage that couldn't be fitted into the boot, 'How are things? What have you been up to Alison?'

I was about to say, 'Nothing at all - I've been too busy trying to sort out this writing project,' when she wagged her finger. 'Don't say nothing. I can tell from your e-mails, brief though they've been, that there's something going on.'

'Yes, there are a few things I want to discuss with you, but I think they'd better wait till we get to the cottage. It's all too complicated.'

'Why am I not surprised,' she sighed, leaning back and bumping her head on the large trunk that was squashed sideways on the back seat.

'Anyway, how about you?' I said brightly, to change the subject. 'What's your news?'

She leaned forward again. 'You'll never guess?'

'Honestly, Susie, there's no way I can make a guess at anything at the moment, but especially what might be happening to you.' There was a glint in her eye that filled me with apprehension. What had she been up to? Every time I looked at her I was astounded by her changed appearance.

'I was going to wait till we were nicely settled with a glass of wine, but I can't bear not to tell you.' She almost bounced up and down in her seat. This was more like the old Susie I remembered.

Better she tell me now. A glass of wine so early in the day, with all the tasks still sitting on my list, might not be a good idea.

There was a note of triumph in her voice as she said, 'Dwayne and I are getting married.'

This surprising announcement caused me to swerve violently and almost let go of the steering wheel, narrowly avoiding veering into the next lane. 'What?' I squeaked, sliding back into my own lane to a loud blast from the horn of the man in the BMW I'd narrowly missed.

'Careful, Alison,' she cautioned, pointing to another car very close in front.

I regained my composure and control of the steering wheel while struggling to remember - who was Dwayne? There had been Bret (a Texan rancher) and Alvin (something in the New York stock exchange) but for the life of me I couldn't remember her ever having mentioned anyone called Dwayne.

'Perhaps we should wait until we get back for the rest of the details,' I said. I'd had quite enough shocks from Susie for the moment.

She ignored this request. 'Yes, but the best part is he's coming over to join me here in Scotland. Just for a short time after he's finished his business in London. But at least you'll be able to meet him.'

'What is it he does?' Nothing Susie now told me would surprise me.

'He's in IT,' said Susie proudly. 'He's really great. He has some contacts in London he wants to catch up with and a conference he wants to attend.'

I said no more than, 'That sounds interesting,' but Susie was in now in full flow and there was no stopping her. No matter how many times I tried to change the subject of the conversation she always managed to steer it back to Dwayne.

'...and I'm sure you'll love him,' she concluded excitedly. 'You'll have plenty of opportunities to meet him, that's for sure.'

We made the four o'clock ferry with only a few moments to spare. Luckily I'd had the foresight to purchase a good supply of tickets which saved a dash to the portacabin that serves as a ticket office at Weymss Bay.

Susie was so delighted to be on her way to Bute again she insisted on going out on to the deck to take full advantage of the journey across the Firth of Clyde, but I stayed indoors in the passenger lounge, nursing a cup of coffee.

She professed herself 'enchanted' to be back on the island, marvelled at the crowded marina, exclaimed at the views on the way to Ascog and even let out a little screech of excitement as we took the road down past Mount Stuart House to our first view of the sweep of Kilchattan Bay.

Apart from the odd murmur of agreement I said little until we at last reached the cottage. I prepared myself for a long evening. What kind of a wedding was Susie planning? Surely it would be a quiet affair? Did she expect me to be a bridesmaid? My only hope was that she'd organise it all with little help from me.

Time was running out and my six weeks on the island devoted entirely to the work essential to the research for this book on the Pavilion wasn't anything like as straightforward as I'd assumed.

NINE

It didn't take long to settle Susie in the little cottage, her many possessions taking up most of the space available, spilling out of her room, cramming the tiny cupboard on the upstairs landing, covering every inch of spare space in the living room. The only room not suffering from a surfeit of Susie's possessions was the kitchen, but I had a feeling that wouldn't last long.

'What on earth are you living on?' she said, peering into the tiny fridge, opening cupboard after cupboard in the kitchen.

'I buy what I need, when I need it,' I said defensively. 'Or I eat out.'

She shook her head. 'I realise there isn't much space, Alison, but we need more than this. All this snacking makes you put on weight.'

I ignored this last remark. If Susie wanted to organise food, that was fine by me, but my preference was to go out to eat as often as possible. Over the next few weeks, cooking would not be high on my agenda. Like all converts, Susie now appeared keen to have me adopt her eating regime, whatever that might be.

As there was nothing in the house that met with Susie's approval to make dinner we agreed to have an early bar meal in the Kingarth Hotel at the far end of the village and walked there, chatting amicably.

'Good choice,' said Susie, gazing round her at the comfortable bar area.

I lifted my glass of red wine. 'Here's to friendship,' I said.

We clinked glasses and went back to studying the menu.

'So,' I said, taking a large gulp of wine, 'how exactly did you meet Dwayne?'

55

As the story progressed I became more and more muddled by the number of people who seemed to have played a part in her romance. More than once I had to stop her in full flow, ask her to repeat something.

'..and that's how I met Dwayne,' she ended, after a long account which seemed to involve several very weird people, a performing dog and a wild pool party at the home of some minor Hollywood star.

'Will you go back to live in the States?' I'd been under the impression Susie was considering coming home for good, but it would appear not.

She shrugged. 'More than likely. Dwayne is coming over to join me soon. He's never been in Scotland before though, like so many Americans, he does have some Scottish ancestry. It'll be a good opportunity to show him round, see if he likes it and maybe find out a little about where his family originally lived.'

'Where did they come from?'

Susie waved her fork in the air. 'Somewhere in Scotland - that's all I know.'

'And what about his job? Do you think he'll find employment here?' I said, thinking of the many people currently out of work.

'Of course not!' she replied in a tone that suggested I'd been suggesting Dwayne might have a future as something quite outrageous, like a trapeze artist. 'He's working with a big IT company at the moment, because he likes a challenge, but he's also a man of independent means, made his money on one of the early dot.com businesses and sold out just in time. He's very clever,' she added, pre-empting any further questions.

'Mmm,' I replied. I'd been here before with Susie: the man who was the love of her life who suddenly disappeared from the scene, to leave her broken hearted.

Before she could raise the subject I said, 'It's going to be very difficult to squeeze him into the tiny cottage here. He might have to find other accommodation.'

She laughed. 'I'm going over to meet him in Glasgow. We'll stay there for a few days, before I bring him over to Bute. And don't worry - we'll book into one of the local hotels.'

I didn't try to persuade her otherwise and we walked back to the cottage in a mellow mood thanks to several glasses of wine, chattering away, catching up on all that had happened since we last met.

That night I slept so soundly I only woke when the alarm rang for the second time. I'd almost forgotten about the dead body in the Pavilion, but not quite. And there were to be more, very unexpected, developments awaiting me.

TEN

The discovery of Ewan Flisch's body had brought the renovation work at the Pavilion to an abrupt halt. No one was allowed in, the blue and white tape clearly marking the area of no entry and when I caught up with Tara next day it was at the Ettrick Bay tearoom.

She was late, very late. I thought perhaps I'd mistaken where we'd agreed to meet and was about to call her when she came rushing in, breathless and dishevelled, banging the door loudly behind her.

I'd left Susie checking her e-mails, with a plan to sort out the kitchen and organise some proper food for us. 'I think I'm still suffering from jet lag,' she said. 'I woke in the middle of the night and couldn't get back to sleep. I expect by four o'clock I'll be ready for a nap.' Thankfully Susie appeared happy to amuse herself at the moment, given my concerns about lack of progress.

In spite of Susie's best efforts, or perhaps because of them, there was little in the way of breakfast goodies in the house, a justification for the full Scottish breakfast I was enjoying when Tara arrived.

'Slow down,' I said as she pulled up a chair, started a garbled apology. 'There's no rush. We have plenty of time. Remember we can't go back to the Pavilion just yet. It may be a few more days before they allow us in.'

'Thank goodness,' she said, sitting down heavily on the seat opposite me. My eyes were drawn in spite of myself to her hair: today the colour was more purple than pink and whether it was my imagination or the light, it seemed to have a tinge of green at the ends. 'I had to go over to the mainland last night and only made the last ferry back from Weymss Bay by the skin of my teeth.'

58

'Well, have something to drink and get yourself together. Then we can talk about what we do for the next few days until we can finish our work at the Pavilion.'

She looked grateful for this suggestion and ordered hot milk, at the last minute adding a large roll with scrambled egg.

'What will the builders do?' she asked as we waited for her order to be made up.

I shrugged. 'They have no option - they have to do the same as the rest of us and wait till the police have finished. Anyway, a few days delay will be of help to us, because it will give you more time to get the photos you need.'

'And we have to set up the rest of these interviews,' she reminded me.

I pulled out my list of names. 'There seem to be quite a number, I'm pleased to say. We should be able to get plenty of material from them.'

Tara frowned. 'There won't be many people alive who remember the opening of the Pavilion, will there?'

'A few, but they would be children at the time so I suppose what they remember will be based on what they heard from parents or grandparents so we'll have to check everything very thoroughly. That will take a fair bit of time.'

'I'm up for that,' she said. 'Something to get my teeth into.' Her eyes sparkled as she spoke. There was one thing about Tara: you couldn't fault her enthusiasm. I counted myself lucky to have her to help me: though occasional niggles of doubt still surfaced from time to time, I'd decided to ignore them. There was so much to do I'd had no time to check out her credentials. Anyway, for the moment her work was more than satisfactory. I'd find out more about her whenever I could spare the time.

We finished up, paid and left the tearoom as one of the many tour buses that visit the island drew up, disgorging an excited and motley crowd of people who made straight for the tearoom without pausing for a moment to admire the view over the bay.

I heard one of them say to her companion, 'What about a walk along the sands before we go in?' but this suggestion was ignored and she meekly followed the others inside. The walk would come later, no doubt, as long as the weather held.

'Where's your car?' I said to Tara, looking round.

'I don't have a car,' she said, as though this was the most obvious thing in the world.

'So how did you get out here?'

'I came on the bus,' she said. 'I usually cycle everywhere on Bute. It's so easy.'

'Well, you'd better come with me,' I said. 'Let's head up to the library and we can start by checking back copies of *The Buteman*. There's sure to be plenty of material there.'

There was almost no traffic on the road between Ettrick Bay and the library in Moat Street in Rothesay, though we did stop off for a few moments at the Post Office in the Port where I bought a birthday card to send to Maura.

'Does you daughter like London?' Tara said as I came out. 'I lived there for a while.'

'We don't see her as often as we would wish,' I replied. 'Though she did say she would try to come up to Bute this summer so that we could catch up. Her partner has a new contract in the Middle East and she's trying to make up her mind whether she should go out there.'

'Difficult,' agreed Tara and we set off again for the library.

As we passed the Pavilion, I noticed a car parked across two of the spaces.

'Let's stop for a minute. That's not a police car,' I said. 'Perhaps they've finished and we can go back in. You can wait here if you like.'

'No way,' said Tara unbuckling her seat belt. 'I'm as curious as you are.'

Together we walked up to the entrance. With little hope I pushed hard at the door. To my surprise it was unlocked and swung open easily.

'Hello,' I called as we crossed the foyer into the hallway.

There was no reply so I called again, louder this time. The blue and white tape still marked the entry to the basement, but otherwise all signs of a police presence had disappeared. 'That's strange, there doesn't appear to be anyone here. Let's check upstairs.'

As we made towards the stairway, the door to the office opened and out came Rufus Beale. 'Can I help you?' He sounded angry.

I was aware of a sharp intake of breath and of Tara shrinking back behind me. 'See you outside,' she said, turning and rushing out through the main door.

Rufus seemed not to notice this sudden departure or if he did he gave no sign.

'I was wondering what was happening, if the police were finished,' I said politely, perplexed by Tara's reaction, wondering what had made her leave so hurriedly.

Rufus shrugged. 'They're not here at the moment, but Gerry will be coming in later this afternoon. He'll be able to help you, update you.'

'Thanks,' I said and turned on my heel, anxious not to prolong the conversation, aware of him staring after me as I left and rejoined Tara who was sitting on the wall outside, staring out over the bay.

'What was all that about?' I said. 'Why did you leave so abruptly?'

For a moment I thought she wasn't going to reply, but then she turned to me, her face pinched and white. 'I recognise that man,' she replied. She was trembling. 'I don't know what on earth he's doing here.'

ELEVEN

In spite of all my coaxing Tara refused to tell me what was wrong, what had upset her. 'It's nothing, it's nothing. Probably of no consequence,' she kept saying and eventually I gave up realising that, at least for the moment, she was unwilling to tell me what was so distressing about Rufus Beale.

Other worries were concerning me: not least the slow pace of our research. Everything was taking much longer than expected and it would seem until we heard from the police, or from Gerry, the Pavilion was out of bounds.

We drove to the library in silence, each of us occupied with our own thoughts and eventually found a parking space outside the Bute museum. Time was when it was possible to abandon the car anywhere on Bute, but now, as with everywhere else, the island has come into the twenty-first century and parking spaces are at a premium.

As we entered the library I said, 'Gosh, this isn't how I remember the place at all.'

'It's been refurbished recently,' Tara said, 'and most people think it's been a vast improvement.' She was smiling, the encounter with Rufus apparently forgotten.

I nodded, gazing round at the banks of shining new computers, the carefully carpeted floor, the redecorated children's section alive with colour, the main desk with its up to date equipment.

'Notice anything about the bookshelves?' said Tara

'Mmm.' I was non-committal, knowing she was keen to tell me.

'They're all on wheels so they can be moved back for a conference or such like.'

'Now that could be useful,' I said, thinking about the launch of our book.

One of the librarians came over, someone I recognised her from my previous visits. 'Good to see you again,' she said. 'How can we help this time?' So she did remember me from my attempts to find out about the house up at Ettrick Bay my friend Susie had inherited.

'Could we have a look at the copies of *The Buteman* …from about 1938 on?'

She called over to one of the other librarians and directed us to a table where a microfiche reader was located. 'Some of the editions we still have in paper format,' she said. 'Would you like those as well?'

'Good idea.' There was nothing like the original version, useful though the microfiches were.

We divided the tasks between us. We started looking for any references to the Pavilion, going back to the 1930s when the project to build it was first suggested. Thank goodness *The Buteman* archive stretched back to the last century.

Tara was happy with my suggestion that she cover the microfiches while I went for the 'real' papers. 'Anything in particular you want to concentrate on?' she asked.

'I suggest we pick out what we can from the early 1930s until the Pavilion was completed. No, perhaps go as far as the opening ceremony and then we'll compare notes.'

'Seems fine by me,' said Tara and she deftly slotted in the microfiche to begin her search.

The distractions of old adverts, interesting stories about island life and photos of important (and not so important) events made it difficult to focus on the work in hand. I had to keep reminding myself we were here for a purpose and interesting though these articles were, they weren't relevant.

So absorbed was I, jotting down everything that could possibly be of use, it was a few moments before I noticed Tara had stopped and was sitting staring at the screen in complete silence.

'Everything okay?' I put my pencil down and leaned over to look at her screen, find out what had disturbed her.

She turned to me, an expression on her face that was hard to read. 'Yes, yes,' she said, 'it's just that I've seen something here.'

I stood up and went round behind her to get a better view. For a moment it appeared she intended to cover it up, or move on. But she didn't. On the screen there was an old photo captioned with a list of some of the men who had been involved in the building of the Pavilion.

'Look at this row of people in the photo,' she said and pointed with a shaking hand.

I scanned the faces quickly. There, right in the front row, was someone who looked remarkably like Rufus Beale.

'That's impossible,' I said. 'It can't be Rufus Beale.' But the closer I looked the more convinced I became that it had to be him: the same broad face, the same high forehead, even the same beard.

'Of course it's impossible,' said Tara, looking round at me, her eyes bright with fear.

'Not unless he's almost a hundred,' I said, trying to make light of it, 'and I'm sure he's not that age.'

I leaned in and peered more closely at the photo, but as it was a rather grainy effort it was difficult to make out the detail. There was certainly an 'R. Beale' listed among the group of workmen, but there was no further information about the individuals in the photo in the accompanying article.

'Those beards make them all look alike,' I said, dismissing her worry. Then, 'Why are you so concerned?'

She shrugged. 'It's nothing really.' She refused to say any more, scrolling down the page quickly.

One of the librarians came over, someone I didn't know, though I'd heard her being called Lisanne. 'Have you found what you wanted?'

'I think we're making progress.'

She looked over my shoulder at the photo only just visible on the screen. 'Mmm,' she said. 'A story or two there.'

This was intriguing. 'What do you mean?'

She shook her head. 'Best to say as little as possible.' And she strode off.

I glanced over at Tara. 'Are you okay?'

She seemed calmer and said, 'Let's go on with this. I'm making a fuss about nothing.'

We worked in silence for a couple of hours, only pausing now and then to check what the other was doing, include or eliminate items of interest.

I found it hard to concentrate. There was something about Rufus Beale, something both Tara and the librarian knew, but refused to tell me.

Ah well, it was probably only a bit of island gossip. Nothing of any consequence for the task in hand.

Or so I thought at the time.

TWELVE

Simon phoned that evening to report on the progress of his business trip around Europe, one of his regular updates. This particular expedition was proving tiring and perhaps the recruitment wasn't as good as he had hoped.

'How are you enjoying the high life?' I asked. Wrong question, as I soon discovered.

'High life? It's really hard work, meeting all these people, trying to engage them, get them to sign up for our courses.' He sounded cross.

'But is it being productive?'

'I guess so, but I'm beginning to long for the rain of a Scottish summer. It's so hot here in Rome at the moment.'

'I wish I'd that problem,' I said, looking out of the window at the rain which had started earlier in the day and was now running down in rivulets, obscuring the view of the bay in a fine mist. The cottage had no central heating and the fire I'd set in the small grate made little impression on the dampness. 'Where are you off to next?'

'Not quite sure. We had a series of meetings set up in Greece but they may have to be cancelled. There's no money for extras there at the moment, given the state of the economy. I'll keep in touch.'

As we signed off, Susie came bouncing into the room.

'That was Simon,' I said before she could ask.

'Missing you, is he?'

'I think he's finding it all much harder work than he thought when he signed up for this six week trip round Europe.'

67

She laughed as she sat down with a thump in the chair opposite me. 'Have you time for a chat about the wedding?'

'I guess so,' I replied, looking over at the pile of notes sitting on the little table which had been moved back to the window in the hope it would make me more productive. 'Though I should make a start on these tonight.'

Susie ignored this comment and moved to the sofa. 'What we need first is a glass of wine.'

'Don't you get up,' I said, 'you look far too comfortable there,' but the sarcasm was lost on her. I went into the kitchen to fetch a couple of glasses of wine.

When I returned a few minutes later, carefully balancing two large glasses of wine and a dish of crisps, she was sitting surrounded by brochures and pamphlets.

'Where did all of this come from?' I said in some astonishment, carefully positioning the glasses so as not to spill the crisps.

'Oh, I have a bag I carry all these bits of information in,' she said, pointing to a large tote bag beside her.

I sat down with a sigh and had a sip of wine. It looked as if it would be a long night ahead, but Susie's excitement was catching.

'First things first,' I said. 'Have you set a date?'

Her eyes took on a faraway look. 'I thought a winter wedding would be good. And Dwayne is as taken as I am with the romantic idea of having it in a Scottish castle. I can just picture it, with all the snow gently falling as we make our way there for the ceremony.'

I didn't want to disillusion her at this early stage, but that sounded a very bad idea to me, very bad indeed. My vision wasn't a romantic one of a wedding in the snow, but more of guests being trapped in a horrendous whiteout or worse still unable to make it to the venue, thwarted by road closures or worse.

'Which castle are you thinking of?' Scotland has no shortage of castles.

She looked at me as though this was a very strange question. 'Why, Rothesay castle of course. What could be better, more appropriate?' She lifted one of the pamphlets from the pile and skimmed through it before beginning to read, "Rothesay Castle is special among the castles of Scotland, not only for its early date, but also for its design. It has had a long association with the Stewarts – after 1371 they became the royal dynasty. In the 19th century the ruined castle was restored to the present state by the Marquesses of Bute and it now provides an excellent venue for all kinds of social occasions." That sounds good.'

'You've obviously being doing lots of historical research,' I said, partly because I couldn't think of anything more encouraging to add. Now I had visions of guests struggling to cope on the ferry, rocking about in winter gales or, even worse, stranded at Weymss Bay, unable to reach the island.

'Dwayne's relatives can stay on the island for a while, get to know the place.'

How would Dwayne's friends and relatives cope with December in Scotland as compared to the balminess of December in Los Angeles where even winter is kind? I dismissed these worries: it was Susie's wedding and it was my task as a friend to support her. 'I'll help you as much as I can, Susie.'

She beamed at me. 'I knew I could count on you.'

As she pulled out yet more leaflets to engage me further, there was a loud pounding at the door.

I jumped up, startled, dropping the pamphlets I'd been scrutinizing. 'Who on earth is that?'

'There's only one way to find out,' said Susie, not unreasonably. 'Open the door.'

There on the doorstep, totally bedraggled, as though she had been out in the rain for a long time, stood Tara.

'Come in, come in,' I said, taking her arm and pulling her in out of the relentless rain. 'What brings you over here in this weather?'

She almost fell in as a gust of wind blew the rain across the front of the house. 'I had to see you, Alison and it's something that couldn't wait until morning.'

'Then it must be very urgent indeed, 'I replied, guiding her to a seat.

She stopped abruptly as she saw Susie sitting there. The expression on Susie's face almost made me burst out laughing.

'I'm sorry, I didn't realise you had a visitor,' said Tara. 'Perhaps I shouldn't have come.' She half turned as though to leave.

'Don't be silly,' was my response and I introduced them. 'Susie is my oldest friend and you can say anything in front of her.'

Susie nodded, as curious as I was about what Tara might have to say that couldn't wait till morning. 'Sit down and I'll fetch you a glass of wine,' she said. Then she hesitated. 'Unless you're driving?'

'I don't drive, I came on my bike.'

'Of course you did,' I said, going in to the kitchen to look for another glass. However as the cottage was really only designed and equipped for two people at the most, Tara had to make do with a tumbler. If she thought this odd, she gave no sign.

'Now, what's all this about?' I asked as soon as she was settled, steaming gently by the fire.

She stared into her glass. 'I'm not sure I can go on with this project,' she said.

This was bad news, very bad news indeed. 'What's wrong?' Then I had an idea. 'It's something to do with Rufus Beale, isn't it?'

She chewed at a ragged nail. 'The company Rufus owns is a new one.'

'Newquixal Renovations? I thought it was a long established family business?'

'Yes, but that's not the name of the original company. I'm sure it was something completely different.'

She took a gulp of her wine and said, choking back a sob, 'I don't want to let you down, but it's very difficult for me.'

This would never do. Unless Tara had a really good reason, I didn't want to lose her from the project.

'You don't need to see him, Tara. You don't need to have anything to do with him. Besides what can be so bad you would have to give up this job?'

'I suppose you're right.'

'I'll help if I can, but you need to tell me what the problem is.'

Out of the corner of my eye I caught Susie sitting open mouthed at this exchange.

Tara seemed not to notice. 'I want to tell you, but not yet.'

'Well, all I can suggest is that you carry on as usual and we'll make sure you don't encounter Rufus. If you don't continue, the project will fall apart. You're good at what you do and besides, it's too late to find someone else now.'

This appeal to her better nature seemed to get results. 'Okay,' she said reluctantly. 'I'll go on and see what happens.'

'That's fine. Don't worry.' I couldn't keep the relief out of my voice. I still had no idea what was troubling her so much. Perhaps when I had the chance to speak to her on my own, she would tell me. She didn't want to say too much in front of Susie, in spite of my assurances.

'I'd best be getting back.'

'I could run you to the flat and you could collect your bike tomorrow.' I held up my glass. 'I've scarcely touched my wine.'

She shook her head. 'Thanks, Alison, but I'll be fine. I'm used to being out in all weathers.'

Susie made an effort to defuse the situation. 'I'm going to be married on the island,' she said. She whipped a photo of Dwayne out of her handbag. 'He's an American.'

Tara appeared to be preoccupied as she took the photo, scarcely glancing at it before saying, 'He's very handsome.'

Susie examined the photo as Tara handed it back. 'Yes, I do miss him.'

Tara stood up. 'Sorry to have bothered you.'

'It's no bother. I only wish I could be of more help.'

I went with her to the front door while Susie went back into the kitchen to fetch the bottle of wine. I'd have to be careful: Susie might be on holiday, but I was still working.

The rain had finally cleared to a sunset of purple and pink streaked skies over Kilchattan Bay, the wet street shimmering in the last of the light. There was the promise of a fine day ahead. A few dog walkers strolled along the sands, taking advantage of the sudden improvement in the weather.

As Tara said goodbye, I said, 'I'll go to the Pavilion first thing in the morning and should be finished by lunchtime. I'll meet up with you in the afternoon and we can review progress.'

'Sounds good,' she said. Then in a burst of enthusiasm, 'I'm so pleased to be working with you, Alison.'

I stood at the door, watching her cycle off towards the end of the village. There was something strange going on and, in spite of Tara's reluctance to tell me, I was determined out find out what it was.

THIRTEEN

Whatever Tara's difficulty, until she was prepared to tell me about it there was no way to help her. I couldn't imagine why she was so upset about Rufus. Certainly I had my own worries about him, but as nothing untoward had happened since that time I'd seen him on the shore at Kilchattan Bay, I'd put it all down to my overactive imagination. Trouble was, how would I go about finding out what was at the root of the problem?

Meanwhile we had to move on with the work on the history of the Pavilion. At the moment I was even further behind with my schedule.

To date our research had revealed that, during the war, Bute (and Rothesay in particular) was a key part of the strategy to defeat the Germans. In spite of the grimness of rationing, blackouts and other deprivations, entertainment continued on the island. The Pavilion boasted one of the best dance floors in the West of Scotland and the stage, with several dressing rooms and special lighting, was ideal for concerts and plays. The venue provided an escape from the worries of the war and many of the Polish, Canadian, English and troops of other nationalities posted to Bute became keen Scottish Country dancers.

There was certainly plenty of material - the problem would be deciding what was relevant. As the history of the Pavilion was so enmeshed with that of the rest of the island we had a difficult task ahead. So the problem about Rufus would have to be low down my list of priorities at the moment.

We'd been interviewed several times about the death of Ewan Flisch. The police were remaining tight-lipped, merely saying 'enquiries were continuing,' but there were plenty of rumours on the island about what had happened and the consensus seemed to be that it was no accident.

Susie was intrigued and bombarded me with questions, but there was little of any substance to tell her. Finally she said, shaking her head, 'I don't understand it, Alison. Nothing you do is simple.'

I had to agree with her.

The Pavilion was a hive of activity when I arrived next morning. Workmen scurried to and fro, calling out to each other, their cheerful banter quite at odds with the terrible event that had happened there so recently. One of the cleaners was walking around in a desultory fashion, clutching a duster, though the usefulness of this in the present circumstances was hard to determine.

The building was in the process of being stripped out, back to its original state, while the overlays of years of additions and so-called improvements, most of which had been either needless or useless, were gradually being dismantled.

Soon we'd be able to see what lay underneath the years of make do and mend. As this might be my last chance for access for a while, I had to make sure nothing was missed, ferret out all the little pieces of information that would enliven the story.

I wanted to speak to Gerry, but according to the cleaner, who seemed to be a mine of information, 'He talks of nothing except the death of Ewan Flisch. He's shut himself in the office, won't answer any requests. I've no idea what I'm supposed to be doing.'

When I did manage to make my way in to see him, I soon discovered the cleaner was right. Ewan's death was all Gerry wanted to talk about. He looked haggard, drawn, as though the death of Ewan Flisch was his responsibility. 'Why would he be down there on his own,' he repeated. 'I can't understand it. None of it makes any sense.' Then defensively, 'It was nothing to do with me. I'd no idea he was there.'

While I could understand that the death of a close colleague would affect him, even if they didn't see eye to eye, his reaction puzzled me. It seemed he protested a bit too much, seemed too ready to profess astonishment that Ewan had ventured into the basement.

Meanwhile I still had a job to do, though any trips to the basement would be off limits for some time and not only because of the police investigation.

Later that afternoon I picked Tara up from the flat where she lived in Rothesay, up a little back street off the High Street. This was one of the old parts of the town, a mix of the original town house of the Stuarts, Victorian tenements and more modern flat-fronted, grey flats. Tara lived in one of the tenements, a stiff climb up a steep winding stair to the top floor where she shared a flat, so I contented myself with using my mobile to let her know I was parked across the street.

She came tearing out of the close, banging the main door behind her, shrugging herself into a voluminous black cardigan as she approached the car. 'I'd have been quite happy to cycle over,' she said, 'it wouldn't...'

'I know, I know.' I interrupted her. 'But having the car will make it easier for us to travel round the island together.'

Although we had agreed to divide out the tasks in the master plan (as Tara called it) we had drawn up previously, there were a number of interviews scheduled in for the morning and for some of them it might be better if we went together. Consistency of approach was essential. At least that's how I sold it to Tara. I didn't want to tell her the truth: I wasn't quite sure how she would do with the interviews and I

76

wanted to reassure myself that she understood the importance of getting it right first time. It would be essential to get all the details correct. There would be plenty of people on the island with long memories, able to pick up on any errors we made. Minimising those was critical.

'The first place we're going is...?' She slid into the passenger seat and pulled a pack of chewing gum from her large bag. 'Like some?'

I declined, frowning as I did so and she hastily put it back.

'A stop for a cup of decent coffee,' I said, as I recollected with a shudder the 'own brand' coffee Susie had purchased with a pile of groceries the day before. You would have thought that after all that time in America she would have appreciated decent coffee but apparently not. '...and some herbal tea for you,' I added, in case she thought I had forgotten her preferences.

'Good idea. I didn't have time to eat.'

Half an hour later, caffeined up (at least I was) and ready to tackle anything, we headed out along the shore Road from Rothesay towards Montford. We had the name of a contact there, someone who remembered, or claimed to remember, the Pavilion during the last war. It was likely some of his stories had been passed on by his parents, so there might be more than a little embroidery here, some disentangling of fact from fiction required. Well, that was one of the things we had to sort out in writing this history - deciding what was true and what was anecdote.

We found the location easily. I'd allowed plenty of time, but we arrived with a good fifteen minutes to spare and sat in the car and chatted. Tara was relaxed, happy and it seemed a good opportunity to probe a little, find out more about her background.

'What made you apply for this job?' I asked her, trying to keep my tone casual.

'Mmm.' She looked away from me, out across the water to watch the ferry make its way towards the harbour. 'I wanted to come back, to stay on the island.'

'So you were away for a while?'

'Yes.'

This conversation wasn't being nearly as productive as I'd hoped. 'It's not an ideal place for a young person like you. Surely there would be more opportunities on the mainland, in one of the cities.'

She turned to face me. Her expression was closed, almost as if she was daring me to ask any more questions. 'It was important to get this job. I really wanted to do it. That's all there was to it.' She laughed, but it was a forced laugh then she said, 'How are we doing for time? Should we go to our first appointment?'

I looked at the car clock. She was right, but that wasn't the reason she wanted us to move, of that I was certain. I switched on the engine and we drove the short distance to Montford. And I was still no wiser about Tara and what she was up to.

FOURTEEN

Bertie Fogle greeted us with old-fashioned courtesy when he eventually shuffled to the door of his large semi-detached house on the main road, facing the sea.

'I'm so pleased to meet you,' he said, peering short-sightedly at one of the business cards I'd bought for such an event as this. 'Come in, come in.'

This was, as we soon realised, easier said than done. The hallway was crammed full of large pieces of solid wooden furniture: an old fashioned hat stand, laden with coats, a mahogany dresser, two large tables, every surface covered with newspapers, letters, boxes and various objects of indeterminate origin. There was only a small passageway to allow us to go through in single file as we followed him, edging in sideways to avoid disturbing anything.

'I keep meaning to clear this out,' he apologised, 'but I never seem to have the time.'

As Bertie must have been at least ninety, I had this feeling any clearing out would have to be done by his relatives after he was gone.

He ushered us into a generously proportioned living room with a huge picture window commanding a magnificent view of the sea. At least it would have been large had there been any space. A bulky telescope stood pointing out over the sea, a common feature of houses on the island as I'd already discovered. True there was a great choice of places to sit, two gigantic sofas and an assortment of chairs including a comfortable looking recliner, all punctuated by solid wood coffee tables, almost one to each seat. Everything was overshadowed by giant ferns in massive stone pots, reminiscent of those which adorned the stairways of the Pavilion.

The room had all the hallmarks of an old fashioned hotel, but I couldn't imagine anyone actually staying here as all the surfaces and most of the seating was covered by books, yellowing newspapers crinkling at the edges and ancient magazines in shaky piles. I resisted the temptation to poke one of them to see if it would actually tip over. In spite of the warmth of the day, a coal fire blazed in the large hearth on the far wall.

Though I tried to disguise the look on my face, I wasn't too successful, because he said hurriedly, lifting a heap of magazines from a couple of the chairs and depositing them on the floor, 'Sorry about this. Do have a seat. I'm in the middle of cataloguing all this stuff, you know. It's quite a task.'

Again this seemed to be an aspiration rather than a likelihood, but after looking round, Tara sat gingerly on the edge of one of the chairs only to leap up with a scream as a large ginger cat that had obviously been snoozing amid the comfort of the pile of papers, suddenly let out a meow of protest at being sat on.

'Sorry, sorry,' muttered Mr Fogle again, 'I try to keep them out of here, but they seem to like it and find their way in no matter what I do.'

How many cats were there, I wondered looking round, before sitting carefully down on a large red leather armchair that had seen better days judging by the little bits of stuffing poking out of it. At least it had the merit of being free from all obstructions.

We had prepared a list of questions, to make sure we asked everyone we interviewed with some consistency, though we had agreed that a little deviation would be fine to allow for personal contributions.

Unfortunately Mr Fogle wasn't in on this plan: he had other ideas. He had a story to tell, but he wanted to tell it his way, no matter how many attempts we made to keep him on track.

'I do remember the Pavilion; I was young then of course...' and he was off on a journey of reminiscences, not all of them relevant.

Several times either Tara or I tried to interrupt the flow, look quickly at our question sheets and ask what we had agreed, but all to no avail. Mr Fogle kept returning to his version of events.

I began to feel exhausted and slightly nauseous, overcome by the stuffiness of the room. If every interview was going to be like this one, we wouldn't have nearly enough time to carry them all out, never mind make sense of them.

Then, as my concentration began to slip yet again and I was wondering if it might be a good idea to cut this session short, he said something that made my ears prick up. '...and of course there was that episode in the 1940s. Terrible that. On a small island there has to be trust and it was awful the way it happened.'

Tara had also perked up at this statement: she was leaning forward eagerly, anxious to hear what Mr Fogle was now saying.

'So there was some kind of problem? That would be the time when there were a lot of soldiers and sailors from overseas on the island?'

Bert Fogle frowned at me. 'Yes, yes. But perhaps I'm speaking out of turn.'

'Then...?'

'I think you should be careful with what you're doing. It could all end in tears.' He wagged his finger at me. 'It's not as simple as you think. There were lots of bad things happened. Including all that trouble with one of the building firms.'

'Such as...?' But this was the wrong thing to say. He looked at me warily. 'It's all in the past now.'

81

He went on before I had the opportunity to ask any more questions. 'So take care.'

This sounded decidedly like a warning... but a warning about what?

FIFTEEN

When I arrived back at the cottage, Susie opened the door before I'd taken my key from my bag. Her eyes were shining and she was almost hopping up and down like a child with excitement as she greeted me. 'Guess what, Alison?'

'I couldn't possibly,' I said, my mind still full of what had happened at Mr Fogle's house and his dark hints of sinister events.

In spite of a lot of prompting (and I do mean a lot), he refused to add anything else, after that first burst of information. 'I'm saying no more about it,' he growled. 'There are people still alive on the island who remember it all,' he added darkly, 'and I don't want to upset anyone. People here have long memories.' He bent to stroke yet another of the cats that had come into the room, meowing loudly. 'Bess and the others need to be fed,' he said as he lifted his head again to look at us, with an expression that said, 'I'm telling you no more.'

There was nothing else to be done but to thank him and leave, but we did so with a feeling of dissatisfaction. Were all the interviews to be like this?

So I wasn't exactly in tune with Susie's enthusiasm, disappointed about what had started out as a promising lead.

'Susie,' I said, 'I'm tired and I've absolutely no idea why you are so excited. I couldn't begin to hazard a guess.'

'It's Dwayne, of course,' she said, deflated by my response. 'What else could it be? I've had an e-mail from him and he's coming straight from his conference in London. He's booked his flight.'

'Did you know he was going to do this?' I was bewildered by this sudden turn of events. Susie had

83

said Dwayne was coming over to Bute, but somehow I hadn't expected him quite so soon.

'You might sound a bit happier for me,' she pouted. 'This will be your chance to find out what a great guy he is. I'm really glad you'll get to meet him at last.'

I sat down on the chair by the window, trying to recollect exactly what Susie had said originally. 'Wasn't the plan that you would meet him on the mainland, go travelling for a bit?' Then before I could stop myself I added, 'Where will he stay?' as the immediate practicalities struck me.

Susie looked at me with some surprise. 'Why, with me of course. Where else would he stay?'

Oh dear, another person to be crammed into this tiny cottage didn't sound like a good idea at all.

'He won't be any trouble,' she said, 'he's such a laid back Californian, he's so easy to please. He'll adapt to anything. And it will only be for a few days, then we'll head off for a proper break. He wants to see as much of Scotland as possible on this trip.' She patted me on the arm.

Yes, but will I, I thought and then aloud I said, 'We'll have to see how it all works out.' I was trying not to sound too ungracious but the thought of another person, delightful as Susie assured me he would be, crammed into this tiny space, did not fill me with any pleasure. How would I get any work done?

'Anyway,' said Susie blithely moving on as though I hadn't spoken, 'as I said, we won't be here long. We'll be doing a fair bit of travelling. Dwayne wants to get a real feel for the country and we'll take in as much of Scotland as we can. His father was in Scotland during the last war or something like that and he says he's heard so much about the country.' As usual, Susie was vague. I guessed there wasn't really much of a plan. If they came for a 'couple of days' as Susie suggested, would they end up staying for a lot longer? I'd heard of people on the island who had come for a short break and never returned to the mainland.

'That sounds a good plan,' I said, 'only staying here for a couple of days. I'm sure Dwayne will love to see as much as possible of the country while he's here.' I tried to be positive. With any luck they'd spend very little time with me and of course I'd be pleased to meet the man who had stolen my best friend's heart. 'I'm sure we'll manage fine, even if it is a squash.'

She looked at me strangely and then she burst out laughing. 'No, no, I don't mean we'll be staying here, Alison. I thought I'd told you we'd book into a hotel.' She smiled. 'You've done well to put up with me for so long.'

I hoped the wave of relief didn't show on my face.

'And,' she went on, 'I want you to get to know him well - after all, he is going to be my husband.'

'Have you now decided what you'll do after you're married?'

'Yes, we'll live in Los Angeles though we'll probably keep a place in Scotland. You would love it there, Alison, it's all so relaxed. And of course there's the sunshine. Once you've experienced that it's very difficult to come back to this unpredictable climate. I have to go back to Strathelder High for a bit of course, do the whole resignation thing properly, give them some notice.''

'I guess California is great,' I said weakly, 'but I don't see Simon and I going out there to live.'

'But you will come and visit - lots?'

'Of course,' I replied, 'I wouldn't neglect my friend.'

'How about I fix us something to eat?' Susie had regained her good humour. 'If we have an early meal

85

we can walk part of the West Island Way before having a glass of wine at the hotel.'

I thought of the work planned for that evening, writing up my notes from our interviews, but then I sighed. That could wait till tomorrow. 'Sounds a good idea,' I said, suddenly realising how hungry I was. I'd had no more than a couple of cups of coffee since breakfast and I was regretting skipping lunch.

Susie disappeared into the kitchen and I picked up the daily newspaper she'd left on the table, but after I'd read the same story several times, laid it aside as my mind wandered. There was so much still to do and I was becoming less and less convinced about being able to do justice to this history of the Pavilion. Perhaps what I needed was a spell off the island? I'd have to return to Glasgow soon. Yes, that was the answer. A few days on the mainland would put everything into perspective.

SIXTEEN

At last everything was sorted out. In his most recent phone call Dwayne had apparently said, 'Of course I'll be happy to stay in a hotel.' I was beginning to warm more and more to this fiancé of Susie, though I had this sneaking suspicion his decision might be as much to do with what Susie had told him about the basic accommodation at the cottage as his desire not to inconvenience me.

Susie and Dwayne had booked into the local hotel at Kilchattan Bay for a couple of days, then they planned to set off on their travels round Scotland.

'He's so looking forward to this holiday. He's heard all about the great walks, the forest trails and the beaches.'

I hoped Susie had warned him about the summer midgies. These tiny insects had felled many a traveller.

Yet I didn't quite have the feeling of relief anticipated when these arrangements were all agreed. My intention had been to have these six weeks on the island, free from all distractions, interviewing, sorting out all the information I'd gathered. To date I'd managed several interviews (at least one of them somewhat dubious), a couple of very disjointed trips to the Pavilion, several revisions of the plan for gathering material and I hadn't even managed to come up with a catchy title, let alone a satisfactory first chapter. I had four weeks left and a feeling of mild panic was beginning to bubble up. When you factored in that business about Ewan Flisch, everything seemed to be spiralling out of control.

I had managed to find time to send off for Tara's original application, but with no hopes it would take me any further forward. Did it matter why she had wanted this job, if she was able to carry it out satisfactorily?

There was no more word on Ewan and I began to relax a little. Surely the rumours were no more than that - rumours - and we'd have word soon his death had been no more than a tragic accident. We'd seen how gloomy that basement was and no matter why he'd been ventured down, the key to the mystery was probably that there was no sign of a torch beside his body. I put the whole episode to the back of my mind.

I'd have to be very firm with myself and ensure minimum disruption to what was left of the schedule. The bright spot in the horizon was that Tara gave every appearance of being more than capable and I could count on her to keep working hard during my short trip to Glasgow.

'I'll manage fine, Alison,' she said. 'Six weeks is a long time to be completely out of touch. I understand.'

'You seem to have managed to clear the decks for the six weeks,' I replied gloomily.

She laughed. 'I'm younger than you and have more stamina. Besides I don't have all the commitments you have. And I live on the island.'

Grateful for her willingness to step in, I ignored these comments and any lingering doubts. 'I'll give you good warning of when exactly I intend to go.'

'I'll pick Dwayne up at the airport,' said Susie on the Wednesday morning he was due in, 'and we'll go straight to the hotel. Perhaps we could arrange to meet up for dinner?'

'Good idea.' Then tentatively, 'Would you like me to cook?'

Much to my relief she waved my offer aside. 'Wouldn't dream of it, it's far too much work for you.' Then she rather spoiled it all by adding, 'Dwayne really likes his food and he's used to a very high standard.'

I could have made a witty remark, but decided not to. Better leave that sort of reply unsaid.

Once Susie had departed for the airport to collect Dwayne from the London flight, the cottage seemed unusually quiet and sad, like a deflated balloon. I'd certainly miss her company.

Then I gave myself a shake. I might miss her cheeriness, her constant chatter, but on the other hand this would give me much more time to get on with the commission for the Pavilion. The interviews we'd managed so far weren't nearly robust enough to make any inroads into the 'personal recollections' section we hoped would be the best bit about the history.

It wasn't that we were slacking, but unfortunately many of the interviews we had conducted had very little substance when we analysed the data. And a number of them had more than a hint of libel in the reminiscences, something we could well do without.

However, after an afternoon glued to my laptop, scarcely stopping for a cup of tea, it all began to look a lot more hopeful. While not all the material was useful, there was enough to give us outlines for a couple of the chapters.

I finished typing up the stories Mr Fogle had told us and sat back, looking at the screen. What had he meant by that story about something connected with the Pavilion happening in the 'forties? In spite of all our prompting, he had refused to say any more. In fact, the way he had tried to distract us gave me the distinct impression he was regretting saying anything.

I closed down the laptop with a sigh. Yes, I had the basis of my section on personal reminiscences, but on re-reading they didn't exactly strike me as riveting. Tara and I would need to come up with a few stories more entertaining than these.

I looked at my watch. Six o'clock! I was supposed to meet Susie and Dwayne at the Kingarth Hotel for dinner at seven. I'd have to move quickly.

After putting the living room to rights in a very perfunctory way, I ran upstairs to change. Not that I was particularly intent on dressing up for this evening out, but at the moment I was in a pair of decidedly old jeans and a shirt inherited from Deborah when she left. Best to make a good impression on Susie's friend if possible.

Did I have time to walk along to the Kingarth, or should I take the car? That was another thing. When I came to Bute to work I'd high hopes of plenty of time for long leisurely walks along the beach and up through the many woodland glades, lots of exercise and fresh air. Unfortunately it wasn't working out like that at all: I was spending most of my time hunched over the computer or drinking cups of very milky coffee in various locations. With the result the waistband of my trousers was beginning to feel decidedly tight. Well, tonight wasn't going to be the night to begin any exercise programme, but if I walked briskly I could just about make it in time. Anyway, I'd never known Susie be on time for anything.

My guess at a twenty minute walk to the hotel turned out to be a wild underestimate and I finally reached the Kingarth ten minutes late. I rushed in through the bar to discover that for once Susie had arrived punctually and was sitting over in the corner of the restaurant with a man who had his back to me.

'Sorry I'm late,' I said, flopping down awkwardly on the chair beside her.

The man got to his feet. He was tall, very tall and very broad, wearing a highly patterned shirt in clashing shades of blue and purple and pale cream chinos. His hair had evidently once been blond, but was now silver, cut very short. He had a striking face, dominated by a large nose, a very broad forehead and a sharp chin, yet the overall impression was one of a handsome man.

A huge smile creased his sun-tanned face as he reached out to shake my hand. His grasp was firm, very firm. So firm it made me wince. 'Sorry,' he said. 'I guess I don't know my own strength.' His blue eyes twinkled at me as though he wasn't at all sorry, but I remained polite, though this didn't make a good first impression on me.

Susie laughed. 'Dwayne still plays basketball. He's very fit.'

Dwayne grinned again as he sat down. 'It's all strictly amateur now of course, but I was one hell of a player in my day.'

That I could well believe but looking at him, all brawn and muscle, I somehow didn't see him as Susie's type. But then, what did I know? Perhaps being out in LA had changed her more than I imagined.

Pleasantries exchanged, we settled down to the serious business of selecting what we would eat from the menu.

Susie patiently explained some of the Scottish dishes to Dwayne but in spite of her earlier comments about his culinary preferences, I was beginning to get the feeling Dwayne would have been happy to settle for a triple cheeseburger with fries. 'Cullen Skink? It's a kind of soup? And you really eat haggis? I was sure that was just a tale.'

As the waitress waited patiently, pencil poised ready above her pad to take our order as soon as we could make a selection, I heard the door open and was aware of someone coming in. I glanced up. It was Rufus Beale. He gazed round for a moment and then walked straight over to our table and stood glaring at us.

I recoiled. What on earth was wrong? Had he deliberately sought us out?

He stood there, swaying slightly as we gazed at him, waiting for him to speak. He leaned over, sending wafts of whisky fumes towards me, then growled, 'What's going on? What old stories are you digging up about what happened at the Pavilion?'

SEVENTEEN

My mouth fell open in astonishment. 'What do you mean?' My mind raced through everything we'd done so far, all our interviews, but couldn't come up with anything that would cause Rufus to behave like this, except that he was drunk.

'I've heard about your investigations. It's all past history, all untrue.'

Dwayne interrupted. 'Now hang on just a minute, sir. Why are you talking like this to Alison?'

Rufus swung round to face Dwayne.' What's it to do with you?' He sounded increasingly aggressive. 'What do you know about it all? Are you involved too?'

Dwayne stood up, towering over the other man as he drew himself up to his full height of over six feet. 'I think you must be making a mistake, my friend. I've never been here before. This is my very first time on the island. My very first time in Scotland, in fact.'

Rufus suddenly backed off, pulling at his beard anxiously. For a moment he looked completely confused. After a moment's silence he said, 'I shouldn't have come.'

'Too darn right,' said Dwayne, but he sounded perfectly calm.

By now Susie had decided she should rush to the defence of her husband to be.

'And who might you be?' she asked also rising to her feet, though at just over five feet she didn't look nearly as impressive as Dwayne. But what she lacked in height she made up for in fierceness.

It was impossible to sit there any longer watching this stand off. All I could think of was to act as normal as possible, ignore this rudeness.

'This is Rufus Beale,' I said, 'he's the owner of the firm commissioned to do the first stage of re-furbishing the Pavilion.'

Dwayne looked at me uncomprehendingly. 'What's that? What's it all about?'

I explained briefly, while Rufus stood silently by, his eyes still fixed on Dwayne. When I'd finished he said, with very little grace considering the upset he had caused, 'I don't want the past to be raked up. I have people on the island who keep me informed about what you're doing. Just remember that.' There was a pause while we all stood there, waiting for someone to make the first move.

'I'm dealing with a history of the people who worked and performed at the Pavilion,' I said, with as much dignity as I could muster. 'I don't know what there is to get upset about.'

'Well, I guess there's no harm done. It could happen to anyone,' said Dwayne, sitting down again, not giving Rufus the opportunity to speak again. 'Would you like to join us folks here for a bite to eat? We haven't ordered yet.'

Rufus looked astonished at this turn of events and for a moment I thought he was about to say yes. There was no way I wanted to spend an entire evening in the company of this dour man.

But he shook his head and said, 'I'm meeting someone here for a drink. I've already eaten.' By the looks of things he'd had enough to drink already. All the aggression seemed to have gone out of him and he stood there, head bowed as he said this.

I turned my attention back to the menu to disguise my rapidly beating heart as he sloped off, like a beaten dog with its tail between its legs. Even so, every time I looked over at the bar, he was watching us, looking away as he caught my glance. And there was no sign of

94

whoever it was he claimed to be meeting. He sat at the far end of the long bar, nursing his pint, ignoring all attempts at conversation.

What on earth did he mean? And what did he think I'd found out that would reflect badly on him? I couldn't think of anything that might make him act like this, but someone had been keeping him informed.

In the end it turned out to be a pleasant evening in spite of this interruption and Dwayne was good company, though Susie behaved like a love-struck teenager, gazing into his eyes and hanging on every word. However, the presence of Rufus in the room, knowing he was there watching us, made me uneasy.

By the time we had reached dessert and coffee (for me) but not for Dwayne ('I only drink decaffeinated and only during the day') I had almost forgotten about Rufus. When I remembered and turned to look at the bar, he was gone. I gazed around the room in case he had merely moved somewhere else, but no, there was no sign of him. That was a relief, even if a temporary one, because I'd have to face him next day at the meeting scheduled at the Pavilion.

We paid the bill and walked out into the gloaming, that half light, half dark of a summer's evening, with the full moon rising over the bay, casting a long shimmering path of light on the water.

Dwayne stopped at the edge of the sands and looked about. 'Gee, this is awesome,' he said. 'In California one minute it's light and the next it's completely dark. We don't get this slow descent into night.' He seemed mesmerised by this phenomenon.

'It is spectacular, especially on a night like this,' agreed Susie as she took his arm. I looked at them, so seemingly happy together. How I hoped this was the beginning of a new chapter in my friend's life, after all the false starts she'd had since the break up of her marriage many years before.

I began to walk ahead, leaving them to the romance of the evening. 'I'll see you back at the cottage for a nightcap,' I called as they headed down on to the beach to stroll back across the sands.

Susie turned and waved to me. 'We won't wait long. This is a late night in Californian terms.'

I waved back. I remembered Susie telling me that about California - how everyone went to bed much earlier than we did in Britain, but then they also rose earlier too.

I began to walk briskly home. Lovely as the evening might be, there was that slight chill in the air as night approached and I hadn't thought to bring a jacket.

In the cottage, I put a match to the fire in the living room and sat down in front of the coals, watching the light flickering back and forth. I was tired, but not yet sleepy and considered making a hot drink, but couldn't face anything more after the meal we'd had.

Now that I had time to relax on my own, to think about what had happened during the evening, it all seemed very strange. Why would Rufus accost me like that in a public place? Unless of course he wanted Dwayne and Susie to hear what was said. That was nonsense: he didn't know either of them. And what did he mean 'someone had told him', was keeping him informed about what was happening?

I had this terrible sinking feeling there was something here that needed explanation. What was worse, I'd concerns that in spite of my initial delight at my good fortune in securing this opportunity to write the history of the Pavilion, there a lot more bubbling under the surface than I could possibly guess.

EIGHTEEN

The next morning Susie and Dwayne decided to set off for their extended trip round Scotland, earlier than first planned. When Susie told me in detail about their itinerary my only comment was, 'That sounds very ambitious.'

'We've bought one of those 'Butterscotch' ferry tickets,' said Dwayne. 'They seem to be good value for money.'

Susie laughed. 'You mean 'Hopscotch' tickets to let us go from island to island.'

He grinned and kissed her on top of her head. 'Of course, honey. It's going to take me some time to get used to this language of yours.'

'We've packed up almost everything,' said Susie. 'When we come back we'll stay in the Four Winds hotel in Rothesay. They've given us a really good deal.'

'I feel a bit mean that I've not been better company, had the time to show you round the island,' I said, but Susie was quick to reply, 'Don't even think about it. We'll be fine and we can have the guided tour of Bute when we come back and you're well on with your project.'

That might be rather optimistic, I thought, but said, 'I hope you'll have a lovely time.'

'Sure will,' said Dwayne. He grinned in that slow way of his. It was easy to see why Susie found him so attractive.

I helped them load up the car, though Dwayne insisted on carrying anything heavy. 'Can't have you gals straining yourselves,' he said. Just as well, as Susie seemed to have brought with her the entire contents of her wardrobe ...and more. The few items she had taken for their short stay at the hotel had given Dwayne a very false impression of the vast amount of luggage she'd brought over from America.

They piled everything into the boot and put the remainder on the back seat, before climbing in. Once again I was struck by the difference in height between them. Next to Dwayne, Susie looked like a little doll. Perhaps that was also part of his attraction.

I waved them off and stood looking out over the bay where the early morning mist was fast disappearing. Another fine day in prospect and it seemed that this spell of good weather was set to continue for a few days, if the most recent weather forecast was to be believed. I was delighted that Dwayne would see the islands of Scotland at their best rather than through a fine summer drizzle, which was the more usual occurrence.

I turned to go indoors: if I hurried through typing up my notes from the previous day there would be time for a long walk along the shore, an opportunity for some fresh air and badly needed exercise.

Not for the first time, I wished Simon was with me. On all the previous occasions when I'd been here on Bute, I'd very much valued his advice, his solid presence. But no matter. I'd have to cope until he had finished his trip in foreign parts and could come over to join me.

As I closed the front door I glimpsed a figure over by the little sailing club hut. He was standing perfectly still, gazing towards the house, but when he realised he'd been spotted, he turned away hurriedly. It was Rufus. What on earth was he doing here? Had he been watching us, watching Dwayne and Susie? I'd gone over everything we'd done so far, but failed to come up with a reason for his outburst last night. He'd known from the beginning I was writing the history of the

Pavilion. What had happened to cause him such concern?

I looked over again, but although he had moved a little way along the shore, Rufus was still there.

Or was I becoming paranoid? It was more than likely he was out for a stroll, enjoying this beautiful morning before setting off for work and had stopped to admire the view, though why he should be looking in my direction rather than out over the bay was a puzzle. Besides it was quite possible he was living here at Kilchattan Bay. That would certainly explain why I'd seen him so often.

Stop all this speculating, Alison, I told myself. There's sure to be a very simple explanation for everything.

I went into the living room to log on to the computer. In spite of my reassurances to myself and in spite of the amount of work still awaiting me, my mind kept drifting back to Rufus. He was such a strange character. I couldn't make any sense of his actions.

Fortunately as I was finishing up recording the last interview the doorbell rang and I opened it to find Tara standing there. 'Hi, Alison,' she said. 'I wondered how you were getting on. Do you fancy a bite to eat out at Ettrick Bay tearoom? We could combine a walk with a chat about the work. It's far too nice a day to be stuck indoors.' She was looking remarkably tidy in a pair of respectable jeans and a pale blue T-shirt, her hair tied up on top of her head instead of floating free as it usually did.

'I couldn't agree more,' I said. 'Let me change my shoes and I'll be with you.'

I ran up the few stairs to the bedroom and left Tara in the living room, idly flicking through the copy of *The Buteman* lying on the coffee table.

As I came downstairs she held the paper up to me. 'Have you seen this bit in the *Bygone Bute* column?' she said.

'I haven't had time this morning to read anything,' I replied. 'Is it something of interest to our project?' I was anxious not to miss anything that might help.

She frowned for a moment, twisting a strand of hair that had come loose round her finger as she went on studying the picture before replying, 'Could be. We'd be able to trace a copy quite easily. This photo shows some of the Canadians who were stationed on Bute. Looks as if it was taken just before they came here.'

'So you think it might be useful? We should be able to find out who owns the copyright of the photo. Any illustration will help pep up the text.'

Tara appeared not to hear me, but kept peering at the page, holding it this way and that. 'Have a proper look and let me know what you think.' She held the paper out to me. 'I'm not sure what the quality would be like, but we could enhance it if we have the original.'

The picture was rather faded and I scanned the faces of the Canadian soldiers posing happily for the camera. One of the men in the second row was vaguely familiar.

I passed the paper back to Tara saying, 'If we can find the original it might be worth seeing what you can do with it.'

What a foolish notion, thinking I recognised anyone here. In these old photos it was all too easy to imagine resemblances to people we knew. Look what had happened with the photo of the workers outside the Pavilion we'd spotted in the library.

Was that why I said nothing to Tara? Later I was to wonder why I didn't trust my judgment. But at the time I thought there was no point in saying the man in the photo bore a strong resemblance to Dwayne.

100

NINETEEN

At the Pavilion, the renovation project was now properly re-started; the builders were working hard to make up for lost time.

We were on our way back to the library before heading out to Ascog to conduct more interviews. On a whim I'd decided we should stop by the Pavilion to see what was happening, what progress had been made. That was the excuse: the real reason was to find out if there was any news about Ewan Flisch.

There were building materials everywhere. 'Maybe this wasn't a good idea,' said Tara. 'I don't think they'll let us in, do you?'

'We'll try.' We slowly pushed open the main door, expecting to be told to leave at any minute.

'You're not allowed in here.' One of the senior workmen, identified by his badge as Brian Jameson, came striding towards us.

'We only want to have a quick look. It won't take long,' I said. 'We need to see what's underneath all the years of neglect if our book is to give a full account of the place.'

He evidently didn't recognise me - or chose not to - and scrutinised the business card I handed over with some suspicion. He hesitated for a moment and that was enough for Tara. 'We won't disturb anyone, promise,' she said.

'You'll have to wear hard hats,' he said firmly. 'I don't want to risk any accidents here. There have been enough accidents already.'

Eager to take advantage of this evidence of a change of heart we nodded. 'Of course, of course.'

'I suppose it'll be okay,' he growled, 'but be very careful. On this kind of building site there's always lots

101

of stuff lying about. Keep to the designated path and don't stray off. We've already had one accident this week.'

'Another one,' I said in horror, imagining the worst.

He didn't pick up on this, but said, 'Fortunately no more than cuts and bruises, but it means we're one man down in the team for a few days while he recovers. Something we could well do without, given we're already behind schedule.'

'We'll be very careful,' I said, with every intention of making the most of this opportunity. Soon only the workmen would be allowed to come and go here.

'Come on, Tara,' I said walking ahead before Brian could change his mind. He stood looking after us as if he was already regretting his decision. 'Wait, wait,' he called.

I turned round. Surely he wasn't going to change his mind? To my relief all he said was 'Make sure you pick up a couple of hard hats from the pile at the bottom of the stairs.'

A series of broad wooden planks created a pathway through the main hallway and the stairs were shrouded in thick tarpaulins, making walking up them more than a bit hazardous. There might not be much to see after all.

We poked around in the little room off the main hallway where the floor was currently still intact, but the walls were shrouded in plastic sheeting. If we'd hoped this stage of the renovation would give us a good idea of what the Pavilion looked like in its heyday, we were to be sadly disappointed. For a start there was too much dust everywhere and most of the original fittings had been covered up or taken to storage, presumably to clean them properly before restoring them at a later date.

'Not much to see, is there?' said Tara, echoing my thoughts. 'It's all a bit like any other building site.'

'I'm afraid you're right. Even so, it might be well worthwhile taking a few photos of the building works. If they turn out not to be useful, there's no harm done.'

'That's fine,' said Tara, taking her camera from her capacious bag and beginning to click.

I held up my hand. 'Wait a minute, 'I said. 'Let's do this in a systematic way, follow the shape of the building. If we do the inside now, we can concentrate on the outside once they start on that.'

The logical place to begin would be at the very top of the building but at the moment there appeared to be workmen everywhere and Brian was nowhere in sight.

'I think we should begin in the main hall,' I said. 'There doesn't seem to be much sign of activity there - only one or two workmen. Then we can ask Brian about access to other parts of the building.' Not that I anticipated a positive response: he was more likely to ask us to leave.

The workmen had been busy in this part of the Pavilion. The old café/bar had been demolished, the roof partially stripped back. Tara took out her camera, but her attempts were half-hearted.

'Listen,' I said, stopping in the middle of the floor.

From below us came murmurs of voices, rising and falling, though it was impossible to hear what exactly was being said.

'What's down there?' said Tara, tapping her foot on the floor.

'That's another part of the basement, under the stage. They must be working on that. I guess it's where they kept the props in the old days. There might be something worth photographing.'

'Do you think we should go down there again,' Tara shuddered, 'after what happened?'

103

'No, this isn't the basement where we saw poor Ewan Flisch. According to the plans this has a separate entrance directly under the stage.'

Tara appeared only slightly reassured. 'As long as you don't want me to go near that other part,' she said, putting her camera back in her bag.

'Hello,' I called out as we made our way across the stage and down through the door at the side, my voice echoing in the empty hall. 'I expect they intend to strip out everything. They can do a lot with it as it's so accessible from the stage.'

I called out again, hearing the muttering of voices from downstairs, now sounding louder as we approached. 'Probably they're far too busy to pay attention,' I said. Overcome by my natural curiosity I added, 'Let's go down and see what's happening.'

Tara followed me slowly, increasingly lagging behind me.

'It's okay, honestly. We're nowhere near where Ewan Flisch was found.'

'It's still very spooky,' she whispered, grabbing my arm as she came up beside me.

The door at the far end of the stage led down a long flight of steps, illuminated by a series of temporary lights strung up across the wall. In the far corner, in the midst of several huge, broken wicker baskets, faded scenery with peeling paint, tattered costumes, their colours bleached by age, two workmen were on their knees in the dust. A large, moveable partition was propped up, leaning drunkenly against the far wall. Faded posters from long forgotten shows lay in heaps on the floor.

'Hi,' I said and one of the men sprang to his feet, a look of alarm on his face.

'What a fright you gave me,' he said, mopping his brow. He picked up the shovel he'd dropped on my approach.

'I did call out, but you seemed very busy. I hope we're not interrupting.' I was about to give the usual explanation about who we were and why we were here, but the look on his face stopped me in mid sentence.

'We need to fetch Gerry down here at once,' he said. 'This is terrible.'

The other man also stood up, his face equally grim. As he stood aside he revealed a series of wires and pipes. The partition wall they had pulled down to gain access lay in pieces on the floor and there was a large pile of earth to the side where they had been digging. Something could be seen in the bright light of the arc lamps rigged up in this part of the room, something sticking out of the ground. I moved forward to get a better view, ignoring the shout of, 'Don't go near there,' from the first man.

Surely it couldn't be what I thought? But it was. It was clearly only part of something much bigger, something that looked very much like part of a human skeleton.

TWENTY

There was a moment of complete silence, then everyone started to talk at once.

'It must be an animal of some kind,' said the taller of the workmen, lifting his safety helmet to scratch a head almost devoid of hair.

His companion shuffled his feet, shifting his weight from one foot to another. 'What is it? Surely it's not human?' Tara squeaked.

'Looks like it to me. I've buried enough corpses in my time...and uncovered enough skeletons,' the second workman said. He grinned as he saw the look on Tara's face. 'I worked for the Council for years as a gravedigger.'

The taller workman said nothing, but shook his head as he turned again to peer at the partially uncovered skeleton.

I stood well back, surveying this find with some horror. If this was a human skeleton, the original body must have been buried here a long time ago.

As though he could read my mind the second workman said, 'It was pretty well hidden,' and he pointed to the far corner, 'deep down. If we hadn't had to dig up this bit to get at the underground cables, we might never have found it. Must have taken some effort to bury it here.' He moved and bent down to get a better view, gingerly poking the object and shifting some of the dirt with the steel cap of his boot.

'Don't do that,' I said, lifting my hand to stop him.

But the taller workman wasn't to be deterred from his belief it was an animal of some kind, in spite of his companion's claimed expertise. 'It might be a dog that crawled in there and couldn't get out again, whose yelping couldn't be heard upstairs. Perhaps because of the music.' He seemed ready to continue to embroider on this theory but his companion was having none of it.

'Don't be daft, Malkie.' The second man looked scornful. 'When did you ever see a dog with hands?'

The taller workman wasn't to be deterred. 'It might be an ape, mind you, from one of the shows. They have hands.'

'Who would take the trouble to bury it? No, no, I'm telling you, Malkie, these are human bones.'

Danny moved forward again. 'We could move it out and see what it's really like. If there's much more of it, like. There's still a lot of earth around it.'

Stepping forward in front of him, I held up my hand and shouted, 'Stop! Don't touch anything. Leave it all as it is. It might be a crime scene.'

'A crime scene? Why would you think that? It's more likely to be one of the old props they used when they performed plays here. Look at all this stuff that's been left lying around.' It was hard to judge if Malkie was trying to convince us or convince himself. He seemed determined to prove these bones weren't human.

We'd delayed long enough. 'Best let Gerry know about this. The police will want to secure the area.'

Danny nodded. 'Aye, she's right. I've seen it on the telly. That's what they do, put that blue and white tape round the place and keep everyone out.'

'So you think it looks like a murder? It couldn't be someone came down here and was trapped?' The workmen had gone back to talking to each other, ignoring Tara and me.

'And who would be able to come down here and bury himself behind a partition wall? What else could it be but murder? It's not likely to have been an accident.' There was a certain ghoulish relish in Danny's voice as he spoke.

107

As neither gave any sign of summoning help, I said in my best school teacher voice, 'Come on, let's go now - all of us. We have to report this.'

If they were surprised at this command, they showed no sign of it. They trooped meekly behind Tara and me, casting the occasional glance backwards as we made our way upstairs to find Gerry.

Not only did it take some time to locate him, but making him understand what we had discovered was far from easy. He wasn't in his office, wasn't in the staffroom. Finally the cleaner, still flapping her duster about in the same ineffectual manner, called over to us, 'If you're looking for Gerry, he's out the back, trying to sort out some kind of office for himself while this place is being done.'

She might not be any great shakes as a cleaner, but she was great as a source of information. 'Thanks,' I said and the others followed me out, round to the grassy patch at the back of the building.

Gerry was apparently arguing with a couple of the workmen as all three stood looking at a small Portacabin perched somewhat precariously on the side of the hill.

'How can I possibly work there,' he was saying. 'There's no way you can get it level on this part of the site. You'll have to move it over to the other side.'

The workmen were equally determined. 'Our orders were to site it here,' said one of them, pointing to a sheet of paper in his hand.

'I don't care what your orders are,' Gerry shouted, 'there's no way I can carry out my job at a slant on the side of a hill.'

This was an argument that could run and run, but what I had to say couldn't wait. As I tapped him on the shoulder and he spun round, I was shocked by the change in his appearance. His face was the colour of

108

putty, his eyes red rimmed and bloodshot as though he hadn't slept in weeks.

'What's wrong? What's happened now?' There was a look of real fear in his eyes. What was he expecting? He couldn't know about the skeleton, surely?

I wasn't to be allowed tell the tale, however, as the workmen, Malkie and Danny, had come up behind me and were now anxious to have the limelight, talking loudly, one trying to outdo the other, one contradicting what the other said.

'I found it first, saw the wee bit bone poking out as we started to dig once we'd dismantled the old partition wall,' said Danny.

'No, you didn't,' said Malkie. 'I saw it first and asked you to help me pull it out. You were busy looking at those wooden truckles and wondering how we could get such big pieces of equipment out of the way.'

'Rubbish, Malkie. Of course I realised what it was. You thought it was the remains of a dog, for goodness sake.'

'Only because you pulled me away and I couldn't see properly till we got more of it uncovered.'

Gerry held up his hand. 'Look, this isn't making any sense.' He turned to me. 'Do you know what they're talking about, Alison?'

There was no easy way to say this. 'There appears to be a human skeleton in the basement, buried behind the partition wall where all the pipes and wires are concealed.'

Was I imagining things again or was his first look one of relief? 'How on earth could that be? Who would put a skeleton there?' Then he paused, as though thinking this strange event through. 'Wait a minute. That's where all those old props were kept. It'll be

109

something from the theatricals. Nothing to worry about.'

Malkie spoke. 'That's exactly what I said.'

'Nonsense, it's a real skeleton, I'm telling you.' Danny's face was red with anger.

'It's a matter for the police,' I said quickly before the row escalated. 'You should phone them at once, have it checked out.'

For a moment it appeared Gerry was going to refuse. He looked from one workman to another as though expecting a definitive answer.

'If you won't, I'll have to.' Not that I wanted to be involved in this.

This seemed to rouse him and he said, 'Okay, if it'll keep you happy. But I won't take the blame when they find out it's no more than a stage prop. You'll look really stupid then.'

'We'll look even more stupid if it does turn out to be the remains of a body.'

'But if the police become involved they'll seal up the whole place and the work will be held up even more - and it may all be for nothing. ' Ah, that was what was bothering him. A look of distress crossed his face and for a brief moment I felt a twinge of sympathy for him. The plans for the renovation of the Pavilion were turning out to be a lot more complicated than first appeared.

'That's as may be,' I replied. 'But unless you decide to ignore it, pretend it hasn't happened, there's nothing else you can do. They need to find out exactly what it is and how it came to be buried under the stage.'

As he hesitated again, I said, 'This is getting us nowhere,' pulling my mobile from my bag, but Gerry stopped me. 'All right, all right. I'll phone the police. It really is my responsibility.'

110

He gave a great sigh and we all trooped behind him to his office in the Pavilion. A few minutes later we could hear him speaking into the phone, his side of the conversation indicating the police were as incredulous about the event as we had been.

He came out of the office, sighing again. 'The police are on their way and they've asked us not to touch anything at all. We all have to stay here until they arrive.'

'I'll just nip out for a fag,' said Malkie. He was chalk white.

Gerry waved his hand in the general direction of the upstairs. 'This is another hold up. Goodness knows how long this will take to sort out. We can't afford that kind of slippage on the project. We're far enough behind as it is. And it will all be for nothing, let me tell you.' He scowled at me. 'It seems that every time you appear, something happens. I don't know how to account for that.'

Neither do I, I thought grimly. It might be best to cancel the interviews planned for the afternoon, explain to people why we were re-scheduling, without giving too much away.

Whoever this skeleton turned out to be, I had this awful feeling many of our plans were about to be disrupted yet again.

TWENTY-ONE

'What do we do now?' asked Tara as we left the Pavilion together. The police had arrived promptly, had questioned us all about finding the skeleton and had organised for the remains to be fully disinterred. It was over now to the pathologist or anthropologist for extensive forensic examination. We were free, at least temporarily, to get on with our work though they'd asked us very politely to stay in touch for 'more questions later.'

'We've cancelled all the interviews for this afternoon,' I said glumly. 'I suppose we could try phoning a couple of them to see if we could still go along to talk to them.' The initial police questions hadn't taken quite as long as anticipated, though the young constable said, 'You seem to have a knack for getting involved in this kind of thing, Mrs Cameron.' He said it with a smile, so I had to assume I wasn't being considered as a suspect.

Tara didn't look too happy at the suggestion of trying to call up our intended interviewees, but she, like me, hated to think of a wasted afternoon.

We sat on the little wall outside the Pavilion and she pulled up her list of names. 'I'll do these in order,' she said, punching the first number into her mobile phone. After five attempts at contacting people, she gave up. 'This is hopeless,' she said. 'Either there's no reply or they've made other arrangements. Do you really want me to go through the whole list?'

I shook my head. 'There's no point in doing that. We may as well call it a day, have some free time. What would you like to do?'

Tara sighed. 'Truth to tell, I could do with some time to help Meg clear up the flat and get in some shopping. Everything's been more than a bit neglected of late.'

'Off you go then,' I said, 'and I'll see you bright and early tomorrow. We'll meet at the first interview scheduled for nine thirty.'

Tara stood up quickly as though worried I'd change my mind. 'I'll be there in good time. I can go on with some of the research at home this afternoon.'

I watched her walk slowly towards the town. She had lost her usual ebullience but whatever was going on, she refused to tell me. An afternoon of working on her own might help her sort out her problems.

What was I to do? Without the slightest inclination to return to the cottage and to my computer, I was at a bit of a loss. Besides, it was an absolutely glorious day, the best day of the year so far. There was no more than the slightest breeze drifting in across the bay, enough to keep you comfortable but not to chill you and the sky was that peculiar shade of intense blue only found in northern countries. Down at the shore, some children had ventured into the water, splashing and paddling about, their shrieks of laughter drifting towards me.

This section of Rothesay was once known as Children's Corner and though the structure had long since been demolished as unsafe, it was good to see this part of the beach still had its attractions. I thought about Bute, how it had once been a firm favourite with tourists from Glasgow who thronged to the island on the many paddle steamers plying their trade up and down the west coast. In those days the promenade would have been thronged with holidaymakers, not the few mainly day-trippers seen from my vantage point at the Pavilion. Yet, on a day like today, with blue skies and bright sunlight, there was nowhere on earth better than this little corner of Scotland.

I'd have to make a move, do something to fill up the afternoon. After all, I was supposed to be working and even if the idea of being stuck indoors on such a glorious afternoon didn't appeal, there must be some way of progressing the project.

Of course! One of the places associated with the heyday of Bute was the Winter Gardens, now the tourist office. I could go along and chat to the staff there, view the various films and artefacts they had as reminders of the old days. My car was parked in one of the spaces outside the Pavilion and after a moment or two considering whether to take it the short distance, I decided to walk. The car would be stiflingly hot and besides, the exercise would do me good.

I set off along the shore road, stopping every now and then to lean over the recently painted bright blue railings on the promenade and look out over the water, enjoying the feel of the coolness on my face. Could this wonderful weather last for the remainder of my time here? I realised with a jolt that already over three weeks had passed, half way through my time on the island and my progress wasn't nearly as great as I'd intended. There was still so much to do, so many people to interview.

I looked back at the Pavilion, square set slightly back from the road, its balconies stripped of the usual flourish of blooms now that the work had started in earnest.

There was someone on the upper balcony. I strained my eyes to see who it was, trying to identify the figure by taking off my sunglasses. It looked very like Rufus Beale. Where had he come from? I was sure he hadn't been in the Pavilion when we were there.

As I watched, someone else emerged from the shadows. This was interesting. The balconies were supposed to be strictly out of bounds to everyone while

114

the work was taking place. They were far too dangerous, but it seemed someone had a good reason for taking a risk.

As the sunlight glinted on his glasses, I recognised Gerry as the other person. Rufus turned away, then lifted his arm as though to strike.

I waited for a moment, continuing to watch this scene being played out in front of me with a mounting feeling of horror. On the still air the voices carried down and although it was impossible to make out what they were saying, the tone of their voices indicated the argument was very serious indeed. Were my eyes deceiving me? Was the bright sunlight distorting my view? Gerry moved back into the shadows by the balcony doorway and Rufus moved after him. Whatever was going on between them, something was making them very unhappy indeed.

TWENTY-TWO

Tara and I had managed to arrange several meetings for the next day, some individually, some together, in a desperate effort to make best use of our time. I was now sure Tara was more than able to conduct interviews on her own: in spite of her odd appearance she had a real knack of getting the best out of people.

A hearty breakfast was essential: goodness knew when I'd have the chance to eat again. The schedule for the day was completely full. Without Susie, the store cupboard had gone back to its usual meagre rations. I'd have to try to fit in a trip to the Co-op in Rothesay - and soon.

The sunshine had penetrated even the gloom of the cottage and it was all too easy to linger, persuade myself another cup of coffee would be a good idea, but eventually there was no option but to make a move.

I gathered my papers, put them in my briefcase, applied a quick dab of lipstick, shrugged on my jacket and I was off. There might be the promise of another fine summer's day in the haze over Kilchattan Bay, but at this time of the morning there was a chill in the air.

I sped down the road towards Rothesay, reaching the town as the ferry disgorged another complement of holidaymakers on to the island - some in cars, some on cycles, but many on foot. Everyone was in good spirits. In spite of a few rainy days, the weather forecasters were predicting a record summer of sunshine and the optimism was catching. Whatever the story about this skeleton, it was nothing to do with me, though I had to admit a strong curiosity about how it had come to be in the Pavilion.

Tara was waiting at the foot of the stairs to her flat, chatting animatedly to the postman. She broke off when she saw me and came running over.

'Have you heard the news?' she said as she settled herself into the passenger seat.

'What news?'

'Gerry's been arrested on suspicion of murder.'

'So they've found out who the skeleton was? That was very quick.'

She stared at me. 'No. He's been taken in for questioning about the murder of Ewan Flisch.'

Of course. How could Gerry possibly have anything to do with this age old skeleton? He wouldn't even have been born at the time whoever it was had been killed. 'Gerry? Why would he murder Ewan Flisch?'

Tara shrugged. 'He did want the job for himself and they didn't get on.'

'Would you murder someone for that?' It didn't seem likely, but Tara didn't seem to find this reason surprising.

'Murder has been done over a sixpence,' she said primly, quoting some source.

Unwilling to be involved in this discussion, I replied, 'Well, we'll see.'

This morning she seemed to have made a big effort to look respectable and was wearing a denim skirt and an overlong T-shirt, though the casual summer effect was rather spoiled by the long boots, more suitable as winter wear, encasing her legs. She seemed as calm as ever and if I'd expected her to confide in me about whatever was troubling her, I was sadly disappointed. Perhaps there would be an opportunity to introduce the subject casually at some point in the day, but for the moment I couldn't think how to frame the question.

Instead I concentrated on the matter in hand. 'I thought we'd start off at that house out at Straad, the

117

one beside the hotel. Mrs Ferrin who lives there worked at the Pavilion in the 1940s. We should be able to get some information from her that would be useful.'

Tara frowned. 'Mmm...I suppose so. But we're not having much luck with the very early days, are we? And that's probably what's more interesting to people who will read the history, who'll want to know what was happening during the war.'

'That's as may be,' I replied, more tartly than intended, partly because I also had some concerns, 'But if you do the sums, anyone who was alive in 1938 and working there when the Pavilion opened would have to be in their nineties by now. We'll be lucky to find even one of that sort of age.'

Truth was, I knew Tara was right. This commission wasn't nearly as easy as I'd first thought. I'd imagined a relaxing summer on Bute, interviewing people with interesting anecdotes to tell, spending time in the library at the Moat Centre; leisurely searching through the records and back copies of *The Buteman* when the weather was inclement; passing the evenings typing up any notes before having a walk along the shore and the occasional meal in one of the local restaurants.

Or even better, supervising much of the research Tara would do. Unfortunately it wasn't working out that way and we seemed to be spending a lot of time going out together with me left to do all the summarising of our findings. There was something not quite right with this arrangement. She was enthusiastic, well able to conduct the interviews, but the problem was when we did them individually it took ages to discuss them, agree what we should put in and what we should leave out.

I'd have to take some action, come up with some solution, but for the moment we were going together to see Mrs Ferrin. And there was no doubt Tara was good company. She knew the island well, knew the people on it and was a source of a host of amusing stories about the place. She seemed to have a wealth of friends, each more eccentric than the other and I was well entertained on the journey out to Straad.

'… and that was why we all ended up at Kames Bay at midnight,' she concluded her latest story about an escapade with a boat belonging to the father of one of her friends.

'You're lucky you didn't get into serious trouble,' I said, then realised as she looked at me in astonishment, how fussy that sounded.

We had by now reached the little village of Straad, once a thriving community but now no more than a few houses, some old, some brand new, dotted along the road leading down to St Ninian's Bay. The village school had long since closed and the 'big house' was now a hotel, popular with visitors as it gave direct access to the beach. We parked on the little road outside one of the original houses where Mrs Ferrin lived.

As we got out the car I said, 'Let her talk, don't ask too many questions…and don't fill in.' This last because Tara had a tendency to chatter and if not held in check was likely to take up the whole conversation, thereby defeating the purpose of the exercise. One of the other reasons we were still going to some of the interviews together.

I rang the bell, but it made no sound, so I resorted to the large well-polished brass knocker in the shape of a hand that adorned the pale blue front door. The house was large, too large to be called a cottage in spite of the climbing roses of red and pink round the door and the mullioned windows. The black and white nameplate on the wall beside the door said Honey Cottage and I looked round nervously for any sign of bees, but there

119

was only one, busily engaged in sipping nectar from the row of hollyhocks in the border by the wooden gate.

I put my ear to the door and heard someone shuffling down the hallway. The door opened a fraction and a little white-haired lady peeped round.

'Hello,' I said, producing my identification card. 'I'm Alison Cameron and this is my assistant Tara McKenna. You said we could come to speak to you about the Pavilion? We're writing a history of the place.'

For a moment I thought she had forgotten who we were, had forgotten the appointment, but suddenly her face lost its pinched and tired look and lit up as she opened the door wide. 'Of course, of course. I've been expecting you. Do come in.'

The inside wasn't at all as I expected. She motioned us down the hallway surprisingly lightly decorated in cream and white, empty apart from a slim ash wood table with a large lamp and the telephone. She ushered us into a large airy sitting room made even lighter by the spare Scandinavian style furniture, overlooking a beautifully tended garden with a distant view of the sands of St Ninian's Bay and the ancient ruined chapel.

'Please sit down. Can I get you some tea? I have it all ready.'

How could we refuse, though we hadn't expected her to produce such a lavish spread. Small sandwiches, home made cake and biscuits came on the tray with a pot of tea and very beautifully patterned pink and pale green china.

I could see Tara was about to launch into her, 'I don't drink regular tea,' routine but a glance from me and she said, 'Only a small cup for me.' The last thing I wanted to do was to upset our hostess so early in the proceedings.

'Now,' said Mrs Ferrin, as she and I sipped our tea and Tara made a pretence of sipping hers, 'how can I help you?'

'We're trying to gather as much information as possible about the Pavilion,' I said and briefly explained the purpose of our visit.

'Oh, dear,' Mrs Ferrin replied. 'I'm not sure I can give you very much information. I didn't actually work there very long, you see. I only filled in for someone who was on holiday.'

Oh, no. Surely this wasn't going to be a wasted trip? I thought about the paucity of our notes so far. Already over three weeks into the project and we had scarcely enough to fill a chapter, never mind a whole book.

'Don't look so upset,' she chuckled. 'I might not be able to help much, but my cousin can.'

'Where does your cousin live?' I asked, wondering how quickly we could terminate this visit without seeming to be rude. If she had said her sister lived in Australia it wouldn't have surprised me one bit, given our recent run of luck.

Mrs Ferrin stood up. 'Oh, she lives here with me,' she said. 'I'll go and fetch her. She is my elder cousin so she takes some time to get ready in the mornings. But she's usually up by now.'

I could feel my confidence rising. This could be exactly what we wanted. Perhaps at long last we were about to have some solid information from someone who knew the Pavilion well. I certainly hoped so.

TWENTY-THREE

I could scarcely stop my mouth falling open in surprise when Mrs Ferrin's cousin shuffled into the room, leaning heavily on a cloisonné patterned walking stick.

'This is Lydia,' she said. I stood up to give me a moment or two to take in the strange apparition before me.

While Mrs Ferrin was a typical lady in her eighties, dressed in a pleated skirt and pale blue jumper, her older cousin was most certainly not. For one thing she was much taller, for another she was made up with rouge, eyeliner and bright red lipstick under a mass of frizzy black hair. Was it a wig, I wondered, or merely dyed? Whatever the answer, it was no wonder it took her so long to get dressed in the mornings. She was wearing a pair of tight fitting jeans and a sparkly top proclaiming 'I'm the One' but the one what I couldn't begin to imagine. All made even more bizarre by the fact she was wearing stout brogues and seemed to be very much in need of the walking stick.

She took my hand, exhibiting long, red painted nails. 'How are you?' she said in a low husky voice.

'Fine,' I replied, but it came out as a squeak. Out of the corner of my eye I could see Tara was struck dumb by this sight, almost unable to move. 'This is Tara,' I said, but though she moved forward to shake Lydia's hand she didn't utter a word. Here was someone more outlandishly dressed than she was.

Mrs Ferrin however, didn't seem to think there was anything unusual about this cousin of hers.

'Tea, Lydia?' she asked.

Lydia motioned the proffered cup away with a regal wave of her hand. 'You know I never drink tea at this time of the morning. Very bad for the complexion.'

She sat down in the chair by the window and took a pair of oversized spectacles from the case on one of the side tables.

I gazed at her wrinkled face, where the make-up had settled into tiny fissures, wondering unkindly how she thought not drinking tea would help. I tried to guess her age, thinking her about ninety but as though she read my thoughts she smirked. 'You wouldn't think I was ninety five, would you? I was the eldest of five and now they've all gone. The only relative I have left now is my dear cousin.' The way she said it made me think she planned to outlive her cousin if possible.

I made some kind of non-committal answer, finding it difficult to know what to say without being rude or lying.

Tara was less inhibited. 'Gosh,' she said. 'You're really ancient.'

The look on Lydia's face indicated her strong displeasure at this outburst and I tried desperately to cover up by jumping in to say, 'But you don't look anything like that age.'

This seemed to pacify her, at least for the moment. She appeared to be a woman who, in her time, had commanded a fair share of compliments and didn't expect them to stop no matter how old she was.

She sat back in her chair and began to tap her stick on the floor. 'So how do you think I could help you with this history of yours?'

I explained once again the purpose of our visit, why we were interviewing people who had some connection with the Pavilion, the book we hoped to publish in time for the unveiling of the renovated building.

She seemed to hesitate for a moment, then she leaned back and closed her eyes. Good heavens, I thought, surely she hasn't fallen asleep?

I was about to speak when Mrs Ferrin lifted her hand to stop me. 'She does this for dramatic effect,' she whispered, leaning over to whisper in my ear. 'She'll reply in a moment or two.'

Sure enough, after a short pause, Lydia opened her eyes and leaned forward. 'I don't know how I can help you,' she said. 'Indeed, I'm not at all sure I should help you.'

I tried to sneak a glance at my watch. I couldn't possibly leave here empty-handed and we had already spent over an hour sitting in this room, resulting in exactly nothing in my notebook.

So I said, 'Anything you feel you can tell me would be helpful. We're trying to collect all kinds of snippets of information, anything at all you remember about the place. It doesn't have to be racy.'

She raised an eyebrow at this last remark. 'You youngsters think that we lived very staid lives, but let me tell you there were some goings on, especially during the war.'

I tried to move her on a little, catch her mood. 'You must have had some good times there. You must know some really interesting stories and you'll be able to check your contribution before we publish.'

She continued to look at me as though weighing up what she should say, if anything.

I went on, 'Most of the local people on Bute are delighted about the re-furbishment and our book will be a permanent reminder of the Pavilion in the old days. What exactly did you do there?'

Then Tara spoke, her voice enlivened by enthusiasm. 'It's all important history, you know. We don't want it to be lost. That's why I've brought this,' lifting her recorder, 'so that we can make sure anything we write is one hundred per cent accurate.'

Lydia seemed to consider this for a moment, flexing her fingers blue veined through, I suspected, arthritis.

'I was one of the players, one of the top stars. I sang well and I was one of the best dancers, though you might not think it to look at me now.'

She leaned back again, lost in the past.

'Any stories you might have would help make the book really exciting. We don't want it to be totally factual: that wouldn't interest people at all.'

Her response took me by surprise. 'I don't know if I should help you. Why would you want to dig all that up again? What possible help can that be to people, all that raking over the past?'

I was puzzled. What on earth did she mean? All I was asking for was her memories of the Pavilion. Did she think I knew more than I did - some secret she wanted to keep to herself? Now really intrigued by her response, I said, 'But it's all important history, information that shouldn't be lost. Lots of people will be interested in stories of the old days.'

She gave a laugh that was more like a cackle. 'It may be history to you, but to some of us it's just like yesterday. In spite of what you say, there are a lot of local people who wouldn't want all that business from the past dredged up. They'd prefer to keep it buried, where it should be.'

She tapped her stick impatiently on the floor. 'Isn't it enough he's been found at last?'

TWENTY-FOUR

Whatever I'd expected Lydia to say, it wasn't that. 'What do you mean?' I said.

A sly look came over her face as she put her stick to one side and folded her hands in her lap. 'They found a skeleton when they started on the Pavilion renovations.' She pursed her lips.

'Indeed.' Did she know I'd been there when it was found? I wasn't going to say anything, not just yet. Better to find out what she had to tell me first.

But it was as though she had suddenly decided she had already given away too much. 'I heard about it from somewhere,' she said evading my gaze, fiddling with the case of her spectacles.

Her cousin looked astonished. 'You didn't say anything to me about it, Lydia. Who was it who told you? A skeleton in the Pavilion? What on earth could have happened?'

'I don't recall who it was that told me. I can't remember everything at my age,' she replied crossly.

Mrs Ferrin turned to me. 'Did you know about this? Who was it? It must have been there a very long time if it's now a skeleton.' This wasn't an act: she appeared genuinely astonished.

There was no point in becoming involved in this skirmish between them: let Lydia tell her what she knew, what she'd heard. All Lydia said was, 'How should I know who it was? I daresay they'll be able to find out one way or another through this GNA or whatever it is they use nowadays.'

'I think you mean DNA,' Tara corrected her, only to be met with a glare.

'Does it matter what they call it, young lady? All I'm saying is that they will be able to find out exactly who the skeleton is after they've done the appropriate tests. That may take some time.'

Did I detect a note of hope in her voice as she said this? Certain that Lydia wasn't telling the whole truth, I had this strange feeling she knew exactly who it was, had almost been expecting it. Problem was, I couldn't think of any way to persuade her to tell me. She was one very determined old lady.

Tara jumped in to the silence that followed Lydia's last words. 'Would you remember that person? I mean, once he or she has been properly identified?'

'What a silly question. How could I possibly answer that without the information?'

None of this was relevant to our Memories of the Pavilion book and I could see Mrs Ferrin was becoming more and more agitated. Her hand shook as she reached for her tea cup, her face registering surprise as she realised it was empty. What exactly was her relationship with her cousin? She seemed almost afraid of her.

'Can I make anyone more tea?' she said, rising to her feet, but keeping her head bowed.

Making more tea was an excuse. She was still upset, wanted out of the way for some reason and this might be the opportunity to persuade Lydia to tell us more. So although the last thing I wanted was yet more tea, I said, 'I'd love another cup, thanks.'

Perhaps once Mrs Ferrin was out of earshot Lydia would be more forthcoming. It was worth trying: the morning was rolling on and we'd achieved nothing. The blank page of my notebook stared reproachfully at me.

Mrs Ferrin bustled out and the three of us sat in an uncomfortable silence until I plucked up courage to say, 'If there's anything you'd like to tell us, anything you remember?'

127

For a moment she considered this request and then she said, 'I suppose you want to know about my time working in the Pavilion?' I'd been right then. Whatever she had to say, she didn't want to say in front of her cousin. The question was left hanging in the air, waiting for her to make the first move.

'Mmm, I suppose there are a number of stories you might find of interest. Though they might have to be anonymous.' She tapped her stick on the floor again. 'Do you want me to answer some questions?'

We were now on firmer ground. 'Yes,' I said eagerly, anxious not to lose the momentum. 'We've a set number of questions we ask and then usually people we interview just tell us what they remember. Or perhaps you've remembered who told you about the skeleton?'

For a moment it appeared she wasn't going to help us, that the mention of the skeleton had unnerved her, but she was evidently made of sterner stuff.

We had to move quickly. It wouldn't be long before her cousin returned with fresh tea and even if her plan was deliberately to keep out of the way for a while, she couldn't linger in the kitchen for ever. In this relationship it was clear Lydia had the upper hand.

'How many people have you interviewed so far?' This wasn't what I'd expected.

'Several,' I replied, trying to appear as vague as possible. Then, in case she had concerns about our sources, I added, 'Everything is very confidential. I hope that will reassure you.'

Tara waved her recorder. 'Do you mind if we record this interview? It will be much easier for us later when we come to writing it all up.'

A moment's further hesitation and then Lydia nodded graciously. 'Of course, if that will make your task easier.'

128

I opened my notebook and started with the simple question. 'What exactly did you do at the Pavilion?' Then I could hopefully lead back to the skeleton.

'I was there for several years,' she said. 'As I said, I was the star of many of the shows, but it all depended how busy they were. Sometimes I worked in the box office, other times I was in the office. I had excellent typing skills, though to look at me now you would almost not believe it.'

She clenched and unclenched her hands and I saw again the purple swollen veins. Mmm, perhaps there was some exaggeration about her starring role? If she had been such a big player, surely she wouldn't have had to take on some of the other jobs she described?

'You must have met some very interesting people during your time there?'

For the first time since we'd entered the house, she smiled. 'I did indeed. I met and often worked with all the big names. It was a great attraction then, in the early days. Many of the big stars came down from Glasgow...and even from London. That and the Winter Gardens. You have to remember that the island and Rothesay in particular was very, very busy. The Glasgow Fair fortnight was the best - you couldn't find a place to stay for love nor money, not unless you'd booked well in advance. And of course during the war, the Pavilion was one of the favourite venues. You could always be sure of having a good time there.' This was a long speech for her and she sat back, breathing heavily.

I tried to bring her back to the point, concerned she might begin to drift into general reminiscences about war time on Bute. It was more urgent to find out about the interesting (I hoped they would be interesting) people she had met through her job at the Pavilion. Important though the building was architecturally, it

129

was becoming evident our book would be more entertaining if it concentrated on the star names of the period.

Tara must have guessed something was troubling me because she leaned over and said encouragingly, 'You must have met some very important artists then? Can you give us more detail about some of them? Any interesting or funny stories you remember?'

Lydia smiled again, her heavy make-up a sheen of sweat in the heat of the room as the sun streamed in through the window. 'Ah, yes, indeed. I had the chance to meet many of them. They all played the Pavilion.'

By dint of gentle coaxing and guided questions, between us Tara and I managed to elicit a number of potentially useful stories from Lydia, some of which would most surely make it into our book.

As the pages in my notebook became filled with scribbles, my spirits rose, though I was grateful Tara was recording everything. Some of my notes might be difficult to decipher later. And yet... whenever I tried to focus on the 1940s, Lydia neatly sidestepped the questions with another anecdote about later years. It was as though she wanted to blank out that era of her life.

'That's been very helpful,' I said to her, closing up my notebook and putting it back in my bag as Tara clicked off the recorder.

'Not sure if that's what you wanted.' She appeared to be about to say something more, but all she said was, 'If I recollect anything else is there a way of getting in touch with you?'

I fished in my bag for a card. 'That's my phone details and I'm staying at one of the cottages at Kilchattan Bay while I'm on the island.'

'And you, young lady, do you have a card?'

'Not really,' said Tara, looking surprised at this request. But anxious for Lydia to make any kind of contact again, I passed one of my cards to Tara. 'Write your details on the back of that,' I said.

Lydia scrutinised both cards carefully, peering at them short-sightedly. 'I don't expect I will remember anything else,' she warned us, 'at least not about my time working, but I may have something to tell you.'

I was about to say, 'Can you not tell us now...' when, as though on cue, Mrs Ferrin came bustling in with a pot of tea.

'Where did you go for the tea?' asked Lydia. 'India?'

Mrs Ferrin ignored this cutting remark. I had the impression she was well used to this kind of sharp barb from her cousin. 'I thought I'd be better to leave you in peace for a while,' she said. 'Oh, are you going already?'

Oh dear. We were packed up and ready to go. I'd no inclination to sit here any longer drinking tea, with the watchful Lydia eyeing our every move. On the other hand, keeping good relationships was an important part of the job we had to do. And there was a little chance Mrs Ferrin might in the end prove the key to getting Lydia to talk about the skeleton. Lydia might just give something away, give us some clue. Not that this was in any way relevant to our task, it was all curiosity on my part, nothing more.

So I said, 'A quick cup would be lovely, before,' looking pointedly at my watch, 'we have to move on to our next appointment. We have another couple of calls to do today before we finish.'

I could see Tara was about to say something, most likely, 'What other appointment?' but fortunately she saw the warning expression on my face and quickly

131

subsided, pretending to be hugely interested in what was in her bag.

I drank the tea hurriedly, the hot liquid burning the back of my mouth in my haste to be gone. Idle chit chat about the weather, the demise of Rothesay as a tourist destination and the price of everything from food to clothes filled in the time as we sat there.

Tara refused a second cup. She hadn't even touched the first one, though she reached over and lifted a lavishly-buttered piece of fruit cake from the plate of home baking Mrs Ferrin had provided.

At last we were released and left in a flurry of goodbyes. I wasn't too sure about Lydia, but I suspected Mrs Ferrin was glad to have visitors; living with the formidable Lydia couldn't be easy.

As we got in to the car Tara stopped and said, 'What was that all about? That business with the skeleton? You think she knows something, don't you? She doesn't seem keen to tell us. If not, why did she mention it at all?'

I paused, my hand on the door. 'She knows something, that's for sure. Trouble is, I'm not sure why she's keeping it to herself.'

'Perhaps she doesn't want to say who it is in case she's proved wrong when they do the DNA tests? She strikes me as the kind of person who always has to be right.'

As a theory, this was a possibility. Lydia was certainly a woman who knew her own mind, aged as she might be. But that wasn't the cause of her reluctance to talk to us about the skeleton. I had a strong hunch I knew exactly why she had clammed up when she did.

I shook my head. We were both now obsessed with finding out exactly what Lydia knew, whether it was relevant or not to our history of the Pavilion.

132

'There's more to it than that, Tara. She knows exactly who it is. The problem is, how are we going to encourage her to tell us?'

TWENTY-FIVE

It was late afternoon when I came back to the cottage, hot, sticky and tired out, looking forward to sitting down for a while in the cool interior. After our visit to Mrs Ferrin we had to sort through all the information we had so far, try to sift what was useful, discard the dross. A lot easier to say than to do.

To take the edge off our disappointment we elected to adjourn to the tearoom at Ettrick Bay before heading for home: a cold drink sounded attractive and we were lucky enough to find a small table in the far corner out of the way of the hungry holidaymakers taking advantage of the selection of tempting food on offer.

As the tables filled up, I beckoned the waitress over. 'I hope we're not taking up too much room?'

She grinned. Young and slim, she was evidently someone else who was working over the summer to make some money. 'No, it's fine. I've seen you here before. You're a regular, aren't you?'

I'd never considered myself as a regular at the Ettrick Bay tearoom, but on thinking about it, I'd been here lots of times over the past few years.

We spread our 'plan of campaign' out on the table, nudging aside the empty tumblers and spent the next hour reviewing our options, aware there was now some urgency to the situation.

'The joint interviews aren't time effective, are they?' said Tara as we surveyed the dwindled heap of notes on the table.

'No, they're not. What do you think we have in the way of chapters?'

'Let's see.' Tara lifted the first few pages. 'Apart from all the anecdotal stuff, we have an introduction of sorts, all that information about the building of the

Pavilion, the competition the council held, the bit about the main contractor going bust, the problems of trying to control the budget and the competition from the Empire Exhibition in Glasgow which was held at the same time. Oh,' as I made to comment, 'there's that photo of the special jetty they built for offloading supplies.'

All of which seemed, to be frank, deadly dull. 'There's not enough meat in it,' I said. 'We need some hook, something that will make people want to read it.'

'So we have to work faster? Why don't you use a recorder like mine?'

'Yes...I'll have to abandon my notebook and use a recorder.' I'd do this very reluctantly, as I much prefer the old technology for this kind of thing, but the recordings Tara had made were a lot easier to understand than my undecipherable scrawls.

'I'll phone you later tonight,' I said, 'once I've been through all this and then I'll e-mail you a copy. If you could send back some comments to-night?'

'Sounds a good plan,' said Tara. Did I detect a note of relief that she was finally to be trusted entirely on her own, without me looking over her shoulder?

As we packed up to leave, I thought again about the previous evening and Tara's reaction to meeting Rufus. It had nagged away at me all day, bubbling just below the surface. Several times I'd the impression she was about to say something about it, explain why she had reacted so badly, but each time she had retreated, moved on to something else. Now it was too late - the opportunity had been missed. I couldn't introduce it now without appearing to be very nosey.

Business done, we left and I dropped Tara off in the town before heading for the shops to stock up on some provisions. I walked down the main street, Montague Street, breathing in the hot, sugary smell of fresh

135

doughnuts at the Electric Bakery, the heady scent of banks of summer flowers displayed at the front door of the florist's.

I stopped outside the fishmonger's, tempted by the range of fresh fish lying in neat rows on the cool slabs in the window. Salmon would be easy to cook, with a cake for dessert. There was still some fruit and cheese at the cottage as far as I remembered.

The fishmonger's was crowded. I wasn't the only person who had decided on a simple supper for a summer's night. As I stood in the queue, thinking about our visit to Straad, I couldn't help but overhear the two women in front of me talking. Neither of them looked familiar, though they didn't look like holidaymakers in spite of their casual attire. The older of the two, a woman in her seventies with long grey streaked hair piled up on top of her head, was chattering animatedly to the younger woman beside her who merely nodded, sending her blonde ponytail flying from side to side.

'They say that the identity will be known next week at the latest.'

This was interesting. They could only have been talking about the skeleton found in the Pavilion and I edged closer to hear what they were saying, under cover of inspecting the fish on the counter.

'…and there's been some talk about that man who went missing in the 1940s. Do you think it could be him?'

'That's what they're saying round the island,' the young woman muttered. 'It's all very strange.' She continued to nod, but contributed nothing more to the conversation.

'If it turns out to be him…' said the other woman and then she turned, noticed me watching them and regarded me with pursed lips. She lowered her voice. 'I can tell you more later.'

Drat! Just as I was considering making up some cover story to find out what she knew, but it was evident from the way she suddenly clammed up she didn't want to share this interesting piece of news. Another opportunity lost, but then it was probably no more than island gossip. We'd know the truth of the matter when the examination of the skeleton had been completed.

Even so, this was a lead I hadn't anticipated. It would surely be easy enough to find out who had gone missing in the 'forties. There must be a record somewhere.

I almost turned to go out and consider something else for dinner, but fortunately the assistant called 'Next, please,' and the older woman's attention was distracted.

Purchases complete, I drove straight back to the cottage, but my mind was going over all I'd learned at Straad, not to mention the conversation in the fishmonger's.

At this time of year the evenings are long and the temptation to linger outdoors until the gloaming fades into night, watching the sunset over the bay, is hard to resist, but there was work to be done.

Refreshed by a quick shower, I spent the next hour reviewing and revising our schedule until it was in a state to e-mail over to Tara. I thought it looked very much better now, much more structured and pleased with my work I added the file before hitting the 'send 'button. I sat back, confident Tara would be able to provide some quick feedback, feeling much more optimistic about the whole venture. Another job done.

Then I busied myself preparing the meal, putting the potatoes ready to boil and encasing the salmon in foil. Such fresh food wouldn't take long to cook.

I should phone Tara, tell her about the conversation that I'd overheard in the fishmonger's, but by the time everything was cleared up it was dark enough outside to put on the lamp.

I checked my e-mails but there was nothing from Tara. That was strange. I'd stressed the urgency of a quick reply, especially as we weren't due to meet again for a couple of days.

Better to phone her rather than send another e-mail. There was no answer and then the call went to voicemail. Very unusual. I tried again in case I'd pressed the wrong button, but for a second time it went to voicemail. Stop being so impatient, I rebuked myself. No doubt something more exciting than reading my e-mail had come up and she would sit up most of the night making up lost time, as young people do.

Well, I wasn't waiting up in the hope. I was tired and bed beckoned. After quickly texting Simon to let him know how the day had gone, I went straight upstairs, crashing out into a deep sleep within a few minutes.

It must have been no more than an hour later when something made me waken with a start. I sat up in bed, listening for any sound, but there was none. Strangely, the street light seemed to be shifting, moving around. In my half awake, half asleep state, I couldn't understand it.

Still groggy with sleep, I pulled on a dressing gown and crept downstairs to the living room, realising as I did so that the curtains were open. And this was no streetlight: it was the beam of a torch roving round the room.

Was it a burglar? So many of these houses were holiday homes, unoccupied for much of the time. Had someone noticed the curtains were open and assumed the place was empty?

138

As I shrank back into the shadows, wondering if this merited a phone call to the police, the light suddenly went out. Drat! My mobile was upstairs beside the bed, so even had I wanted to, there was no way to phone anyone. I sidled round, keeping as close as possible to the wall to reach the window and the cover of the curtain.

The torch sprang into action again, its beam sweeping through the room quickly, as though the person had a good idea about what he or she was looking for. It could only be a burglar. The security in the cottage was hardly good. In fact there was none. Crime was a rarity on the island; few homes boasted an alarm.

As I stood shivering with fright, the light suddenly went out again and a moment or two later there was the sound of footsteps fading into the distance.

My courage was at low ebb, but I had to see who had been outside. It was dark, but there was enough light from the street lamps to let me to make out the distinctive shape of someone heading at a brisk pace round the curve of the road, out of the village. I was certain it was Rufus Beale. Did he want me to know he'd been watching me? What on earth was he after?

TWENTY-SIX

The sun streamed in early through the thin curtains on the window of the bedroom at the front of the cottage. Used to our room at the house in Glasgow where the thick curtains kept out any vestige of daylight, I found it hard to go back to sleep once wakened. I would start to drift off, only to awaken with a jolt, remembering what had happened. Eventually, finding sleep impossible, I rose and dressed.

Once in the car, I dialled Tara's number, but in spite of several attempts there was no reply. Initial annoyance was now giving way to anger. What on earth was Tara doing that she had switched off her phone, especially when she was supposed to be working?

There was nothing else for it. I'd have to begin my round of interviews and hope she would turn up some time during the day with a very good excuse.

My first interview was with a war veteran, now living in a flat at the back of Port Bannatyne, but as that involved driving through Rothesay, I made a sudden decision to stop off and call in at Tara's flat. Hopefully she might be out and about, in a part of the island where the mobile signal wasn't good, but even so, surely she would have checked her voicemail and replied to my messages? Worse still, there had been no response to my e-mail and the write up of our last interview from the night before.

On reaching the High Street, I slid into a parking space right across from Tara's flat and scrabbled in my bag for my notebook, intending to put a note through the door if there was no reply. A brief message would be enough, but when we did meet up I'd have to remind her the success of this venture depended entirely on our being able to work as a team.

The postman was coming out as I reached the main door, which saved me trying one of the many other doorbells and becoming involved in a long explanation. On a whim, as he said a polite, 'Good morning,' I stopped him.

'Any word yet about Gerry Nutall?'

At first he looked as though he was about to tell me to mind my own business, but instead he smiled and said, 'Ah, you're the woman who's working with Tara?'

Not quite how I would have put it I thought before saying, 'Yes, that's right; we're working together on a history of the Pavilion.'

A huge grin lit up his weather-beaten face. 'He's been released meantime, but he's saying nothing about it.' He tapped the side of his nose. 'No doubt there'll be more word soon. Hard to keep anything secret.'

This reluctance on the part of Gerry to provide full details was probably a source of great disappointment to many.

With a quick 'Goodbye,' I started to toil up the four flights of steep stairs to Tara's flat, pausing half way to catch my breath. On reaching the top I waited a moment or two before ringing the doorbell. This really brought home my lack of fitness and I mentally added 'exercise' to my list of things to do. It was becoming a very long list.

There was, exactly as anticipated, no reply to my knocking, (I suspected after a few tries that the bell was broken) so she must have left. I was about to scribble a note and put it through the letterbox when the door was suddenly flung open and a young woman who could only have been Tara's flatmate stood there. She was small and mousy, clad in a scruffy T-shirt and a pair of

141

track suit bottoms which had also seen better days. A smell of paint, so strong I could almost taste it, wafted from the room at the end of the hallway.

'Did you forget your key? I'm in the middle of finishing off the paintwork,' she said and then almost at the same time, 'Oh, I thought you were Tara.'

'I'm certainly looking for Tara,' I said. 'I'm Alison Cameron.'

She tried to peer behind me, as though I might be concealing her friend and then her face registered dismay. She wiped her hands on her trousers saying, 'Have you seen Tara?'

'No, I haven't,' I replied. 'That's why I'm here.'

This was not the answer she wanted. 'I'm Meg, Tara's flatmate. I think you'd better come in,' she said.

TWENTY-SEVEN

Meg looked close to tears as she ushered me down the hallway and into the kitchen. 'This is the only room that's presentable at the moment,' she said gruffly. 'We're - or rather I'm - trying to do the flat up a bit. Tara is too busy with the Pavilion project so I've kind of taken on the work.'

Even in the kitchen, where it would appear most of the contents of the main room had been dumped, the smell of gloss paint was overpowering. Meg went over and yanked at the window, pulling it open. A welcome gust of fresh air blew in.

'You haven't seen Tara? Had any word from her?'

'I thought Tara might be with you,' she said. 'It's not like her to go off without telling me what she's doing.'

'I haven't seen here since yesterday afternoon and she hasn't replied to any of my calls. That's why I'm puzzled.' If Meg was her friend she must surely have some idea of what Tara was up to.

Meg looked as if she was weighing up what to tell me. I said nothing, waiting for her response and finally she said all in a rush, 'She had a phone call about nine last night and then went out, saying she wouldn't be long, but she wasn't back by the time I went to bed at twelve. I didn't think anything of it till this morning when she wasn't around. She's usually up well before me.'

'Who was the phone call from?'

Meg shook her head and pushed back the mousey brown lock of hair that had fallen over her eyes. Where Tara was dramatic, someone you would notice in a crowd, her flat mate was the opposite: pale and slightly plump, her paint spattered outfit far from flattering. But perhaps this wasn't doing her justice. You could hardly expect her to be working on the flat in her best clothes.

Action was needed. 'Did you check her bedroom? Has her bed been slept in?'

Meg looked at me doubtfully. 'We could do that if you want, but somehow I don't think it will help.'

'Worth a try,' I said and she turned to lead me down the hallway to the room at the end. She pushed open the door. 'This is Tara's bedroom.'

One glance at the room and I understood Meg's problem. It was difficult, if not impossible, to tell if Tara had been here last night. The bed was unmade, the duvet half on the floor, the pillows askew, but that might only have been because she didn't usually bother to make it up. And as for the rest of the room, it had all the appearance of a place recently burgled. Not a single surface was left uncovered and there was no order anywhere. Papers and books were strewn in random order all over the little desk by the window, spilling on to the carpet, piled up in the corner.

The dressing table hosted a range of cosmetics that would have done justice to the Superdrug store in town and the wardrobe door stood ajar, clothes haphazardly arranged on hangers crushed in together or hanging on the outside door.

I looked around, words failing me for a moment. I had complained often enough in the past about my daughter Deborah's untidiness, but this was of a different order entirely.

'I see what you mean,' I said. 'Is it always like this?'

'Mmm,' said Meg, obviously torn between loyalty to her friend and a desire to tell the truth. Then she added hastily, 'She might be very untidy, but she's very organised as far as work is concerned.' She bit her lip. 'What do you think we should do?'

'There may be a perfectly simple explanation,' I said to reassure her, but for the life of me I couldn't think what it was. Tara was well aware of our work schedule; of the timetable we had to keep to if we were ever to complete this book on the Pavilion, so I couldn't possibly imagine why she would suddenly take off, unless there was a very pressing reason.

'Do you think we should phone the police?' Meg gazed anxiously at me. 'She is missing after all. Anything could have happened to her.'

I said, 'It's early days yet. Why don't we wait and see if she turns up some time today? Phone me later this afternoon or sooner if you hear from her. If there's been no word we can go to the police then.'

She nodded, relief that someone else had made the decision evident in her expression. 'I have to go to work soon but I'll pop back whenever I get a break. I work shifts in the Bute Fabrics factory. I still don't understand where she could have gone.'

'I'll keep trying her phone,' I said, trying to sound very positive. 'I'm sure there's nothing really wrong, that she'll turn up safe and sound.' I sounded a lot more confident than I felt, not at all sure she was safe and sound. It was difficult to come up with a plausible reason for her taking off as she had.

Meg walked down with me to the front door. She touched me lightly on the arm as we reached it. 'You don't think anything awful has happened to her, do you?'

'Of course not. Try not to worry.'

I left after giving her yet more reassurances and went back down to the car. There was no option but to continue with the interviews for the day and try to cover Tara's appointments as well as my own. In spite of having plenty to keep me busy, what might have happened to Tara wouldn't be far from my thoughts. I should, of course, have checked her out at the beginning, as soon as my suspicions surfaced, but with everything else that was going on, I'd not made the time. Something I now regretted.

At Port Bannatyne, driving up Castle Street towards Kames Terrace where my next interview with a certain Tom Barber was scheduled for ten o'clock, I tried to concentrate, get the questions for the interview straight in my head. This was probably a great fuss about nothing. Tara was sensible; it wasn't likely she would have come to any harm.

What had started out as an interesting commission on the Pavilion, something to set me on the road to a new career after teaching and give me an enjoyable six weeks on the island of Bute was rapidly taking on all the aspects of a nightmare.

First the death of Ewan Flisch, then the discovery of the as yet unidentified skeleton and now Tara's disappearance. And there was the puzzle about Rufus Beale. What was he up to? Was he trying to frighten me? There were plenty of questions, but no answers.

I switched off the engine and sat for a few moments. Was it possible all these events were in some way connected? Surely not. My imagination was at work as usual, that was all. When Tara did come back, I'd make it very clear to her that this was no way to behave if she wanted to continue working on this project. It was still hard to quell the niggling doubts.

There was too much to think about at the moment. I had to get through this interview and hope Tara would turn up safe and well...with a good explanation.

TWENTY-EIGHT

Tom Barber was primed and ready for the interview, although the reaction to his first sight of me was obviously disappointment.

'Is there no one else?' he said as he opened the door to his first floor flat, peering to see behind me as he did so. 'Are you alone?'

I had my identification all ready to show him, but he didn't seem the least bit interested. 'Didn't you bring a photographer with you?'

Suddenly I understood why he was dressed so smartly in a formal dark blue suit, crisp white shirt and a navy tie with some kind of crest on it, his shoes so highly polished they almost sparkled. His grey hair was cut very short, making him look almost bald and his stiffness of posture betrayed his time in the services.

He stood aside to let me in, bowing a little as he did so. 'Please come through.'

'I'll be taking the photos,' I said with a flash of inspiration, rooting in my bag for my camera, hoping I hadn't left it back at the cottage. If Tara enhanced them with the computer package she used with such ease, at least one of them should be passable.

Tom seemed only slightly mollified at the sight of the camera. 'I suppose you know what you're doing,' he said grudgingly, 'but I always thought a professional camera was much bigger than that, had a tripod.'

'Oh, it's amazing what you can do now with these digital cameras,' I responded, laughing to cover my confusion, but he continued to look at me suspiciously.

His flat was a revelation, especially after coming from Tara's place. It was neat to the point of obsession. Tiny as it was, here was a man who believed in 'a place for everything and everything in its place.' No newspapers cluttered the small tables and the few books on the shelves seemed to be arranged by height and by colour.

The only concession to frippery was a large glass bottle containing a model of a many masted sailing ship and three brass ornaments which on closer inspection looked as if they were momentoes from a vessel of some kind.

'Gosh, that's quite a feat,' I said looking more closely at the ship in a bottle, carefully labelled in copperplate writing *S.S. Bulwhot*.

He glared at me suspiciously for a moment, perhaps thinking I was being sarcastic but then he seemed to soften and said, ' Yes, it took me a good few months to do that, but the winters can be long here, especially if you're confined to the house.'

'Were you ill?'

'You could say that, but thankfully I can get along just fine now. Have a seat.'

There was no offer of tea or coffee, thank goodness. With the number of cups I was drinking, I was beginning to feel decidedly shaky.

I took out my notebook and the recorder. 'Do you mind if I record our chat? It makes everything so much easier.'

'What about the photo?' he said gruffly and I leapt to my feet and switched on the camera, taking several photos in various poses, over by the window, holding his ship in a bottle, sitting beside his treasures from his time at sea. All in an effort to keep him happy, make him feel I was treating the task in a professional way. I'd no real hopes they would be of a high enough quality, at least not without some work, but when I'd finished to my surprise he said, 'Let me see them. You can do that, can't you on those new fangled cameras?'

'Of course, of course,' I replied and showed him how to use it, crossing my fingers he'd be pleased with at least one of them.

He lingered over the shots, moving back and forwards, inspecting each one carefully before saying, 'That's the best one of me. Use that one.'

'Absolutely.' I took the camera from him and made to shut it down.

'Aren't you going to have another look at the one I've selected?'

'Yes, of course, of course.' Oh dear, this interview wasn't going at all well. No matter what I did I seemed to get it wrong. His reply to my first question didn't improve matters any.

'So how were you involved with the Pavilion?' I asked in as upbeat a tone as I could muster, given the circumstances, putting the camera back in my bag.

'Haven't you done your homework?' he growled. 'I was in the navy and when we had shore leave the Pavilion was our favourite destination.'

'Ah, so you were one of the regular customers? Did you meet friends there?'

For a moment he gazed into the distance as though seeing ghosts from his past and eventually he spoke, the expression on his face softening as the memories returned. 'Yes, we had a great time and the girls went mad for anyone in a uniform. That was the best bit.' He paused while he chuckled to himself. I didn't dare ask what was so amusing him and I held my breath, not wanting to interrupt the flow. 'I remember one shore leave in particular. I met this girl at the dance on the Saturday and walked her home. It was hard to get away with any hanky panky in those days - at least not without the whole island knowing - though it did happen of course. I made sure it wouldn't happen to me; have to marry someone after one mistake. Anyway

149

this girl was from Glasgow, living with an aunt on the island for the duration of the war, so that was entirely different.' He winked as he said 'Glasgow'. Did he mean me to understand that as she was from the city she would be more willing than the local girls?

'And?' I said in what I hoped was an encouraging tone as he hesitated, his eyes fixed again on some event from the past.

'What was I saying? Oh, yes, the girl I met at the Pavilion. She was a sparky wee thing - a fall of long blonde hair - what was it they called that style? Oh yes, 'peek-a-boo' and she had the brightest blue eyes you could imagine. She looked a lot like that film star that was so popular at the time - Veronica Lake.'

I had no idea who he meant by Veronica Lake, but nodded in agreement as though I did. It would be easy to check her out later on the internet.

He went on, 'I arranged to take her to Scalpsie Bay: I'd borrowed a bike from someone I knew.'

'Gosh, it would be hard work pedalling round to Scalpsie from Rothesay,' I said, imagining Tom and his girlfriend puffing and panting on a tandem.

He looked surprised at this suggestion. 'It wasn't a push bike - it was a motor bike. Someone I knew worked in the garage in town, could get a bit of petrol in spite of the rationing. It was one of those really hot days - the summers were much better then, of course. None of this nonsense about global warming or whatever.'

I could see him drifting off again into a tirade about the changing weather patterns and tried to bring him back on track. 'You had a good day out?'

'What? Oh, yes. Well of course I had been at sea a long time, so a kiss and a cuddle, if you get my meaning, was well on the cards, or so I thought. Even though the island was crowded as it was in those days, with holidaymakers, you could always find a quiet spot out at Scalpsie. Her being from Glasgow, from the city, I guessed I was in with a chance.' He stopped and winked again at me.

'What happened?' I didn't see what any of this would have to do with the history of the Pavilion, but perhaps when he got to the point there would be a story of some use.

'What happened? Well, we found the secluded spot, right down by the beach, in a little cove no one knew about, surrounded by huge rocks that gave us all the privacy we needed.'

He chuckled again. What was coming next?

'I told you it was a hot afternoon? One of the hottest of that very hot summer. We settled ourselves down on the rug in the sunshine, I put my arm round her...and we both fell asleep.'

I burst out laughing. 'You both fell asleep?'

There was a twinkle in his eye as he said, 'Yes, hard to believe, isn't it? But we'd been working so hard on the last watch and I'd had very little sleep, so what with the heat and all, not to mention the couple of drinks we'd had before we went over to Scalpsie...'

This was a good story and very funny, but I didn't have any idea how I could use it in the book.

'So that was it?'

'Oh, yes, as far as my romance with that girl was concerned. When I woke the sun was setting over the bay and she was gone. Walked up to the road and hitched a lift from someone I guess.'

'You never saw her again?'

He frowned at me as though I had said something really odd. 'Of course I saw her again. That was the whole point of the story. I had nothing more to do with her, didn't even speak to her again, but I heard later

151

she'd been back at the Pavilion the next night. Someone else had more luck than I had.'

He paused for effect, knowing what he was going to say next would intrigue me...and it did.

'I didn't have anything more to do with her but someone on the island did. She met this Canadian and there was a right load of trouble.'

'I see,' I said, but I didn't.

'Oh, a real lot of trouble. You see what I didn't know at the time was that she was also seeing Willie Flisch and he didn't take too kindly to this Canadian muscling in.'

'Flisch? Isn't that the name of the manager of the Pavilion? The one who was found dead?'

A cunning look came across his face. 'The very one. Willie was his great-uncle. Strange, isn't it, how life works out? And Willie was very upset indeed about the Canadian muscling in. Though,' a shrug of the shoulders, 'he must have known what she was really like.'

'What happened to her?' I said.

He leaned back. 'She married Willie of course, he was besotted with her, but that was only after the Canadian left her in the lurch.'

TWENTY-NINE

I drove back to the cottage, my head buzzing with the information from Tom Barber, determined to write up this interview while it was still fresh in my mind, even if some of it couldn't be used. There was little time before the rest of the interviews scheduled for the afternoon.

In the end he had given me several useful pieces of information, some interesting anecdotes about the heyday of the Pavilion, most of which would sit very nicely in the chapters we were planning on personal reminiscences.

But it was the story of Willie Flisch and the Canadian that intrigued me. Was it relevant in any way to what had happened at the Pavilion - Ewan Flisch's death, the discovery of the skeleton and perhaps even Tara's disappearance? It might be a long shot, but a little idea niggled away at me, told me they were connected. But how?

It was strange that Willie Flisch should be Ewan's great-uncle and even stranger no one had mentioned it before now. Was I way off track by trying to link all these episodes together? As the interviews progressed, more and more of these stories were likely to surface. In a small place like this, lots of people were related and with many years' experience of island life I should no longer be surprised at the complexity of any relationships, family and friends.

What I had most surely discovered was a reluctance to rake up any bad stories about the past. Oh, everyone was willing to talk about the dances, the well known stars who played there, the amusing anecdotes about lost loves. It might well be I was one of the few people who didn't know about Willie Flisch and his wife.

My natural curiosity wouldn't let this rest. There had to be some way of finding out what progress had been made on identifying the skeleton, even if it was time away from the work in progress.

There were still more questions than answers. If the skeleton was the elusive Canadian, why would he have been murdered? Willie had been willing enough to marry this girl Tom talked about (though he refused to give me her name, claiming he 'couldn't remember') and the Canadian would have had only some brief leave. Surely even in those days, it wasn't a motive for murder? Because, no matter how you looked at it, there was no way the body, to become the skeleton, could have got wedged down there in the basement, buried behind the partition wall, of its own accord.

Meanwhile I was heading for Kilchattan Bay, determined that an afternoon of work would be the best way to banish all these confusing thoughts. Having heard Tom's story, I was more than a little curious about the location of the very private cove he had told me about. Given this was Bute, it was still likely to be there and still be as private many years on from his original escapade.

Tempted to delay for a few moments, I went over and sat on the bench on the beach straight across from the cottage and lifted my face to the sun, closing my eyes against the glare, relishing the warmth. As I was reluctantly considering going indoors to make a start on writing up my notes, my phone rang. It was Susie.

'Hi, Alison. Had to tell you the good news.' She paused.

'Well, out with it.' What had she been doing?

'Remember we said we might go and have a look at Rothesay Castle as a venue for the wedding? We've done more than that, we've gone ahead and booked it and they confirmed it by e-mail this morning.'

154

I sat bolt upright. 'You've done what? Without looking at anywhere else?' Then recollecting I was supposed to be delighted by the fact they had decided to get married, not to mention that they were now adults and under no obligation to consult me about any of their decisions, I hastily covered my tracks by saying, 'That's great news. When is it to be? What date have you decided on?'

'Next summer, June 14th to be precise,' said Susie.

Thank goodness they'd given up the idea of a winter wedding. 'Are you happy with that...with the venue, I mean? It will be a fair way for some of the guests to travel.'

'Nonsense. 'Susie dismissed my concerns. 'It's no more than an hour and a half from Glasgow, less from the airport,' completely ignoring that it would take some time to get from California to Glasgow in the first place.

'But I thought the place was a ruin?' From the way Susie had described it, it didn't sound too promising.

'No, no,' was her reply, 'the grounds are lovely and great for photos. We'll be able to have a proper look round once we come back to the island.'

'How many people were you thinking of inviting?'

'It will be a small wedding,' said Susie firmly. 'Not more than fifty. We only want to have people we know well.'

'I'm delighted it's all worked out for you. We'll have a chance to catch up properly when I see you again. Sadly, in the meantime, I've loads of work to do,' and I rang off before there could be any discussion about bridesmaids.

I crossed the road to the cottage, deep in thought, narrowly missed by a car whose driver hooted impatiently at me. I hadn't mentioned Tara's disappearance to Susie, anticipating she would turn up soon with a perfectly sensible explanation about where she had been. Even so, concern gnawed away at me.

Once inside, before switching on the computer, I tried her number. Again it rang out before going to voicemail. Now past being cross, I was deeply concerned.

I sat down on the chair at the computer, staring at the blank screen. Meg had been right. We would have to contact the police, report Tara missing. Where on earth could she be? She must have had some reason for leaving so abruptly. And who had made that mysterious phone call to her?

THIRTY

The Rothesay Police were, as ever, both helpful and polite. Unfortunately the constable on duty was someone I recognised. He didn't bat an eyelid as he said, 'Ah, yes, Mrs Cameron, we have had dealings before.'

I was surprised he didn't suggest I should be banned from the island because each time we met seemed to coincide with trouble of some kind. But he was much more professional than that and pulled out the report form without another word.

Meg had insisted on coming with me. 'I need to know what's happening.' I didn't want to argue with her, so before going into the station I went over to the flat to collect her, a bit of me hoping she wouldn't be there. Then I could say I'd tried. But she was ready and waiting.

'We'll organise a missing persons notice,' said the constable once we'd explained the problem, 'and if she hasn't turned up within the next twenty four hours we'll send it out and then put stage one of our procedures in place.' He sounded less than concerned, probably thinking this was a lot of fuss about nothing. She was an adult, after all and scarcely any time had elapsed since she had last been seen.

He wrote something on the form and then said, 'Has it occurred to you she might simply have gone off the island for some reason of her own?' What he was saying was did we want to initiate a full scale search when the explanation for Tara's so-called disappearance might be a very simple one indeed?

'But we're in the middle of a very important piece of work,' I protested. 'She knows how much there is still to do.'

'She wouldn't have left without saying where she was going. She always tells me.' Meg shook her head at this suggestion. 'I think she was worried about something, especially after that phone call the night before.'

The constable raised his head. 'What phone call? You didn't mention any phone call.'

Meg blushed. 'No, I didn't think it was important at the time, but straight after she went out and that was the last I saw of her.'

'Who was the call from?'

'No idea. She didn't say. But come to think of it she's been acting a bit strange these last few days.' Meg looked close to tears.

I turned to her in astonishment. 'Are you sure? What do you mean 'strange'? She seemed perfectly fine to me, anxious to get on with the work in hand.'

'That's because you didn't know her very well,' said Meg, biting her lower lip. 'Tara can seem perfectly normal on the surface but underneath she can be worried about all kinds of things. She's one of those people who's always cheerful to the outside world.'

This was news to me. Tara seemed one of the most laid back people I'd ever met. It was possible, not knowing her very well, I'd misjudged her.

'If you'll excuse me,' said the constable, interrupting our conversation, 'we can get as many details as possible on the information sheet and then I'll action it.'

'Sorry, sorry,' we both said at the same time and Meg finished giving details about Tara as far as she could remember them. I'd nothing to add except I couldn't imagine why she would disappear off when everything seemed to be going so well.

There was nothing more to be done for the moment, so we said goodbye and came out into the sunshine, blinking in the glare.

'What are your plans now?' I asked Meg as we stood outside the Police station, at a loss what to do next.

'Going back to work. There's absolutely nothing else I can do at the moment. I can only hope that constable is right and for some reason Tara has decided to go off the island for some reason we don't know about.'

Why was Meg even considering this as an option? As she and the constable knew only too well, even in summer the last ferry from Bute over to the mainland at Weymss Bay leaves at ten past nine in the evening so if Tara had rushed out after the phone call, there was no way she could have managed to get off the island that night. And if she'd waited till the next day, where had she been, why had she not come back to the flat?

I stood staring after Meg as she walked down the High Street towards the centre of town. How little I really knew about Tara, even less about Meg and it hadn't occurred to me to ask. Stupid I know, but my head was so full of everything that was going on I'd forgotten even to ask for her mobile number.

I looked at my watch. I'd have to hurry or I'd be late for my next appointment. In spite of all that was happening, I had to keep the project going.

To my great delight the two appointments I had that afternoon proved to be very helpful, so much so I came away feeling perhaps at last my luck had changed and even without Tara I might manage to make some progress on a couple of the chapters.

Bara McLuskie had worked behind the booking office all through the 1950s and gave me lots of anecdotes about the place and the people. What's more she was able to suggest a few more people on the island who had strong connections to the Pavilion and who would be 'delighted' as she put it, to be interviewed for the book. I made a note of several names and phone numbers.

And Drew Dobson had been one of the assistant managers for almost ten years immediately after the Pavilion opened so he could fill in a lot of background about the earliest days.

I left him soon after four o'clock, much cheered in spite of knowing that until Tara returned I'd have to do her interviews as well as my own.

With an hour or so to spare, I headed for the Pavilion hoping it might be possible to pick up some gossip. According to *The Buteman*, Gerry Nutall had lost his temporary status and had now been asked to stay on to supervise the remainder of the building works, in spite of his visit to the police station.

'I was only asked to go in to help with their enquiries,' he said to anyone who would listen.

No one believed him. It made a much better story that he had actually been arrested for the murder of Ewan Flisch.

He greeted me less than enthusiastically as I made my way into the building. I'd rung beforehand so he had made sure there was a clear path, free of all obstacles, to the office, but he was in the portacabin (the cleaner was again the source of information), now steadily set at the very far end of the green where the ground was more level.

'The men are working at the moment in the upper part, making good progress with the main hall and the little hall,' he said. 'This whole business of the body and now this skeleton is really holding us up. We still can't get access to the basements. Apparently the forensic people have other tests they want to carry out so we've all been strictly forbidden to go near the place. I don't understand it really. It's been over two weeks since poor Ewan was discovered there and a week since the skeleton was found.'

'These things move slowly,' I said, trying to placate him. 'And they want to be sure they have gathered all the evidence. Is there any more word on who the skeleton might be?'

He narrowed his eyes. 'Beyond confirmation that it's a male, there's nothing I can tell you at the moment. There are all kinds of rumours flying about, but nothing definite.'

His shifty gaze made me think he knew much more than he was saying.

'Will the remains of any clothes that were found be a help in the identification?'

'Possibly. If they find any.' He dismissed this line of enquiry. 'That's nothing to do with me.'

'So no idea about the age of the skeleton or how long it's been there?' I probed, but to no avail.

'If they do know, they're not telling me. I wish I'd never heard about this job.' He looked gloomy at the thought of yet more delays and changed the subject. 'All this is costing money, you know. Every day that we can't work on the place is another day men aren't employed.'

'I'm sure the police understand all of that,' I replied. 'There's bound to be news soon.' I wasn't at all sure that this was true. After all, wouldn't it very much depend on what the police and the forensic team had found at the site? I'd have to phone one of my friends who knew more about this kind of work than I did, try to get some information. Though it was none of my business really. I'd plenty to do with writing the history of the place without worrying about what else had been happening.

161

I became aware that Gerry was talking to me again. 'So what do you think, Alison?' He waited for my response, peering through his thick pebble glasses.

'Mmm...it all depends.' I stalled for time, not wanting him to realise I hadn't been paying attention.

He licked his finger and fiddled with a stain on his cuff, avoiding looking directly at me. 'I don't think there's any argument about it. Either we ask to postpone the publication or we realise it's going to be a long while before the Pavilion is re-opened.'

Good heavens! I thought. Surely he's not going to suggest to the committee that the writing of the history is put back until the place is ready? The investigation could take a long time.

Sad as I was about the circumstances, I didn't want to find out my commission had been put on hold or even worse, revoked. I'd not exactly given up my teaching post because of this, but having something to start me off had made the decision so much easier. If it was all to come to nothing I'd no idea what I'd do, where I'd find other work.

I had to say something to Gerry, but what? The best I could come up was, 'But wouldn't it be better if the publication was ready to go, all finished? Then you could be sure it would be available for the re-opening of the Pavilion.'

I tried to think of exactly how much of the book was in a reasonable form, give him some idea of the structure of it to date. 'I'll make sure you have a draft copy as soon as it's ready. That way you can have some input.'

As there was no reply to this, I added, 'We will of course give you a credit for your help.' Would an appeal to his vanity help sway the decision?

He said nothing for a moment, drummed his fingers on the desk, took his glasses off, put them back on

162

again. What was going on? I didn't think this long silence boded well.

He cleared his throat before he replied, 'That's as maybe, Alison, but what if the Pavilion doesn't re-open?'

This was something I hadn't even considered.

THIRTY-ONE

There was no point in lingering much longer at the Pavilion with Gerry, fretting at the idea of all my efforts coming to nothing, all the work we'd done being wasted. And what would I say to all those people I'd interviewed, promised a spot in the book?

It was small consolation when Gerry added hastily, 'Of course you'd be paid for the time and effort you've invested to date.'

There was another problem. Without something big, something substantial to show to prospective clients it would be hard, if not impossible, in the present climate to secure further commissions. I could see a return to teaching - and supply teaching at that - looming and I didn't fancy the prospect one little bit.

There had been no news of Tara and back at Kilchattan Bay in a gloomy frame of mind, I sat at the computer to review progress. If that was the right word for it. The word count was substantial, but it needed more work, a lot more work. Should I go ahead, continue with the interviews with Bute residents or instead have a trip off the island? I'd been promising myself a couple of nights back home for some time now.

That might work on both counts. I could pursue a couple of contacts in Glasgow and have a trip to the Mitchell Library for some general background about the island as a favourite destination in days gone by when the paddle steamers and then the bigger steamers had plied their way down from the Broomielaw in Glasgow to Rothesay, disgorging huge numbers on to the island for their annual holiday. Tom was right: either the weather had been better in those days or else they were a hardier crew, able to enjoy themselves rain or shine.

I saved the new material into the folder labelled 'Pavilion: second draft' and sat staring at the screen for a few moments. My mind was made up - I'd head for the mainland for a couple of days.

I'd go back to Glasgow, check on our house, check on our cat, Motley; both being looked after by a kindly neighbour. And there'd be a chance to meet up with Deborah, now returned from her art course in Italy. There might even be time to do some shopping in the city. The more I thought about it, the more cheerful I became. After all it would only be a few days away. Surely nothing could go wrong in my absence?

*   *   *   *   *   *   *   *   *

The journey next day across a calm Firth of Clyde gave me a chance to think about what to do. Scarcely a breath of wind ruffled the surface: fine for those on the ferry but less than satisfying for the yachts whose drooping white sails showed they were engaged, or trying to engage, in a race down the Kyles of Bute.

Trippers crowded the ferry, returning after a day out on the island. Some very young children scampered about the passenger lounge, excited by the big adventure of being on a boat. They ran backwards and forwards, chased by harassed parents, probably wishing they had caught an earlier ferry. It was long past bedtime for many of these youngsters.

The house in Glasgow was strangely quiet. It was hot here in the city, hotter than on Bute and as I opened the door to the lounge, dust motes danced in the shafts of late sunlight coming in through the none-too-clean windows, a sign of how long it had been since a duster had touched any of the surfaces. Well, I certainly

165

wasn't going to start now. I was far too tired. It was something that could wait until morning.

Motley came stalking out from the kitchen and looked at me disdainfully before sitting down and beginning to groom himself. My words of greeting were completely ignored. It appeared he hadn't forgiven me for abandoning him for the summer, though I knew he was having a great time going between our house and my neighbour's where he'd be completely spoiled.

He padded off upstairs, probably to find a comfortable spot on one of the beds (which was completely forbidden), but I was in no mood to stop him.

I kicked off my shoes and flopped down on to the sofa, using the remote lying on the coffee table to switch on the television. I'd watch the news, make a cup of tea and then phone Deborah but in the meantime I'd put my head back for a few minutes, relax a little to cool down after my journey.

Ten minutes later I was sound asleep and awakened to the orange glow of the street lights casting an eerie light over everything in the room. For a moment I was disorientated, unsure where I was, then looked at my watch, scarcely able to believe I'd been asleep for a couple of hours.

I swung my legs round and sat up. At least it wasn't too late to phone Deborah. If I was to be on the mainland for only a few days, I did want to catch up with her, hear all about her course in Italy and also if there were any prospects of her getting a job, any job, as a result. Much as I loved my younger daughter, her forays into the world of work had been less than successful, in spite of the many qualifications she seemed to have amassed. This was partly because she saw herself as a member of the art world where you need luck as well as talent to succeed. I lived in hope that one day she would indeed strike it lucky. In the meantime she sometimes lived with various friends, in a paid flat when she was in work, as a favour when she wasn't. And when life was really difficult, she came back home. I wasn't quite sure which of these it was at the moment though, by the tidy state of the house, it was most likely she was living with friends in Glasgow.

I pressed her speed dial number and prepared to wait, but she came on almost immediately. 'Hi, mum, how are you? And where are you?' At least I think that was what she said because the noise in the background rendered her almost unintelligible.

'Are you in the pub?'

'What made you think that?'

'Oh, just a hunch.' I tried to talk to her, but had to repeat myself so often that eventually I gave up. 'Look, are you free for lunch tomorrow? If you are I'll meet you in town at the Café Vita in George Street.'

'Sounds good,' she said, 'I'm staying with Pam at her flat on Great Western Road so I can get the subway in to town.'

At least we now had an arrangement to meet and I could catch up with all her gossip then. She rang off, agreeing to text me when she was on her way.

Was it too late to phone Simon, to update him on all that had happened on the island? I missed his advice very much because although it wasn't always welcome, it was always practical and he had got me out of more than one scrape. The call went to voicemail and I had to content myself with leaving a brief message. Probably just as well. I was too tired to go into lengthy explanations about everything that had been going on and, in spite of my long nap on the sofa, still exhausted. Besides, everything would look better in the morning, it usually does. Unfortunately not on this occasion.

THIRTY-TWO

The next morning, after a lot of discussion in innumerable phone calls and texts, I arranged to meet Deborah in town, but not at our original venue. My trip home had to be a quick one, because, with no Tara to help, there was a pile of work waiting for me on Bute. I'd fit in a trip to the Mitchell Library after lunch with Deborah, then look out some information about Bute from the filing cabinet in my study. At least I hoped that's where it was.

'I have to be at the hairdresser's at ten o'clock and after that I'm meeting Sally in the West End. She's broken up with her latest boyfriend and she needs a shoulder to cry on. She's very down about it all, though I think she's well rid of him.'

I knew Sally only from Deborah's tales about her, but from memory she was always changing boyfriends. Now whenever Deborah mentioned Sally and her woes, I mentally tuned out.

'So it would be best if we could meet around one o'clock at that place at Kelvinbridge. Forever Green it's called.'

I didn't like the sound of this one little bit. It's difficult enough having a daughter who's a vegetarian even if nowadays most restaurants provide a good menu to cater for them, leaving us carnivores to have a choice as well. Forever Green sounded as if it might be wholly vegetarian. 'Is it a new place?' I asked tentatively.

'I've been there a couple of times. I know you prefer meat dishes, but honestly the standard of cooking is so good I'm sure you'll love it.'

This didn't reassure me, but now wasn't the time to argue. If all else failed, hopefully they would do a decent omelette.

I called on my neighbour, Ella, to check all was well and to thank her for continuing to look after the house and also Motley. After a night spent on my bed and waking me at the crack of dawn by scratching at my face, he was probably huffed I'd shouted at him and had gone to find better company. Sure enough, there he was, happily ensconced on the rug in Ella's living room, fully stretched out to take advantage of the sun streaming in through the window.

'He's here a lot and we love having him,' said Ella. 'When our own cat died we didn't get round to closing up the cat flap and it's proved really useful as Motley can come and go as he pleases.' She looked at him fondly and he began to purr. Judging by the way he was getting the best of attention here he might elect to stay with Ella: cats have no loyalty.

By the time I'd caught up on the gossip, what had been happening in the neighbourhood while I'd been on Bute (very little as it turned out and certainly nothing as exciting as the events at the Pavilion), it was time to meet Deborah. It took me some time to locate the restaurant - which had a tiny frontage on to Woodlands Road - and even longer to find a parking place, as most of the street were either resident parking permits only, or already taken. Eventually, after going round in circles for ten minutes, I was lucky to spot someone coming out and waited to slide into the vacant space. Or rather park there after several attempts because the space was very tight. I clicked the mirror in, hoping that would deter anyone from bumping the front of the car which was sticking out slightly more than was safe.

Parking ticket secured, I hurried back to the restaurant with a few minutes to spare, though as

Deborah is never on time for anything, I was first to arrive.

The restaurant was compact, no more than twelve tables each covered with newspaper instead of a cloth and there was a faint musty smell in the air of long dried lentils, bunches of herbs and other stuff I could only guess at. The chairs had evidently been purchased from a junk shop or found in a skip because none of them matched and no attempt had been made to paint them, though it was difficult to see in the dim light. Too eco-unfriendly, I guessed. After the glare of the sun outside, it took me a minute to accustom my eyes to the interior of the restaurant. But there was no sign of Deborah.

A young waitress came bustling over. At least I assumed she was a waitress though it was difficult to tell from her flowing dress of many colours and her frizz of long hair. 'Can I help you?' she said, smiling broadly.

'I'm here to meet someone, but I don't think she's arrived yet.'

'Then why don't you have a seat at one of the tables and relax until she appears.'

'Good idea.' I looked round. The tables by the window were taken but there was one in the far corner that looked promising and would allow us to chat in peace.

I sat down and began to read the newspaper table cover. Using these instead of an ordinary table cover wasn't such a bad idea after all.

A few minutes later, as I was in the middle of a very interesting story about a well-known personality who was suing for divorce, the door to the restaurant flew open and Deborah came hurtling into the room in her usual frantic manner.

'Gosh, I'm not late, am I,' she said as she rushed over and threw herself into the chair opposite.

For a moment I couldn't speak. Then I croaked, 'What on earth have you done to your hair?'

Deborah has, or had, long black curly hair but now her hair was short, very short and a peculiar shade of dark red.

She laughed as she ran her fingers through it. 'Don't you like it? It's a complete change. I decided I needed a new image, something to make me look entirely different.'

'It's certainly that,' I replied, eventually finding my voice.

'Don't worry. If I don't like it I can grow it again.'

I kept staring at her in fascination as she said, 'Let's look at the menu. They can sometimes take a while to bring your order.'

This at least, gave me some cover, but I couldn't help but steal furtive glances at her from time to time as she devoted herself to perusing the very long menu, trying to get used to this new image of my daughter.

The menu was even more disappointing than feared, but not wanting to upset Deborah by making a fuss, I settled on a nut and nettle roast with a tomato sauce, hoping I could do it justice.

We chatted about this and that and she was happy and bubbly with news of the prospect of a job. 'I know it's not what you might want for me, but it's an opportunity to show some of my own work if I take up this post in the craft village. It really does have potential.'

'Yes, but does it pay?'

She shrugged. 'I'll get paid for everything of my own I sell and a small commission on any other goods.'

It didn't sound too positive to me. I mentally ran through all the jobs Deborah had had in recent years

171

and none of them had amounted to very much, unfortunately. This one didn't look any more promising, in spite of her enthusiasm. I don't know where Deborah inherited these artistic genes: there wasn't anyone on either side of the family who had been the least bit artistic.

The waitress eventually arrived with our order and I had to admit it was far tastier than I'd anticipated, moist and succulent and the sauce was so superb I ate every bit.

All Deborah wanted to talk about was the forthcoming job, how many of her friends would be joining her in the craft village, how she hoped she'd be able to choose her preferred spot ('You have to make sure you're in a position where customers see you as they come in and out'), how long it would take her to build up stock ('I'll have to work round the clock and then some') until eventually I tuned out and let my mind drift away to my proposed research at the Mitchell Library.

We decided to skip dessert and opt for coffee (or what passed for coffee) and I said, 'It's been good to catch up with you, but I'll have to head soon to the Mitchell Library.' The restaurant was by now very crowded and lively; it was evidently the haunt of a group of young people who used it on a regular basis, a local meeting place.

As the door opened yet again to admit another group, I said to Deborah, 'I think we should pay the bill and leave. There are people waiting.' I bent down to lift my bag when something, or rather someone, caught my eye. Coming into the restaurant, looking about her to spot whoever it was she intended to meet, was someone I recognised. It was Tara.

I sprang to my feet, spilling the contents of my bag over the floor. 'Tara,' I called, waving over to her. She

172

looked round, scanning faces to identify the source of the call, but when she spotted me the smile froze on her face. Without a word she turned and almost ran from the restaurant, slamming the door behind her.

'What's wrong, mum?' said Deborah as I leapt to my feet to follow Tara out.

'Won't be a minute,' I said. 'Wait here.'

Out in the street there was no sign of Tara. I looked left and right, up and down the main road, but the warren of streets around the restaurant made it impossible to be sure about which way she had gone.

I went back slowly into the restaurant where Deborah was sitting, looking extremely puzzled, holding my bag on her lap.

'Sorry about that. It's someone I know, someone I've been looking for. I thought something terrible had happened to her.'

'Why were you looking for Tara?'

'What! You know her?'

'Of course I do,' said Deborah, 'that's Tara McKenna. I know her well.'

THIRTY-THREE

The first thing I did was phone the Rothesay Police and then Meg (whose phone number I'd finally remembered to obtain) from my mobile. She sounded so relieved I thought she was about to burst into tears. 'You're sure she's okay?'

'As far as I can tell,' I admitted. 'I didn't actually speak to her, but she looked perfectly fine. I'll meet up with you when I'm back on the island.'

And once on Bute I'd have to go straight to the police station to confirm I'd seen Tara and to all intents and purposes she was alive and well.

'Where does she live?' I'd asked Deborah as I sat down opposite her again after my unsuccessful attempt to catch up with Tara.

'On Bute, of course. Is that how you know her?'

I then had to explain (as briefly as I could) about Tara being my researcher, how she had disappeared without a word and how we imagined all sorts of terrible things might have befallen her.

Deborah looked thoughtful after I had finished this story. 'Well, I first met her at art college. She was bright, but she didn't seem to think that was what she really wanted to do. She was very indecisive and left at least twice to my knowledge. I think her real interest was photography rather than art.'

This helped tell me something about Tara but didn't explain her sudden departure from the project. 'That's as maybe, but she left me in the lurch without a word.'

Deborah shrugged. 'I wish I could help you more, but I didn't keep up with her.'

So when I returned to Bute I'd have to make a decision. Should I wait a little to see if Tara came back with a good explanation or try to recruit someone else to assist me? I certainly couldn't do it all myself. Not only because there was a lot of work, a lot of interviews, but because in any project like this it's important to have someone else to discuss progress, exchange ideas.

Meg had sounded confused when I phoned her again to mull over the news. 'Why would she do that? Why would she disappear so suddenly,' she kept repeating, but I'd no answer.

'All I can think of is that it was something to do with the phone call she got, but exactly what I've no idea.' I didn't mention the ferries, that she must have spent the night somewhere on the island.

We had to leave the discussion there, secure in the knowledge that at least Tara was safe.

Meantime it was back to work, keeping up with all the developments at the Pavilion, interviewing as many of the locals as possible, spending my evenings writing up my notes. I was more grateful than ever Tara had suggested using the recorder: it made everything so much simpler. There was no more news about Ewan Flisch, nor about the skeleton, but being so busy, I'd no time to feel frustrated at the lack of information.

This solitary existence wasn't suiting me one little bit. Thank goodness Susie and Dwayne were due back soon and even if they were staying in a hotel, I'd enjoy their company of an evening.

Susie had been on the phone again about their wedding plans and I'd a sneaking suspicion she was waiting for me to volunteer my help. 'You are on the spot, Alison, so perhaps if we need anything checked out, you could do it?'

'Thanks for that,' I replied, but the sarcasm was completely lost on her. I'd little experience of weddings, but I knew from friends there was much more to it than booking the date and choosing the outfit. Still, all that was in the future. At the moment there was work to do and now I'd no excuses.

Then she took me by surprise. 'We thought we'd come back over to Bute tomorrow. Dwayne is interested in what you're doing at the Pavilion and all this excitement there seems to be. Honestly, Alison, you always seem to get yourself involved in a heap of trouble.'

'I only told you because you're a friend. I didn't expect you'd be scolding me: I don't see how you can think it's my fault.'

'Whatever,' said Susie. 'Well, unfortunately I mentioned it to Dwayne and he seems very interested indeed.'

I sighed. 'There's not much I can tell you about it all. From what I've heard the forensics team are still busy and there's very little likelihood I'll be among the first to know what they've found out.' Susie might be sorry she'd told Dwayne, but I was very sorry indeed I'd mentioned it to Susie.

'I don't know why he's so keen,' admitted Susie. 'And he won't say. It's not like Dwayne to be ghoulish.'

'Didn't you say he thought he had some Scottish ancestry?' It was all I could think of though as far as I remembered he hadn't to date expressed the slightest interest in the history of Bute.

'Mmm, possibly. But I don't think his interest is anything to do with Bute. I'll ask him.'

I put questions about Dwayne's ancestry to the back of my mind, being much more concerned about Tara's continuing absence than about Dwayne's interest in the skeleton at the Pavilion. Apart from being worried, I was more than a little hurt that she'd made off like that without a word when, as far as I could tell, we were

176

getting on well together. But it would appear there had been problems I'd not been aware of.

Still, I was pleased to see Susie again when they arrived late next evening, looking fit and well after their trip round the islands.

'We went to Mull, Coll and Tiree and then we managed a few days in Skye,' she said.

'And the Cuillins were pretty good,' added Dwayne, though he pronounced it 'Quillins'.

'So you did some climbing?' I didn't think Susie was the least bit interested in the great outdoors though Dwayne might have persuaded her to make the attempt.

They looked at each other and smiled. 'We didn't actually climb to the top,' admitted Susie, 'just a little way up.'

We spent the evening sharing a bottle of wine and hearing about their adventures on the various islands, including nearly missing the ferry that only ran once every three days, something which seemed to give them a great deal of mirth. 'You should have seen Susie waving frantically from the pier, trying to persuade the captain to turn back,' said Dwayne, laughing heartily.

Susie glared at him and for the first time I detected a little frisson in their relationship. 'I wasn't the one who misread the timetable,' she said frostily.

This didn't upset Dwayne one little bit. 'Anyone can make a mistake,' he said, 'and besides it was no hardship to stay on for a couple of days.' He leaned over to give her a kiss on the cheek and she smiled.

Had it been me I'd have been fretting all morning about being in time to get to the ferry terminal, but during her time out in Los Angeles Susie seemed to have become even more laid back than she was before she left. How I envied her that.

But all through our conversation my mind was on Lydia out at Straad and her hints that she knew

177

something about the skeleton. In spite of taking my number, there had been no phone call from her. I'd have to find an excuse to go back to Straad and tease out more information without upsetting her or her cousin.

Then I hit on the bright idea of saying we wanted to beef up the chapters about the kind of employment the Pavilion provided for people on the island in addition to all the anecdotes we had about famous people. Given the previous stories she had been able to provide, she would hopefully by now have remembered others.

Next morning I phoned the house and fortunately spoke to Mrs Ferrin, but she hesitated on hearing my request. 'I don't know if Lydia will be up to seeing anyone at the moment. She's had a really bad cold and it's worn her down.'

I have to see her again, I thought, remembering with some affection her very odd appearance, her claim to have been one of the stars at the Pavilion.

Now I'd made up my mind, I didn't want to let the opportunity slip. And besides, at Lydia's advanced age there was a strong possibility she might not be with us for much longer and there was something important she knew. 'I'll be very careful,' I promised. 'I won't wait long and I won't tire her out.'

'I suppose you could pop round today after lunch, about two o'clock. But only for a short time.' Mrs Ferrin sounded very uncertain. Perhaps she was afraid of Lydia's reaction to unexpected guests as much as of the effect of visitors on Lydia's health.

This arrangement wasn't terribly suitable. The next day would have been preferable as I'd another interview lined up for two thirty. But confident I could push my arrangement back to three o' clock, I said, 'That would be fine. I'll be prompt.'

After a hasty phone call to my afternoon interviewee and a quick trip to the shops to stock up on some essentials, I was ready to go round to Straad.

'I'll see you later,' I said to Susie who was sitting by the window, watching Dwayne as he set off for a walk along the shore. In spite of living in a hotel, they spent a lot of time at the cottage.

There had been no opportunity so far to bring up the subject of the skeleton with him. I hadn't said anything, waiting for him to make the first move, but there was no indication he'd any real interest. Perhaps Susie had imagined it all. Sometimes Susie seizes on a casual, throwaway remark as though it's the most important thing in the world.

'We'll head back to the hotel soon,' said Susie, 'and I'll call you about dinner tonight.'

Mrs Ferrin greeted me at the door to their house, even before I'd had the chance to knock. 'Lydia's resting at the moment,' she said, placing a finger on her lips, 'but you can go in if you don't stay long.'

There was nothing wrong with Lydia's hearing and no sooner was I indoors than she began calling from her room upstairs. 'Who's that at the door? What's going on?'

'Nothing much wrong with her then,' I said, more frostily than intended.

Mrs Ferrin had the grace to laugh. 'Nothing much wrong with her at all, if you ask, but we have to be careful at our age.'

'I'll be in the kitchen if you need me,' said Mrs Ferrin. 'I'm doing some baking for the church sale of work this weekend.'

Indeed the aroma of freshly baked scones wafted from the far end of the house as I climbed the stairs to Lydia's bedroom and knocked on her door. She was lying back on a bank of pillows as rosy cheeked as

179

ever, though whether that was her natural colour or the application of rouge was hard to decide at this distance and in the gloom, because the curtains were tightly drawn across the windows.

'Come in, come in,' she said, struggling up to a sitting position, 'It's not often I have unexpected visitors.'

'I've been told not to keep you long, not to tire you out.'

'Stuff and nonsense. There's not much wrong with me. It's only a slight cold. My cousin makes too much fuss. Put on that light by the little table.'

I did as she asked and a soft glow lit the room.

Her eyes were as sharp as ever as she said, 'What did you want to see me about?'

I started on my prepared speech about trying to put together a chapter about the employees at the Pavilion, but was no more than half way through when she held up her hand. 'Don't give me all that stuff. I told you as much as I could about that last time you were here. You've come about that skeleton, haven't you? You want me to tell you what I know.'

Stunned by this more than direct approach, I struggled for the right words but at last all I could say was, 'Yes, I suppose I do. In this case any information is helpful.'

'But none of it is of any use in a history of the Pavilion, is it? You want to know because you're curious. Go on, admit it.'

Lydia was sharp, very sharp and I couldn't tell a direct lie, so I contented myself with nodding my head, waiting for her next words.

She eyed me thoughtfully for a few moments as though weighing up what she should say. 'I'll tell you what I think, though of course I've no proof. The 'experts' may be better able to tell you than I am.' It was evident she had scant regard for those who might consider themselves 'experts'.

'I guess you know the story?'

She took a deep breath and looked into the distance as though what she had to say was there. 'There was a lot went on at the Pavilion during the war, more than people care to admit you know. It wasn't all grim, you know, but everyone was aware we might be living on borrowed time and people had to enjoy themselves where they could. There were a lot of army and navy personnel on the island then. They were billeted in any spare rooms available. Even the Kyles Hydropathic Hotel was commandeered as a headquarters for one of the submarines flotillas.' She stopped. 'It seemed the dying would never end. And you'll have seen the memorial garden out at Port Bannatyne, all those poor young men?'

She shuddered and then paused, her eyes fixed on some distant memory.

I waited, saying nothing.

Taking a deep breath, she said, 'The local girls loved all the excitement, especially those who were inclined to be a bit flighty, believe anything they were told.' Her tone of voice made it clear she didn't include herself in this number. 'They were so glamorous, from another world and they brought exotic gifts, nylons, chocolate, chewing gum. Their rations were a lot better than our boys got.' There was a trace of bitterness in her voice.

'And...' I said. I didn't want her to go off into a long history about the distribution of rations during the war. Much of that I could glean from other sources, other interviews. I wanted her to tell me what she knew about the skeleton.

She seemed to recollect herself. 'Where was I? Oh, yes, the way those from Canada seemed to lack

181

nothing. There were a lot of problems with our own boys of course. Well, you can understand that, can't you? They came over here with all their slick ways and fancy goods and put the local lads right out of joint. There were more than a few fights, let me tell you.'

'You think the skeleton was something to do with this?'

She looked at me as though weighing up exactly what she should say. 'There was one lad, a Canadian who got involved with one of the local girls. She was a bit of a catch and she'd set more than a few hearts racing. She loved it of course, all the attention and even more so when this man began to court her. Her boyfriend wasn't at all happy and by that time they were almost engaged so he was really upset.'

'Was she by any chance from Glasgow originally?' Could this be the same girl Tom had told me about?

'Yes, she was as it happens, though she'd been living and working on the island for some time. Her aunt and uncle had a farm here. She fancied herself as a bit of an actress, always dolled up to the nines.' Lydia sniffed. 'Of course the men all fell for that sort of thing.'

I could feel my spine begin to tingle. 'Who was she engaged to?' and I waited with bated breath for the answer.

'Oh, not just engaged. She married him. She married Willie Flisch. But that was after the Canadian disappeared. Left her with a bun in the oven, as they say.'

Lydia used this expression in a very posh voice, so much so that I had to turn away to hide my laughter.

If Lydia noticed this she made no comment on it and I turned back as she said, 'The story was he had been recalled, gone missing in action. But I think he never left the island.'

182

THIRTY-FOUR

It was as though Lydia, having told me this story, didn't want to say anything more. In spite of my coaxing all she would add was, 'That's only my guess, take it how you will. All I'm saying is that it was very strange that the Canadian disappeared suddenly like that, without even saying goodbye to her.'

'Didn't that happen a lot during the war? No one knew from one minute to the next quite what was going to be happening. Or where they were about to be posted. Wasn't it all supposed to be secret? People were sworn to secrecy about where they had been assigned to.'

She pursed her lips. 'You may well be right, but I was there and I know what went on in that affair. I knew her well, really well. We worked together at the Pavilion for a while, before she moved to the Winter Gardens. She told me everything, well almost everything. How he wanted to take her back to Canada with him after the war was over, promised her a great life like she'd seen in the pictures. What girl wouldn't have had her head turned by that?'

Something about the way she said this made me pause. 'Willie Flisch married her soon after the Canadian left?'

'Very soon after. They wasted no time, but then they wouldn't in the circumstances, would they?'

An idea was beginning to form in my mind. 'Was that the reason they married so soon after? She was pregnant by this Canadian and wanted to avoid a scandal?'

Lydia turned away from me. 'Who knows? It's all over now; it's all in the past.'

183

Intrigued as I was, this wasn't really much to do with the history of the Pavilion: I didn't see where it could be included. But it had everything to do with my inability to let a mystery remain unsolved. I had to find out what was being said about this skeleton, who he really was, what information had come to light. There was a very strong chance that Lydia was right. If the skeleton was this elusive Canadian, there might have been a very good reason why he hadn't left the island.

I was about to ask Lydia if she remembered the name of this Canadian when the door opened and Mrs Ferrin put her head round. 'I hope she's not tiring you out, Lydia?'

Lydia waved regally. 'I'm fine, stop fussing.' Mrs Ferrin retreated sharply.

I was bemused by the relationship between these cousins. Lydia was obviously queen in the household and this visit confirmed my opinion that Mrs Ferrin acted like a mother hen. She fretted and worried, though I was sure Lydia was a great deal more robust than anyone thought, in spite of her age.

I stood up. 'I must be going,' I said. 'I've another appointment up at Kilmory. Thank you for agreeing to see me at such short notice and I hope you recover soon.' I'd many more questions, but no hope of receiving an answer from Lydia at the moment. That would have to wait until another day. It was no more than a suspicion, but perhaps Lydia was enjoying stringing this story out, keeping me guessing. 'Perhaps I could call and see you again soon?'

But Lydia had closed her eyes and apparently drifted off to sleep. Which left me with the problem about what to do: go to the police and tell them this story, or wait until I had more proof?

I tiptoed from the room to join Mrs Ferrin on the landing. 'I hope I haven't tired her out,' I said.

She shook her head. 'She always has a nap about this time every day.' But her eyes looked sad and she might only be saying that to make me feel better.

We went downstairs and said goodbye. Mrs Ferrin remained standing at the door as I walked over to my car, musing over the information Lydia had given me. There was no doubt now in my mind that the skeleton found in the Pavilion must be that of the mysterious Canadian, but surely the police must know by now? If Lydia had her suspicions there would be other people on the island who also had an idea about his identity. Someone with more proof than she had.

There had been no public information beyond that first news about the discovery. Why? Was there some connection with the murder of Ewan Flisch? Nonsense: they were two quite separate incidents. Separated by time as much as anything.

The only coincidence was that they had been found in the same place. And if the Pavilion renovation hadn't started, the skeleton might have lain there forever, with no one any the wiser. It had all been so long ago, Lydia was right. Even if it was this Canadian and he had been murdered, the murderer was also likely to be long dead.

Even so, I'd no idea how I'd be able to concentrate on my next appointment. Curiosity cannot easily be quashed and after I'd finished at Kilmory, I'd go along to the Pavilion to find out if any further information had been released about the skeleton. Gerry would surely have heard some news either from the police or through island gossip. Could I come up with a good excuse to make him tell me what he knew?

And I was still no further forward with a plausible reason for the behaviour of Rufus Beale. I could think of nothing I'd found out that would cause him problems.

If Simon had been here he would most likely have said, 'It's none of your concern, Alison. Concentrate on the work in hand.'

This was all good and well, but there was no way I could rest until I'd got to the bottom of this story. After all, I tried to persuade myself, it might have some bearing on the history I was writing. Some bearing that, for the moment, I couldn't quite work out.

THIRTY-FIVE

Back at the Pavilion the blue tape had gone and the renovations were once again under way. Scaffolding barred my way into the building. 'Sorry, love, you can't come in here. Not allowed,' said the workman I now knew to be Malkie. He pointed to the large notice on the window at the front 'Access Strictly Forbidden.'

'I'm looking for Gerry,' I said.

'Oh, he's still in that temporary office round the back.'

Sure enough I found Gerry in the small portacabin perched in the green space at the back of the building.

'It's not exactly comfortable,' he grumbled. 'It's baking hot now and it'll be freezing in the winter.'

'Perhaps they'll be finished by then?'

He looked at me as if I'd said something outrageous. 'Finished by then? I just hope we don't find any more skeletons...or dead bodies. We've been held up enough as it is.'

He must have seen the look on my face at this rather callous statement, because he added hastily, 'Not least because it's been so dreadful for the people concerned ... all of them...' Then he added, 'You don't need to worry, Alison. The committee met last night and the renovation will go ahead so your little project is quite safe.' He said this with what looked like a sneer, but I ignored him, though I couldn't deny my relief the outcome had been a good one.

He was evidently feeling the heat because he was attired in a loose T-shirt and shorts, sitting on a red plastic chair directly in front of a fan that was going full blast, but sending out bursts of air that were only slightly cooler than the air inside the portacabin.

I pulled forward the only other chair in the room and sat down without being invited as he continued to grumble about the premises. 'They say there's nothing better they can provide. How am I expected to work out of this, I ask you?'

I debated whether to sympathise with him or try to cheer him up. I opted for the latter. 'It will be well worth it when the Pavilion renovations are finished,' I said. 'Just think what an asset the new building will be to everyone, not only on Bute but beyond. It might even get back its former popularity.'

He looked at me doubtfully as though weighing up whether or not this was a joke. 'That's what everyone tells me. I'm not so sure. Besides they still want to advertise the post of project supervisor and there's no guarantee who'll get the job.'

Here was another avenue I didn't want to go down. Surely the post of project supervisor was exactly in his line of work? There was nothing I could do about his situation, either now or in the future. How could I get him back on to the subject of the skeleton without being too direct?

Fortunately I was saved from making this decision as the phone on his desk rang. He lifted the receiver impatiently and spoke into it for a few minutes saying, 'I see. That's very interesting. I'm not sure how I can help. Oh, I see. Well, certainly I'll do that.'

It's always intriguing when you only hear one side of a phone call but I paid little attention, assuming it was something to do with the arrangements for the renovation of the Pavilion.

He looked at me thoughtfully as he replaced the receiver. 'Well, well. Who would have guessed it? Seems they're finding it difficult to make any progress with that skeleton.'

I said nothing, waiting for his next remark, hoping he wouldn't suddenly realise he shouldn't be saying anything to me.

But he was unaware of any problem as he continued. 'There was nothing to identify him. No identity disc, no shreds of clothing. Looks like someone didn't want him to be identified.'

He seemed to consider this information for a moment, rolling the pen in front of him backwards and forwards across the desk. 'I suppose it must have been one of the men stationed here during the war, though how he came to be in the basement of the Pavilion is still a complete mystery.'

Because someone put him there, I thought.

Gerry seemed to have forgotten there was someone else in the room and spoke as if to himself. 'There will be lots of investigations now, into the men who were here during the last war, anyone who went missing. Though I don't remember hearing about anyone going missing on the island. There were some foreign soldiers and sailors who were billeted here for a while or came over to enjoy the delights of Rothesay on the Liberty boats, but it's all a bit of a mystery.'

Then he looked across as though he had only just remembered me sitting there and said briskly, replacing the pen on top of his notepad. 'Anyway, let the police sort it out. There's nothing I can do about it. I have enough to worry about keeping everything in order here. There have been a number of problems with the building itself. Getting all the asbestos out for a start. That's proved a real problem - it's very dangerous stuff, you know.''

He was off again on the same tack and I didn't want to sit and listen to more tales of woe, anxious as I was to leave quickly and think about what he'd said. There was little doubt in my mind that the skeleton was the

Canadian both Lydia and Tom Barber had talked about. Memories are long on the island and there was no reason to doubt theirs. But I had this feeling they'd only told me part of the story: they knew more than they were saying. Should I inform the police about our conversations? And if I did would either of them back me up? It was all so complicated.

Why did I feel this responsibility to find out the truth about the skeleton? Because I knew that however the he had come to be here, it wasn't through chance. Someone had hidden the body in the basement of the building long ago and now all that was left was the bare bones. Then I thought, suppose it wasn't a case of the body being taken down to the basement? What if something had actually happened there? That would make much more sense. Because if the death had happened somewhere else why go to all the bother of burying it in the basement of the Pavilion?

There was no doubt in my mind that those investigating knew it must have been murder. That wasn't the point. Problem was, did Lydia?

THIRTY-SIX

Gerry continued to vent his frustration at what he thought of as everyone trying to thwart him, make his job difficult, but when I did try to steer him back to the phone call he was unwilling to say any more about the skeleton. It was as though he had suddenly realised he shouldn't have said anything at all to me, should have kept the news to himself. Well, too late now.

He stood up and dismissed me with a curt nod. 'Sorry, I have to get on.' Beads of sweat were trickling down his forehead, but whether it was because of the heat of the afternoon or something else was hard to tell.

'That's fine,' I said, also standing up and making for the door. He was far too preoccupied to ask about the reason for my visit, thank goodness.

Once outside, I crossed the road to look back at what was happening. The front of the building was completely covered in scaffolding, the main doors wide open, to reveal yet more scaffolding inside. Up on the balconies boxes and crates were stacked high, but it was impossible from this distance to see what they were for. When the work was finished, the building would be returned to its former glory. At the moment it looked chaotic.

I suddenly realised I was exhausted, as much by the events of the afternoon as by the interviews, so opted to head back to Kilchattan Bay for a long walk along the shore, to clear my tired brain and to cool down.

The weather if anything was even hotter, oppressive in spite of the cooling afternoon breeze from the sea and in the far west there were signs of clouds beginning to gather. It was as though it was gearing up for an almighty thunderstorm, though the sky was still clear blue over the island and the bay sparkled in the

191

sunshine. Bad weather might be on its way and this might be the end of the good spell for some time. For the moment, it was still very hot.

As I opened the car door a wave of heat hit me and I switched on the engine and the air conditioning, trying to avoid the steering wheel until it was cool enough to touch.

At last I judged it was safe to continue and set off, stopping only for a few moments in town at the Electric Bakery to buy an apple pie for afternoon tea. I wasn't sure what Susie had planned for later, but I didn't think I could face another meal out. Apart from the fact I was too weak-willed to resist the desserts, which was doing my waistline no good at all, evenings were the only time available for writing up my notes.

I would be firm - Susie and Dwayne could go out for dinner. I'd make do with a couple of poached eggs on toast, though I'd have a slice of the apple pie with a cup of tea when I reached the cottage. That much I'd earned.

Kilchattan Bay was busy with tourists, the sands along the shore unusually crowded with walkers of all ages. A few people sat down by the edge of the water or paddled about but there was an unusual lethargy about everyone and everything. In spite of all our desires for hot, Mediterranean weather it's clear that as a nation we're very poorly equipped for it. Another few days of this heat and the newspapers would be full of stories about drought, hosepipe bans and requests to share bathwater. It happened every year with a horrible predictability.

I switched off the engine and sat for a moment, people watching. A few boats sailed in the bay, but even they seemed imbued with the lethargy of the day. This part of the island was the haunt of walkers and today the West Island Way at the end of the village seemed to be more popular than ever with those seeking the cool shade of the trees. Where once the old pier had been busy, bustling with ships coming in and out delivering coal, now a long line of cars stretched back to the end of the street.

I roused myself from my daydream. This wouldn't get the work done. I started up the engine again and drove very slowly down the street, looking out for a space as close as possible to the front of the cottage. Several boats were parked along the street on their trailers, one or two looking very much the worse for wear with peeling paint and chipped boards: restoring them would be a labour of love for someone.

I eventually found a tiny space down by the road opposite the old pier and squeezed in, took the apple pie from the car and started to walk back on the shady side of the street, thinking with pleasure of a cup of hot, sweet tea.

As I approached the cottage, I noticed a slightly battered bicycle propped up carelessly against the far wall. There was someone lingering at the door, someone I knew well. I almost dropped the pie in my amazement, but managed to save it just in time.

'What are you doing here? Where have you been?' I said to Tara, trying to contain my anger.

THIRTY-SEVEN

'Don't say a word,' I said, putting my finger to my lips as Tara made to reply. 'Let's go inside.' The last thing I wanted was a full-scale row out here in the street, where everyone could see us.

I fumbled for my key in my bag. 'Hold this,' I said, handing Tara the apple pie.

Once inside the cottage I motioned her to a seat. 'Not yet,' I instructed her, 'not until we're settled with a cup of tea, though I've none of that stuff you drink.'

'Water will be fine,' she said meekly, settling herself into the chair by the door as though ready for an escape if anything went wrong.

'Good. You can have a piece of pie though. I'm going to.' I wasn't in any mood to be kind to her. She had dashed off without a word, had let me down badly and whatever her reason for doing so, it had better be a good one.

I went into the kitchen, my hands trembling so much I could scarcely fill the kettle and the water splashed over the floor. I bent to wipe it up with some kitchen towel. How dare Tara do this? Come waltzing back without a word, as though nothing was wrong, as though she'd merely been on a few days' leave. I took several deep breaths, trying to compose myself, trying hard to think how best to approach the problem.

I took my time in the kitchen, standing at the counter waiting for the kettle to boil, taking down a mug for me and a glass for water for Tara, sectioning the pie and putting a slice on each plate. Now that she was here I couldn't think how to begin, what to say to her. Should I tell her her contract was at an end, that she had effectively terminated it by her behaviour? If I did, I'd be left without an assistant and I'd little idea where I would find someone else, especially one as good as Tara. This was an impossible situation, but there was no point in making a rash decision, at least until I'd heard what she had to say.

Best to let her tell her story, I thought, taking the laden tray through to the living room, silently handing her the glass of water before putting milk and sugar into my tea. She took the proffered slice of pie and a napkin, letting it rest in her lap and staring at it as though it was something strange and exotic.

I sipped my tea and gazed over at her, determined not to be the first to speak, to break this uncomfortable silence.

When she did at last say something, it wasn't at all what I expected. 'Can I still have my job? You haven't recruited anyone else, have you?'

She wasn't going to have it as easy as that. There would have to be a bit of explanation about her behaviour, a pretty good explanation.' That all depends.'

She sighed and nibbled at her slice of pie, sending sugary crumbs cascading down on to the front of her T-shirt. 'I wouldn't blame you if you wanted to fire me. I know I shouldn't have gone off like that, so suddenly.'

'Not to mention running off when I saw you in that restaurant in Glasgow. Apart from anything to do with the job, do you have any idea how worried everyone was about you? Meg was distraught. We had the police alerted and everything, convinced something terrible had happened to you.'

She went bright red and fidgeted in her seat, concentrating on her plate as though she might find some answers there. When she raised her head, her eyes were shining as though she was holding back tears. 'I couldn't speak to you, couldn't tell you. Not then, not when I wasn't sure what was happening myself.'

195

'You could have acknowledged I was there, spoken to me, instead of making off like that.'

'I suppose so,' she mumbled, 'but I didn't want to get into a discussion with you. It was all far too difficult to explain, not till I'd had some confirmation.'

'Well, it must have been something extraordinary to make you leave the island so suddenly, run off like that.' Still I wasn't convinced: she was skirting round the story, whatever it might be.

Then it came to me. Was this something to do with her original application? 'When we first met, you wouldn't say much about your background.' No point in beating about the bush. Now that we were having a heart to heart, I might as well have the whole truth. 'Did you lie on your application? And there were other things. Your reaction when you saw Rufus Beale. What was that all about?'

She looked at me again, biting her lip, looking close to tears. I sighed. Why was I being so hard on her when I hadn't heard the full story? I should give her the benefit of the doubt, give her some help. 'Was it that phone call you had that night? Was it to do with that?'

'It's all so complicated. I don't know where to start.'

'Take your time and tell me about it. I'm willing to help you, but you have to be honest with me.' Any decision to be firm with her faded as I saw how distressed she was.

'It's a long story.'

'I have the time.' Not strictly true as I spent most of my days at the moment anxiously watching the clock, but that was of no consequence.

She took a deep breath. 'You know the firm that Rufus Beale runs? Well, his family have been builders going back several generations.' She stopped.

'Yes, from that article in *The Buteman* at the library we saw his father had been one of the original contractors.'

Tara shook her head. 'There were problems with his father: stories he'd made off with other people's money. And Rufus Beale has had several companies; all of them going into liquidation, leaving the creditors broke. All except Rufus of course.'

This might be a story for the police, but I couldn't see what it was to do with Tara.

Then she said, 'My father was one of those who lost absolutely everything. His was a small firm and he couldn't recover. He died a broken man. Rufus should never have been allowed to set up another company and certainly not to win that contract for the initial work on the Pavilion. Someone helped him.'

'That must have been awful for you.' It explained a lot, but not everything.

She nodded as though not trusting herself to speak.

I leaned forward. 'You can tell me, Tara. Whatever it is, I have to know what happened so that I help you.'

She gulped. 'I wish it was as simple as that.' She seemed to be considering what to say next. 'Have you heard any more about that skeleton, the one found in the Pavilion? You remember?' She said this as though a dozen skeletons had been found recently.

'Yes, I know about it. We were both there when they found it.'

'Any word yet on who it was?'

I hesitated. Should I tell her what I'd found out, little though it was? I decided against this, at least for the moment. 'Mmm, there have been some suggestions and I'm sure the police have some idea,' was as much as I was prepared to say. I wasn't going to repeat what I had heard from Tom Barber, nor from Lydia. Anyway,

197

at the moment there was no way of confirming their suspicions.

This story was going at a snail's pace, so I said impatiently to hurry her along, 'One theory is that he was a Canadian, one of the soldiers on the island during the last war.' I hurried to qualify this. 'At least that's what's being said.'

She nodded, sending her long silver earrings jangling. 'Mmm...that's interesting.' Again she hesitated.

'Look, Tara,' I said, 'sad as this story about what happened to that poor man might be, it's all long ago, all in the past and nothing to do with us.'

I didn't want to sound hard hearted but it did appear that she was displaying an extraordinary concern for something which was really none of our business.

'So what do you intend to do now? Let the police know?'

'I'll try to get more information before I go to the police. It's not easy to get that kind of proof.' She got up. 'I don't expect you'll want me to continue to work with you now?'

But I'd also made up my mind. With only a couple of weeks left to wrap up the research part of this project there was no way I'd manage it all on my own, no matter what Tara had been up to. 'If you want to keep the job, it's fine by me.' Then I put on my sternest look. 'No more running off without telling me. If only you'd explained, it would have saved a lot of grief for everyone.'

She hung her head. 'I promise, Alison. I'll work doubly hard to make up for lost time.'

I wasn't being quite as magnanimous as she thought. In the short time left it would be impossible to recruit someone new and besides, Tara had proved she was very good at research.

198

She came over and hugged me. 'Thank you so much. This job means a lot to me, I really want to do it and I won't let you down again, I promise.'

'That's fine,' I replied, slightly embarrassed by her enthusiasm.

'I'd better start at once. Could we meet this evening to bring me up to date?'

'And let Meg know right now you're back on the island,' I added. 'She's been very worried.'

'I will. I couldn't confide in her, couldn't confide in anyone.' She sounded so young, so vulnerable I felt a wave of pity. If Rufus Beale was the crook she believed he was, no wonder she had been astonished to see him managing the Pavilion renovation.

She lifted her bag and I went with her to the door of the cottage.

'I'll see you this evening about eight o'clock. Come back here.' This arrangement would give me a good excuse for skipping dinner with Dwayne and Susie.

I watched her as she swung herself nimbly on to her bicycle and pedalled off along the street past the stables and towards the end of the village.

I stood by the door in the afternoon sunlight, reluctant to go back into the darkness of the cottage.

Tara's questions made me think again about the skeleton. There was an undercurrent on the island, people had suspicions about what had happened. But no one was willing to come forward. Why not?

And if it was indeed this missing Canadian soldier there were still a lot of questions to be answered. Including who had killed him...and why?

THIRTY-EIGHT

I was in the middle of clearing up when Susie and Dwayne arrived.

'Was that Tara I saw hurtling out of the village on her bicycle?' she said in some astonishment.

'Yes, yes,' I replied, anxious not to become involved in a long discussion, nor a long explanation, about Tara's return. 'Everything's fine. I'll tell you more about it later,' I said to forestall any further questions. Truth was, I felt completely exhausted.

There was something else on Susie's mind and she was almost bouncing with excitement. 'We've got news, we've got news,' she said.

Accustomed as I am to Susie's enthusiasm for anything and everything I didn't expect anything unusual, but I was wrong. 'How about some tea and a slice of apple pie and we can sit down and you can tell me?'

As this offer didn't tempt Susie it must be something very important indeed she had to say

'Okay,' I said. 'What's happened?'

She and Dwayne sat down on the sofa and he held her hand tightly in his.

'We've been over to Rothesay Castle and sorted everything out, confirmed the booking.'

'We just love the place and Susie thinks it would be so romantic to marry here,' said Dwayne.

'Wouldn't it be easier to marry in California?' I said, before adding hastily, in case Susie thought this was a way of trying to upset her plans, 'Simon and I would be delighted to come out for it.'

'It's what Susie wants.' Dwayne squeezed her hand affectionately, 'and I do have some connections with Scotland.'

'I'll think we should have some tea,' I said making for the kitchen to give me time to consider a response.

When I came back they were sorting through a number of brochures spread out on the coffee table in front of them.

Susie was busy, immersed in her task, but as I poured the tea, Dwayne said, 'Any more word on that skeleton in the Pavilion?' It was said casually, as though he was doing no more than making polite conversation, but as I passed the cup to him, he pressed my hand. What was the meaning of this? Did he want me to tell him, but not let Susie know?

Should I tell them what I'd found out? But then Susie said, obviously more tuned in than I'd given her credit for, 'I can see from your face that you've heard something, Alison. Do tell. Dwayne is fascinated by old history, especially anything to do with Bute, now that he's been on the island.'

I'd give them the brief details, but not everything. After all very little was known. Dwayne sipped his tea stoically. I had the distinct impression he would much have preferred coffee, but was too polite to say so. 'Go on, Alison. Don't keep us in suspense any longer.'

I gave a shortened version of what I'd been told by Lydia. 'But take it all with a pinch of salt,' I cautioned. 'It may all be rumour.'

Susie's eyes grew wide as I came to the end of the much abbreviated tale. 'Gosh, that is extraordinary.'

She turned to Dwayne. 'Didn't you say some relative of yours was based on Bute during the war? Wasn't that one of the reasons you were interested when I suggested coming here?'

This was news indeed about Dwayne. 'All you said was that you had some Scottish connection, not that you had anything to do with Bute.' Why hadn't he mentioned this before?

201

Dwayne waved his hand vaguely. 'I guess that's the case. But, gee, it was all a long time ago.'

Alert as I was for any information that would help our history, this sounded interesting. Here might be an opportunity for a view about what happened at the Pavilion from a completely different angle, a perspective that could result in some serious overseas sales. 'And which of your relatives was stationed here?' I fumbled in my bag for my recorder.

Dwayne hesitated when he saw what I was doing, as though deciding how much to tell me, before saying, 'It was my dad who was here on Bute, though I've no idea for how long before he went back into action.' He nodded agreement as I clicked the recorder button, adding, 'He was very young of course back then.'

'And does he still talk about his time on Bute?' Even if his father was no longer alive, there might be some information he'd passed on to Dwayne.

But this was not to be a fruitful source of anecdotes. 'Nope. I know nothing about his time on Bute. He died during the war, left mom with me. Mom married again and I'd a great family, but I've nothing to remember him by except a couple of photos.'

'How sad.' I must confess that although it was a long shot, I felt a real pang of disappointment. An account from one of the men posted to Bute would have added interest.

Then Dwayne said, 'I have a photo here. I always carry it about so it's a bit dog eared by now.' He stood up and reached into his back pocket, bringing out a small, much-creased photo from his wallet. He smoothed it out a bit, then passed it to me. 'That's my dad,' pointing to a man at the back.

I gazed at the very faded photo of a man with sharp chiselled features and blonde hair cut extremely short. He was dressed very casually, not in uniform and it had obviously been taken at some family event in a garden judging by the other people in the photo, some sitting on the veranda, some posed round a smoking barbeque.

'He was a very handsome man,' I said politely - though it was difficult to tell because of the faded quality - as I passed the photo back to him. There was something familiar about Dwayne's father, but I couldn't think what. No doubt it was because there was a strong family resemblance between him and Dwayne.

Dwayne gazed at it again before slipping it back into his wallet. 'Sure was. I'm just sorry I never got to know him.' Then he added, 'Though don't get me wrong. I had a wonderful time as a kid, never knew that my dad wasn't my real father till mom told me many years later.'

The moment passed and Susie said, 'Well, at least you have happy memories of him.' She patted his hand.

There was an awkward silence, thankfully broken by the sound of my phone. It was Simon. Oh dear, I'd been sadly neglecting my husband recently, thinking guilty of the messages he'd left and I hadn't got round to answering.

'I'll go outside to take this,' I said. 'The reception's better.'

'How are you?' Simon's voice was faint, muffled and I moved further along the road.

'All's well,' I said. There was no point in starting to tell him the whole sorry tale about my lack of progress and about Tara's disappearance. That would keep until he was home. Besides, he was more than likely to say to me that I shouldn't get involved in problems that were none of my business.

But what he had to say surprised me. 'The last part of the trip has been cancelled, Alison. We were due to go on to Poland, but it's been decided that we've done enough travelling and recruiting for this year. I can't say I'm sorry. I'll be glad to get home.'

'When will you be back?'

'At the end of this month. I'll keep you posted. At the moment we're trying to re-schedule flights.'

'But I won't be back in Glasgow until the middle of August,' I said. 'I'm all tied up here and there's no way I can leave any earlier.'

'Don't worry about that, Alison. I'll go back to Glasgow for a few days and then I thought I'd join you on Bute.'

'Fine, but I'll be working,' I replied more crossly than intended. The clear summer I'd anticipated to make a good start on the project was rapidly turning into a six weeks of constant interruptions.

'Don't worry about me,' he said with a chuckle. 'There are plenty of golf courses on Bute to keep me busy.'

That much was true. And it would be good to have his company, his steadying influence. Now that Tara had returned eager to make up for lost time, surely everything would go to plan. I'd be able to complete the interviews, finish the research and go back to Glasgow to spend most of the autumn and the winter writing up the publication.

It all sounded too straightforward, too simple...and it was.

THIRTY-NINE

'Guess what they're doing?' said Tara, moving restlessly in her seat. Once again we were meeting in the tearoom at Ettrick Bay. Since her return, Tara had been as good as her word and had worked tirelessly.

Through the window we could see threatening clouds had gathered, moved in across the bay and the lights were on in the tearoom. Suddenly the first drops plopped loudly off the flat roof of the building and for the rest of the afternoon the sun appeared only briefly amid a succession of torrential downpours.

'Let's go through this quickly,' I had said, aware the tearoom was busy, a refuge for a day of unpredictable weather. 'Let's order lunch and press on.' No sooner had we found a table in the far corner when, as though on cue, the main door opened and a family group tumbled in, shaking off the worst of the rain.

Tara seemed to be back to her old self, eager to forget about her flight to Glasgow.

'How are the interviews going?' I wanted facts, not supposition.

'There is a problem,' she said, toying with the piping hot cheese and onion toastie that had just arrived. 'Some of the interviewees seem a lot more interested in what's happening in the present rather than recollecting the past.' Then she sighed. 'But can you guess what's happening.'

She wasn't to be distracted then. 'I couldn't possibly imagine,' I said, not having the faintest idea of what she was talking about. Besides I was still recovering from a very late night. I'd sat up long after Susie and Dwayne had departed in a state of mild panic, reading through the total sum of my work to date. What was worse, even printed off on single pages with double spacing it was perfectly obvious, in spite of all our work, there was no way it would make more than a slim volume. And that was before I edited out all the stories that might be libellous.

'Have you heard the latest about the skeleton in the Pavilion?'

There was no way she was going to let this go. 'Go on, I know you're dying to tell me.'

She paused for a moment, no doubt for effect. 'They've decided to do one of those facial reconstructions, to get a better idea of what he looked like, see if it sparks any memories of people on the island.'

She bit into her toasted sandwich. 'So we'll be able to see what he looked like.'

'When will this happen?'

'They've started already.'

I had to ask. 'But what about DNA tests? Isn't that what they would do first?'

She shrugged. 'No use in this case, from what I hear.'

And in all the excitement, the death of Ewan Flisch seemed to have been almost entirely forgotten. Or perhaps the police had a good idea about what had happened to him, but they wouldn't want to reveal too much information, certainly not to the general public, until they had proof. Gerry hadn't been formally arrested, but any time I saw him he looked more and more haggard.

The door to the tearoom opened suddenly and I glanced up idly, busy as I was trying to shuffle papers, listen to Tara and eat my lunch. Rufus Beale looked around, casting his eyes over every table, lingering on ours for a moment. He obviously didn't see whoever it was he was looking for, because he turned on his heel and went out as suddenly as he had come in.

'He might at least have said hello to you,' muttered Tara, turning away. 'How rude.'

'I think he's that kind of person,' I said, wondering why he'd been here. It seemed that everywhere I went, Rufus Beale turned up. Surely he wasn't stalking me? I dismissed that thought. This was a small island. It was no more than coincidence. Besides, I had other things on my mind apart from Rufus.

'I have to go along to the Hereuse nursing home this afternoon,' I said.' A couple of the residents there might have some interesting stories.'

'And I'm going up to the museum - they have a series of documents that will shed light on the very early days, before the Pavilion was built,' Tara said.

'Good idea, 'I replied. 'That will give us a nice intro about what was on the site before 1938.' This was an angle I hadn't thought of and one of the reasons I was so pleased to have Tara back. Young and resourceful, she could come at the project from a different perspective.

We'd been interviewed yet again about the murder of Ewan Flisch but there was absolutely nothing more we could tell the police. I shivered to think that the murderer might still be here on the island. There was no definite word, merely that, 'Enquiries were ongoing'.

I left Tara and headed towards Ascog and the Hereuse nursing home, feeling tightness in my chest as I approached. Last time I'd been here was in less than happy circumstances, but although the structure was still the same - an old house with a new annexe on each side - there had been many changes. For one thing the avenue of gloomy trees lining the driveway up to the main house had been severely pollarded, and some of them had been cut back altogether so that there was a lightness in the approach that hadn't been there before.

The huge front door, repainted a bright shade of red, new curtains at the windows and, inside, carpets replaced by modern flooring all gave the place a decidedly cheerful air. There had been many changes here.

There was a new owner as well, or rather owners, because a young couple had bought the property and Magdela Ottis welcomed me with a firm handshake and a smile. She was tall, slim and very elegant, her dark hair tied up in a chignon with not a stray hair out of place.

'I do hope we can help you,' she said. 'I've heard all about the project of course and I'm sure some of our residents must remember stories about the place. Where would you like to start? Or would you like some tea first?' Although her English was perfect, she spoke with a trace of a foreign accent, an indication she was not a Brandane. More and more the island attracted people to move here, tempted by the quality of life it had to offer.

I declined the offer of tea. 'Perhaps that would be good later.'

'Come with me. I have spoken to them all and there are three residents here who had some connection with the Pavilion many years ago. They are waiting for you in the small lounge at the back of the house, overlooking the gardens.'

Here there was also a surprise. The lounge was decorated in sunshine yellow, dotted with a variety of upright and comfy chairs, the far wall dominated by a huge flat screen television.

'This we call the football room,' grinned Magdela. 'This is where the football fans come to watch the games.'

In the corner two men and a woman sat together at a table, playing cards, but they looked up with interest when Magdela introduced me.

'Ah, you're the woman who's writing the history of the Pavilion,' said one of the men, his quavering voice an indication of his age. News travels fast in all corners of the island and the residents here had also heard about the book on the Pavilion.

'Of course she is. Isn't that why Magdela brought us together?' said the woman, her stooped back making it difficult for her to swivel round.

The other man seemed not to hear. 'What are you talking about?' he said. 'Why have you stopped playing?'

The woman rapped his hand. 'Don't be so rude. This young lady (thank you for that, I thought) has come especially to see us.'

Oh dear, this looked as if it would be hard work. But I'd reckoned without the redoubtable Magdela who drew up a seat for me and one for herself as she said, 'Of course that is quite correct. You all remember Alison has come to ask you what you remember about your days at the Pavilion, when it was first built. Anything you can tell her will be of great help to her. It is very important that she gets material for her history of the place.'

'Why, has it burned down?' said the man with the quavery voice.

'Don't be silly, dear,' said the lady. 'You remember that article in *The Buteman* about how they are going to do a lot of renovations, make the place modern.'

'I don't hold with modern,' said the deaf man darkly.

'No, no, it's not modern - they're going to restore it to the way it was in the beginning.'

'That'll cost a lot of money. We need plenty of other things on the island here before...'

The old lady rapped him on the knuckles again. 'They won't be using your money, Tommy. Not that they'd be able to get a penny out of you.'

This was getting me nowhere fast and I pulled out my recorder in the hope of changing the subject and moving them back on track. 'Perhaps if we could chat about the Pavilion, about anything you can recall. First of all what did each of you do there and when?'

With some coaxing from me and a lot of encouragement from Magdela I managed to get a good hour's worth of material. In fact once they started they were difficult to stop and only the prospect of the tea trolley on its rounds brought a halt to proceedings.

This time I gratefully accepted a cup of tea and a slice of fruit cake and turned to talk of more general matters. Magdela stood up. 'I must apologise, but I have some work to do before the supper time. I am happy to leave you to chat if you wish?'

'That's fine,' I said. 'I've enough material for what I want.'

I turned to the trio of residents who were happily munching away, completely ignoring me as they concentrated on the tea and cakes. 'I'd like to thank you all for your help. It's been great to meet you all and hear your anecdotes. I'm sure I'll be able to use some of them.'

'Of course,' said the deaf man,' if you really want some juicy tales about the Pavilion in the 1940s, you should speak to Iris MacDonald.'

I stopped at the door. 'Who's she? How can she help'

'Because,' said the deaf man patiently, 'she's Violet's sister. The one who was married to Willie Flisch.'

'And where does she live?'

He frowned. 'She used to live in a house up at the back of the Serpentine in Rothesay, but I heard she moved. The hill got too much for her.'

He couldn't enlighten me any further, had no idea where she'd moved to.

This was interesting news indeed. I'd have to try to find her...and soon.

FORTY

The phone call from Tara was unexpected, the high pitch of her voice betraying her excitement. 'It's ready, Alison, the reconstruction of the face of the skeleton is ready. I thought it would take much longer.'

At that moment I was sitting in the cottage, head bent over the computer as I'd been for the past couple of hours, trying to ignore the beginnings of cramp in my feet as well as my fingers. Added to which my brain appeared to have gone numb and I'd typed the same interview up twice, only realising when reading over the last few pages. So this news from Tara was a welcome distraction from my problems. 'So what's the plan to show this reconstruction?'

'There will be a kind of private showing and then there will be posters made and a spot on television including that popular T.V. crime programme. They'll send the pictures to Canada and to the States as well, in fact send them round the world. Once a positive identification is confirmed it will hopefully lead them to some information about what happened or who was responsible for his death. There must be someone out there who knows the true story.'

'We'll be able to see it, see this reconstruction soon?'

'Yes, we can go along to the museum on Friday morning at ten o'clock for the unveiling.' Tara was almost squeaking with excitement.

'And in the meantime?' While it would be very interesting to see what this man had looked like, it wouldn't take us much further forward in the work we still had left to do.

'Don't fret, Alison. I've some other good news,' she said, a note of pride in her voice. 'I've managed to track down some good quality original posters for early events at the Pavilion, some of the dances and the shows and we can use them as long as we acknowledge copyright. I can show them to you tomorrow after we've been to the museum.'

'Good idea.' We chatted for a few more minutes and then I hung up. Tara had done really well again. The pictorial element was very important, it was essential to have as many illustrations as possible in the book and it was looking like we'd been very fortunate indeed, thanks to Tara's hard work. Illustrations would make the book easier to sell for one thing and I toyed briefly with the idea of producing two books: one a lavishly illustrated coffee table tome, the other a more detailed history.

As quickly as I thought about it, I abandoned that idea. We'd enough to do trying to finish one book and there was still all the text to check, to organise before we could pass it over to the editor, never mind getting it published. Editing and proofing would take us to the next summer and we'd be lucky to have everything ready in good time for the proposed grand re-opening in June. Now that the work was underway again, the team of workmen at the Pavilion were pulling out all the stops.

So it was back to work on the computer, reminding myself these notes had to be translated into a format to allow me to work on them when I returned to Glasgow.

Susie and Dwayne had headed off again, this time for a trip to Edinburgh and then they were due to leave for America after a final couple of days on Bute. Or so they said. If all went according to plan they would be here to meet Simon who kept texting me to remind me that he would be joining me on the island. As if I would!

After an overlong stint at the computer, I slept badly that night, in spite of a long walk along the shore before bedtime. The weather had changed yet again; the rain had cleared and there was a promise of more good weather in the days ahead.

My sleep was filled with dreams of skulls and of being trapped in some kind of underground cellar and I wakened just as dawn was breaking, my heart thudding fit to burst. Try as I might, the details of my dream escaped me. Probably as well, but worried the dreams might return, I got up, showered and dressed and walked down into the village for the morning paper.

Several cups of coffee later and I was ready to face the day. There was plenty to keep me busy until we could see the reconstruction of the skeleton's head.

Friday came round quickly and as we weren't due at the museum till ten so I spent an hour reading over the notes from the night before, printing off a hard copy the better to spot any errors.

My mind kept drifting, kept wondering about the skeleton and what it would look like, though it was unlikely to take the quest for the murderer any further forward. It was all so long ago, there was every likelihood the murderer was himself - or herself - dead. And did it matter now, after all this time?

With all these ideas buzzing in my head, I drove to the museum, luckily finding a parking space only a couple of streets away.

I showed my credentials to the member of staff guarding the door. There was more security than I'd thought and he checked everything carefully before allowing me to enter, directing me down the corridor.

A small cluster of people crammed into the main part of the museum, moving about, trying to make the most of the space available. I recognised a couple of the museum staff, one or two voluntary helpers, two men

214

who could only have been police officers, a reporter from *The Buteman* and someone from one of the national dailies.

I looked around for Tara, finally spying the top of her head right at the front of the crowd. She was standing beside a young man I didn't recognise, standing guard at the front over something draped in a white cloth. I felt a shiver of excitement. It must be the skeleton's head.

She waved when she spotted me. 'Isn't this exciting,' she said, pushing her way through the crowd and coming up to join me at the back of the room. 'Don't you want to be down at the front, to see what's happening?'

'Do you want to come with me?'

'No - you go on.'

She smiled and squeezed my arm before starting to push her way back through the throng. The buzz of excitement grew louder as one of the policemen came to the front and stood beside the young man.

'Ladies and gentlemen, if I could have your attention.' The noise abated but didn't quite die away so he tried once more, this time in a much louder voice. 'If we could have silence for a moment.'

This time the room grew quiet, so quiet it was strangely unnerving. The only noise was the soft click of a camera.

'Thank you. I'm going to hand you over to Lenny. His department at the university was responsible for the reconstruction you're about to see so I hope you'll be suitable impressed by the quality of this work.'

Lenny, obviously relishing his moment of fame, looked at the clock on the wall and then exactly at ten o'clock he gave a loud cough to attract our attention.

'Ladies and Gentlemen, I am pleased that you could come along today for this first sight of the

215

reconstruction of the head of the skeleton found in the Pavilion. There were one or two problems, especially as part of the skull was very thin. Parma and her assistants have done a great job in this and we're all looking forward to seeing what he looked like.'

Parma was small and slight and looked as if she was far too fragile to take on something like this, but evidently it wasn't her first time. With a flourish she pulled the covering from the head.

Everyone edged forward, those of us at the back standing unsteadily on tip toe to have a better view.

Here at last was the man who had been found in the basement, so striking it was impossible to believe he was made of clay. They had added details to make him even more lifelike. His piercing blue eyes stared out at us, his blond hair gleamed in the shafts of sunlight coming in through the high windows and his aquiline nose gave him a majestic, stern air.

There was a loud gasp in the room, an intake of breath as the face was revealed. I stared at the apparition in front of me because the gasp from me was loudest of all. This was someone I recognised. With his high forehead, strong chin and long aquiline nose, it could only be the man Dwayne had shown me in the photo of his father.

That was when Tara fainted.

FORTY-ONE

'Are you going to tell me what's going on?'

Tara and I were sitting in a side room of the museum. She sipped at a glass of water, her face still ashen. 'You know something about that skeleton, something you've been keeping secret.'

There seemed to be so many people who knew about the skeleton in the Pavilion, who had some connection to him. If that was the case why was it that no one had done anything about it before this, set the wheels in motion when he first went missing? Or had there been some publicity at the time, something I'd missed? I'd have to go back to the library and check through the copies of *The Buteman* for that period.

This jumble of thoughts was going through my head as I listened quietly to Tara fill in some of the gaps. 'My grandmother was married to Willie Flisch but my father was Canadian - Marvin Tempus. He was stationed here on Bute during the last war and he fell in love with her, or so she believed. She was from Glasgow, but like many people she'd come to the island out of the way of the terrible bombing. Her aunt had a farm so there was plenty of work.'

She took another sip of water before continuing, 'I gather she was quite a beauty in her youth and a number of men on the island were very much in love with her, including Willie. It caused a lot of problems when she fell for Marvin. Of course he promised her the earth, a new life in Canada, all she could ever dream of. She was more than anxious to get away, explore the big world. Trouble was because she had been too long here in the rural backwater of Kammadie farm, one of the smallest farms on the island. If it

217

hadn't been for the war, she'd have gone back to the bright lights of the city.'

She stopped, gazing at me to judge my reaction. Still I waited. There was nothing to be said about this story, not until I'd heard it all.

'It was a disaster, of course, the marriage, I mean. Willie thought he could deal with it, bringing up another man's child, but he couldn't.'

'Ah, so she became pregnant by this Canadian, this Marvin?'

Tara grimaced. 'Yes, Marvin wasn't quite the star turn he pretended to be, that was for sure.'

'What do you mean by that?'

Tara sighed. 'I suppose I should tell you the whole story, why I suddenly disappeared off the island like that?'

'Well, it would be helpful,' I said, but my mind was on other matters. I was again having serious doubts about continuing to use her as my research assistant. Her disappearance had badly shaken me, shaken my belief in her. I needed someone to rely on, someone to trust and this episode had made me very concerned indeed about Tara. Why had she kept her suspicions about the skeleton to herself for all this time? With some difficulty I returned to what she was saying.

'It all started during the war. You know the story about the Canadian 'invasion' of Bute, but I don't think you can begin to imagine, unless you've heard the stories, what an effect that had on the island. As soon as she became pregnant Marvin abandoned her, left the island.'

This puzzled me. 'Wait a minute,' I said. 'I thought he left the island because his time here was up, he went elsewhere?'

'That's why I disappeared so suddenly. The phone call was from Lydia to tell me what she knew about the skeleton.'

'Lydia out at Straad?' This was a surprise. She hadn't mentioned anything about contacting Tara to me. Was that why she'd asked for Tara's number?

Tara ignored this question and went on, 'I had to find out if he'd had left the island so I went to the Mitchell Library for help in tracking him down. It meant a trip to London and I'd just arrived back in Glasgow the day you saw me in the restaurant.'

I hesitated before asking the question. Part of me wanted to hear the answer; another part hoped it would all go away. 'Did you find out what you wanted? Did he rejoin his regiment?'

She shook her head. 'No, the records show he was posted as having deserted, gone missing.'

Suddenly it all made sense. Who else could the skeleton be but Marvin? Even so, the decision about what to do next wasn't mine to make.

'So what do you intend to do now? Let the police know? They'll be able to arrange a DNA test, confirm who he is.'

It appeared that at least one mystery was about to be solved.

FORTY-TWO

I had to speak with Dwayne, had to contact him without delay.

'Are you sure?' Tara sounded more and more concerned as she listened to my theory. 'Old photos can be deceptive. Maybe it was only someone who looked like him? Or it might have been a trick of the light.'

Of course I was certain. Even if the photo was old and faded, there was a strong resemblance to Dwayne in the reconstructed skull, a family resemblance too good to be denied.

Unfortunately I'd been so astonished at the sight of the reconstructed skull that I'd blurted out in front of the whole crowd, 'But that's Dwayne's father.' Every head in the room had swivelled round to look at me, but the distraction of Tara fainting had saved me from having to explain my outburst.

Now that she had recovered from the shock, she picked up on my comment. 'What on earth was that all about, Alison? And who is Dwayne? Do you mean your friend Susie's boyfriend?'

A brief explanation didn't satisfy her so I backtracked a little. 'I need to see that photo again but let's say that I'm ninety nine per cent sure it's him.'

Tara was visibly upset. 'But how could it be? If Marvin was planning to marry my grandmother, how could this Dwayne be his son?'

I had a good idea about this, but wasn't too sure how to tell her.

She took my hesitation for a sign of bad news. 'Go on, Alison. Tell me the truth. You know something, don't you?'

'It's only a guess...'

'Well then, what is your guess?' She stood up in front of me, hands on hips. What harm was there in telling her what I suspected. It would make no difference now.

'It's only a guess, Tara, but probably he already had a family back home,' I said. 'It wasn't all that unusual. Lonely men, away from their wives, not knowing if they would live to see their families again, enjoyed the day. It was a different time. If you thought the next day might be your last you would do almost anything to chat up one of the local girls. It was only when she became pregnant that there was trouble. '

Tara looked astonished by this. 'Do you think that's what happened?'

'Do you know anything about Willie and Violet's marriage date? Or about when your mum was born?'

'I know my mother's birthday, of course,' said Tara. 'I've no idea when my grandmother married.'

'It would be a good idea to find out. That may give us the final clue to what happened.'

'Shouldn't we go to the police, like now?'

'We could tell them what we know, or suspect, but we could do much more with some proof. This is speculation at the moment.'

'I've got all the family papers back at the flat. We could pick them up.'

'Let's do that and then we'll go round to the cottage to try to piece all this together.'

We opened the door and peeped in to take a last look at the head, now surrounded by the audience, Parma and her colleague being subjected to a battery of questions, the intermittent flash of cameras making her blink. There was no doubt in my mind who this man was, but I had to be able to convince other people. Too often in the past I'd gone rushing in, making bold deductions that turned out to be completely wrong. I didn't want it to happen again. Besides, knowing who he was didn't give us any more information about why he'd died, though the mention of the thinness of the skull had been interesting.

We drove to the flat in the High Street. 'I'll wait here,' I said as Tara leapt out of the car, heedless of any traffic and ran over to the close.

She emerged a few minutes later, clutching a slim folder. 'There isn't very much,' she said 'and I'm not even sure the marriage certificate is here.' I didn't say I was astonished she was able to find the information so quickly, given the state of her room. 'Do you have your mother's birth certificate?'

'Yes, it's here.' She patted the folder.

'That will give you the date of your grandparents' marriage,' I said. 'Let's look at that as soon as we get back to the cottage.'

We drove in silence round to Kilchattan Bay, each preoccupied with our own thoughts. Only when we were settled in the living room with the documents spread out in front of us did we start to talk.

Tara's mother's birth certificate was easy to follow and the date of her parents' marriage was given as over a year before her birth.

'But that seems very strange if Violet was pregnant when she married Willie Flisch. Let's look through the rest of the documents.' In spite of several trawls through all the papers, there was no sign of a marriage certificate.

Tara sat back and fiddled with one of her earrings. 'That's very strange indeed. We'll have to try something else.'

'Let's try the internet. We'll be able to find it through Scotland's People.'

Tara looked puzzled.

'It's an online website for all the Scottish genealogical records,' I explained.

It didn't take us long to find what we were looking for. Yes, there it was, the date of their marriage wasn't as recorded on the birth certificate - it was a full year later. Tara's mother had been born only five months after the wedding.

'I can't believe it,' said Tara, staring at the screen, 'and I'm sure my mother didn't know. They were such a devoted couple and my mother always said that Willie worshipped my grandmother, would have done anything for her.'

'There were no other children?'

'No, none. My mother was the only one.'

An idea was beginning to form in my mind, but I didn't know if it was a real possibility. There might be something here, something to link to the murder of Ewan Flisch. Some piece of information was niggling at the back of my mind, only just out of reach.

A sudden burst of inspiration and I realised what it was. 'Tara,' I said,' who was it who told you about the skeleton - that it might be your grandfather?'

For a moment she looked undecided about whether to reveal her source. She avoided my gaze as she said so quietly as to be almost inaudible, 'It was Lydia. She asked me to come to see her, told me the story.'

'So that's who made the phone call that had you rushing off?'

'Yes.' She looked bashful. 'I stayed there overnight. I needed some space after she told me the story.'

Why had I not guessed? This was the connection. Somehow or other Lydia was involved in what had happened all those years ago, why she had asked for a contact number for Tara.

But why didn't she want to tell me about it? Another trip to Straad was called for. There was no way I could rest until I found out what else she knew.

FORTY-THREE

That was very odd. There was a light on in the cottage at Kilchattan Bay. It was summer and the nights were long; there was no need for lights.

It was unusual for me to be out all day: I tried to be back by teatime at the latest. It was fine doing all the interviews, but even with a recorder, I had to write them up as I went along. There were so many anecdotes, so many versions of the same stories. It wasn't merely that people's memories were suspect; even when they remembered an important event there could be as many different versions of it as there were people. It was my task to make sense of it all without offending anyone.

I parked the car in the street and switched off the engine. Perhaps I'd been so pre-occupied that morning I'd forgotten to switch off the light? But that was stupid. At this time of year sunrise was around four o'clock and, even on a dull day, a light wasn't necessary by the time I got up.

I locked the car, took a deep breath and crept along to the front door. No matter how often I told myself this behaviour was foolish, I couldn't stop myself from trembling. Could I peep in? Unfortunately the windows of the cottage, being of a great age, were small, but I sidled up to the front window and darted round to peer in. Only part of the front room was visible, but it appeared absolutely empty.

I crept along the side of the cottage towards the back window into the kitchen, keeping low. I only hoped none of the neighbours were looking out - they would have wondered what on earth I was up to. A swift look through the kitchen window convinced me there was no one there either. What should I do now? Whoever was in the cottage could be anywhere. There was a ladder in the little shed at the bottom of the postage-stamp sized garden but I lacked the courage to retrieve it in order climb up to look in the bedroom windows.

Perhaps I could knock on one of the other doors in the terrace? Make up some story about hearing mice and being afraid of them? Or phone the police station, saying I'd lost my key? That seemed a very poor option: I'd already caused enough trouble. What I really didn't want to do was to go in on my own, but I couldn't stay out here all night.

I took a deep breath and went back round to the front door. I lifted the flap of the letterbox very carefully and peered in, listening for any sound as much as trying to see if there was anyone inside.

'Are you okay?' I stood up quickly at the sound of the voice, almost trapping my fingers in the letterbox as it snapped shut with a loud clunk.

I recognised the tall, gangly young man who was gazing at me with a very puzzled expression as a neighbour who lived a couple of houses down. 'Have you lost your key?'

'No, no,' I said, a little too quickly. Then in what I thought of as a moment of inspiration I said, 'I thought there was something trapped in the letterbox.'

He looked at me suspiciously. 'Mmm...I did wonder what you were doing, creeping round the back of the building. I thought you might be a burglar.'

'Gosh, do I look like a burglar, 'I said with a forced laugh, trying to make light of the episode and not succeeding.

He frowned. He evidently didn't think this remark funny. 'Burglars come in all shapes and sizes,' he said.

I pulled my key from my bag with a flourish and inserted it in the lock. Although he was still looking at me suspiciously, I might as well make use of his presence.

I opened the door and strode in, shouting, 'No, everything is absolutely fine. I'm so glad you're here. It's always good to have a man about the place.'

By now the young man was backing out, a strange look on his face, probably wondering what he had got himself involved in, what was going on.

I stopped and listened. Silence. There was no sound, no one came rushing down to the front door, tried to escape through the kitchen. There was no one else in the house.

The young man was still regarding me, his mouth open in amazement, as I closed the door on him with a 'Thanks, I'll be fine now,' and leaned back heavily against it, waiting for my heart to stop beating so loudly.

After a few minutes I felt able to look carefully round the living room. In the far corner, beside the computer, the desk lamp burned. Even if I'd switched on a light earlier in the morning, in a half awake state, there was no way I would have switched on this lamp, strictly for use when working on writing up my notes.

I began to examine every surface, seeking evidence that it wasn't my imagination, that someone had been here. But there was no obvious sign of an intruder. My notes lay in a somewhat haphazard pile, but then that looked very much like the way I'd left them, though I could go through them more carefully later. And how could anyone access the information on the computer without a password? I'd been extra careful to devise a password that would be difficult to guess. It was all a puzzle, yet I had this feeling someone had been in the room.

A cursory inspection of the rest of the house told the same story. There was nothing missing, nothing out of place as far as I could tell. I sat down on the bed and thought about it. Who would want to break in here? I was writing a history of the Pavilion, for goodness sake, not engaged in some kind of espionage.

I went down into the kitchen to make some supper, though whether I'd be able to eat anything with this tight knot in my stomach was a moot point. I switched on the television for the distraction of the news and sat down, moving a pile of folders to do so. Then I noticed it. The blue folder, the one that held all our photos, wasn't properly closed. It wasn't very noticeable, but enough for me. I began to flick rapidly through the photos. There were so many it took me a few moments to realise that there was indeed a photo missing: the photo of the group of workers outside the Pavilion when it was being built. I searched again, in case I'd missed it, in case it had become stuck behind another photo.

It most certainly wasn't there. And unfortunately, with everything else I'd had to do, I hadn't got round to scanning this set of photos into the computer.

FORTY-FOUR

Why would someone steal the photo? Although it was, as far as I knew, the only original in existence of this particular event, it wasn't of any value. No, whoever had taken it had had another reason for stealing it.

Should I phone Tara? But although it was very unlikely she was the culprit, I was still suspicious about her. When I thought about it in my quieter moments, why would a young girl like her want to undertake a commission like this one? And I'd been so busy I hadn't had time to have a good look at her application. It had gone on the 'to do' pile and then I'd promptly forgotten about it.

I ran through the list of people in my head: anyone who might have an interest in this old story. There was Gerry, of course. He seemed to know more than he said. While he claimed to be the 'new boy' evidence suggested he had connections with the Pavilion going back a long way. Then there was Rufus: he seemed to be more than a little interested in anything I found out. His father's company had long associations with the island. Was he concerned I'd find out that the story about his father running off with money was true?

And of course there was Dwayne. Unfortunately, apart from the fact that he was American rather than Canadian - a distinction he had pointed out to me on more than one occasion since we'd discussed the skeleton - he had no known connections to Bute. He certainly wouldn't have come to the island if it hadn't been for Susie.

That left Tara. Was she strong enough to have murdered Ewan? But what motive could she possibly have had?

No matter which way I tried it, I couldn't come up with a solution. And Ewan's death, as so often happens, had dropped to the very bottom of the news items.

The police would be working hard behind the scenes, no doubt they had suspects, but they weren't going to share that kind of information with me.

If Simon had been here, he would have told me to get on with the task in hand and not concern myself with other matters. Which was all very well to say, but unfortunately there was still that business of the missing photo. It was scarcely the kind of crime the police would be interested in, in spite of my increasing conviction that Rufus was stalking me.

The phone rang, making me jump. 'Hello,' I said.

'Gosh, Alison,' said Susie. 'You sound very far away. Are you okay?'

'Fine,' I said, perhaps a little too quickly to convince her.

'You sound worried about something.'

There was no point in starting to tell Susie about what had happened, not over the phone. I sidestepped the question.' How are you? And more important, where are you?'

She chuckled. 'We're in Glasgow sorting out all the details for the wedding.'

'Why are you doing that in Glasgow if you are planning to get married on Bute? Surely you would have to make all the arrangements here?'

'Well, yes, but I have to think about what I'll wear.'

'Did you find something?'

'Not quite decided. I'd like your opinion.' Then she changed tack. 'But that's not why I'm phoning you. We've decided to come over to Bute again for a couple of days before we go back to L.A. It would be good to see you again and we can have a couple of days relaxing on the island. Don't worry,' she added before I

230

could speak, 'we won't be staying with you. We've booked into the same hotel as last time.'

'Are you sure?' I said a pang of guilt, but secretly hoping she would indeed refuse any offer of accommodation at the cottage, thinking of the amount of work still to do.

'Absolutely. I'll text you when we're on our way.'

'I'll meet you at the ferry.'

'No need, we've hired a car.'

I set to work to type up my notes from the day's interviews, but from time to time I would pause, thinking again about who might been in the cottage.

I'd this feeling that Ewan's death and the discovery of the skeleton were at the centre of the puzzle, that the two were connected, but I didn't have the faintest idea how.

FORTY-FIVE

I met Simon at the ferry. 'No point in bringing over my car if you're going to be there,' he'd said.

In vain I said to him, as I'd said so often to others, 'I'm working.' His reply was, 'Oh, surely you'll be able to give me a lift to the golf course before you go off on your jaunts each morning.' Why did I get the impression he wasn't taking any of this seriously? I debated telling him about my suspicions about someone being in the cottage, stealing the photo, but in the end decided he'd only worry even more about me. After all, I could go back to the library, check the details and order up a copy of the photo perfectly easily. It didn't make sense.

We returned to the cottage to meet up with Susie and Dwayne, both enjoying their last few days on the island before returning to the States. I still hadn't come up with a way of telling Dwayne what I knew, though as soon as he read the local paper he was bound to find out.

It seemed such a convoluted story and I'd harshly declined Tara's offer to come over and meet him. 'Let me talk to him first,' I said, determined to find some way. 'Once he knows and has had time to think about it all, then you can meet him.'

'Good we all managed to meet before we go back to L.A.,' said Susie, proudly introducing Dwayne, whose firm grip and 'Howdy,' took Simon by surprise.

We had a pleasant evening walking down to the Kingarth after supper and we each in our own way brought Simon up to speed with what had been happening. Actually I'd have preferred to say as little as possible to him, but Susie was as ever bubbling with the story. I could see him frowning as he listened to the details of the discovery of the skeleton in the Pavilion, the death of the manager Ewan Flisch. Eventually he turned to me and said, 'I thought, Alison, this was to be a simple commission, something less stressful than teaching.'

'It is,' I said, avoiding his gaze. 'It's just that a lot has been going on. None of it has been my doing.'

'But it appears you're involved in it.'

'Oops,' said Susie, 'have I said too much? I thought Simon would want to hear the full story.'

'And I daresay that Alison would have given me a very abbreviated account if it had been left to her.'

'That's not fair,' I protested.

This precipitated my decision. I couldn't let Susie and Dwayne leave without knowing the full story. When we returned to the cottage I thought, It's now or never and said, 'I think we should all sit down with a drink. I've something to tell you, Dwayne.'

Whether he was surprised I'd something to tell him or was surprised by the offer of yet another drink, all he said was, 'Yeah?'

A deep breath. 'You remember I told you I was going to the Bute museum, that they were doing a reconstruction of the face of the skeleton found in the Pavilion?'

'Uh...hu,' said Dwayne, a note of caution in his voice.

How to say it tactfully? 'Look, Dwayne, this isn't easy, but from the photo you showed me of your father, I suspect the skeleton might have been him.'

Simon stared at me as if to say, 'I knew I shouldn't have left you on your own here,' but wisely he made no comment.

Dwayne also seemed lost for words, but Susie jumped in. 'That's not possible. Dwayne is American and the skeleton is Canadian, so it's very...'

Dwayne held up his hand to interrupt her. 'Not exactly, honey. My mother was American, from Kansas originally, but my dad was Canadian. They decided to move to America, to be near my mum's folks while he was away in action.'

There was a silence in the room. Dwayne looked as if he was about to add something more, but several times he hesitated.

'So there's something about all of this bothering you?' There was something else weighing on his mind.

'I guess I didn't tell you the whole story,' he said. 'I only learned it myself from my mom just before she died.' He took the photo from his wallet. 'All my life I was told what a hero my dad was, how he had died for his country, fighting evil, so that we could all be free. Then on her deathbed my mom said she had to tell me the truth. He hadn't been such a hero: he'd been a deserter. Had come to Bute and when he was on leave had made off. Can you imagine how I felt, and how bad I felt when Susie wanted to come here, then wanted to get married here?'

Susie lifted his hand and squeezed it affectionately. 'Why didn't you tell me, Dwayne? It doesn't matter one bit where we get married.'

'Dwayne patted her hand. 'No one likes to have their childhood dreams shattered. Most of the time I wished mom hadn't told me the truth. I'm only sorry she isn't here to find out what really happened to him.'

He looked round at us all. 'Guess that wasn't true either? He didn't return to duty because someone killed him.' He turned to me. 'What happens now?'

'We go to the police as soon as we have a new copy of the photo and tell them what we know. No doubt they'll be able to do a DNA test with you and confirm everything.'

234

'But we're supposed to be going back to Los Angeles tomorrow,' wailed Susie.

'That's a mite tough, honey, but don't you think this merits staying here for a couple more days?'

Susie had the grace to look ashamed at this. 'I guess you're right.'

'There may be no option,' I said. 'The police will want all the details and that may take some time.'

I heard a great sigh from the corner of the room. 'Why didn't I stay on in Glasgow?' Simon was shaking his head as though in sorrow.

It was too late now. We had to go along to the police station, tell them what we knew, give them the details. Perhaps then they would be able to re-open the case properly, decide what to do. They might even identify the murderer.

More than ever I was convinced someone on the island knew exactly what had happened that night at the Pavilion...and who had a motive for murder.

FORTY-SIX

I had to talk to Lydia. She was the one who held the key to this puzzle about the skeleton. She had some information, something she didn't want to reveal. I could only guess she must have a good reason, but every time I thought I'd come up with an answer, there was some vital piece missing, persuading me I must be wrong.

On the way I called in at the library, to check the details and order another copy of the photo that was missing.

'Is Lisanne in today?' I asked the librarian at the desk. As she had given me so much help last time, it would be easier to approach her.

'No, she's not here. She's taken special leave for a few days,' said the librarian. 'Can I help?'

I squinted at her badge. 'Thanks, Clara,' and explained my problem.

Together we went over to the microfiche and she deftly inserted the roll of film.

'That's it, just there,' I said, as the photo of those working on the Pavilion came up.

'Ah,' said Clara. 'You know that Lisanne is a member of the Beale family? I think she's been upset by all this business, finding out what happened with her grandfather.'

'And what was that exactly?'

'Well, the story he was less than honest.' She scrolled further down. There was the paragraph I'd noticed last time, but I hadn't attached any significance to it. A confirmation of what Tara had said.

I noted the details, but it was unlikely I'd be able to use this material, except in the most oblique way. Still, it was part of the early history and couldn't be left out entirely.

I thanked her, went down to order a copy of the photo from *The Buteman* office and then headed straight for Straad. On the drive over I rehearsed various ways of approaching Lydia, ways to persuade her to reveal exactly what she knew. Would she believe I needed to fill out a chapter about the beginning of the war, about the various Canadians on Bute and their exploits?

All my ideas sounded too lame, too implausible. In the end I opted for relying on her sense of good will, her understanding of how important it was to tell the truth after all these years, give Dwayne and Tara back their past.

To my surprise there was a dark blue car parked out side the door, a car I didn't recognise. If there were visitors there would be no chance of speaking to Lydia privately. I'd have to come back, though right now I couldn't think of another excuse for a visit.

I knocked loudly, but it was a few minutes before the door was flung open. Mrs Ferrin stood there, clutching and unclutching the apron she was wearing, her eyes reddened from crying.

'What's wrong?' I said in alarm, guessing it could only be something to do with Lydia.

She stifled a sob. 'Oh, Mrs Cameron, the doctor's with her, with Lydia now. She took a turn for the worse this morning and I had to send for him, though she tried to insist she'd be fine.'

I stood there awkwardly on the doorstep, not knowing whether to wait or to turn and leave. I certainly couldn't insist on seeing Lydia, not if she might be really ill, might even be close to death.

I bit my lip. This was not a time to be thinking about what had happened all those years ago at the Pavilion, what was over and done with. 'Is there anything I can do? Anything you need?' I couldn't leave her like this, so distressed.

She wiped her eyes. 'I can't think straight, to tell you the truth. It's all too much at the moment, Lydia was always the strong one, the...'

Before she could finish, the doctor, a brisk young man with thinning fair hair came downstairs in some haste, clutching a shiny bag. 'She's asleep,' he said, 'so let her be for a while. I've left a prescription beside her bed.' He took his coat from the peg beside the door and smiled re-assuringly at Mrs Ferrin.

'You're not going to move her to hospital?' It was hard to tell if this was something Mrs Ferrin wanted or something she feared.

He shook his head. 'There's no need for that. She's not that ill. It really is no more than a heavy cold. I suspect it's all because she hasn't been sleeping well and it's all caught up with her.'

'Oh, I'm so relieved.' I thought Mrs Ferrin was about to burst into tears, but she held back, gulping.

The doctor patted her arm. 'Now you look after yourself as well and if there's any change in your sister, let me know. Understood, Iris? And try not to worry - she's a tough old lady.'

Mrs Ferrin nodded again. 'Thank you,' she said softly as he strode out to his car at a great pace and coiled his long legs into the driver's seat.

I couldn't say a word, but stood staring at her. She was certainly about the right age, even though her name wasn't Flisch but Ferrin. Why had I not thought of this, wondered about her first name? She had married of course and changed her name, as had Violet. She and her sister must both have been MacDonalds. It might be too much of a coincidence, but was Mrs Ferrin Violet Flisch's sister?

238

FORTY-SEVEN

The moon was peeping through the clouds, illuminating the waters of the bay in shades of pewter and silver as I headed back to the cottage. It had been a long day and I was exhausted, over tired. Thank goodness this was almost the end of my time on the island, at least for the present.

Simon had gone over to the mainland. 'I'll call in at college and bring my car down from Glasgow. With all the stuff you seem to have collected, Alison, we'd be better with two cars.' I was certainly looking forward to heading up to Glasgow and home. 'Then I can take Dwayne and Susie to the airport.'

I'd grown fond of the cottage at Kilchattan Bay as my little bolthole and in many ways I'd be sorry to leave it, leave the peace of this little corner of Bute, but it would be good to be home again, perhaps even have time to catch up with friends and family, pace myself to write up my research. Tara would be here on the island, of course, to tie up any loose ends, sort out any questions I might have.

The skeleton, poor Marvin, would soon be laid to rest. Dwayne had arranged for his father's remains to be taken back to Canada. 'It's what he would have wanted,' he said. In many ways it was good that Willie Flisch was also dead. The evidence was most clearly that it had all been a terrible accident, though I couldn't understand why Lydia hadn't spoken up earlier.

I thought back to my last conversation with her. At last I'd realised that, as an islander, she didn't want to stir up old ghosts. Finally I'd said to her, 'But don't you owe it to them all to clear it up?'

239

'I guess so,' she had said in a whisper. 'But it's not for me to speak ill of the dead.' I was under strict instructions not to tire her out, but this couldn't wait.

She leaned over and grasped my hand. 'Call my cousin in.'

I went downstairs to find Iris. She was in the kitchen, kneading furiously at a pile of bread dough.

'Lydia thinks we should have a chat.'

Her eyes filled with tears. 'I knew it would all come out one day, but at least they're all dead.'

She wiped her hands on a tea towel and we went up to Lydia's room.

'Oh, Lydia,' she said. 'What a mess.'

Lydia struggled into a sitting position and I leapt forward to adjust her pillows. 'Isn't it better that everyone knows the truth now?'

'What really happened?' I urged her gently.

Iris sighed. 'You know the story; know that my sister Violet was pregnant?'

'Yes,' I said, 'I know all about that bit of it. What I don't know is how the skeleton came to be in the Pavilion basement.'

'The thing about Willie Flisch was that he had a terrible temper. But he was mad about Violet, would have done anything for her. Or so he thought in the beginning. What he couldn't get over was the way Marvin had betrayed her. He arranged to meet Marvin backstage after one of the performances. Willie helped from time to time with the heavy work of moving scenery and that kind of thing.'

There was a silence. I held my breath.

She sighed. 'Of course there was a fight and according to Willie, Marvin fell and banged his head. There was nothing Willie could do to revive him. He knew the Pavilion well, knew that that part wasn't used, so he hid the body there.'

240

'All on his own?'

Iris shrugged. 'As far as I know. He was very strong.'

Surely not strong enough to dig a grave and seal it up behind the partition without any help. 'So how did you find out?'

'He told Violet I about it. Seems he was in a terrible state.'

'Why didn't they go to the police? It was an accident.'

'Things were different in those days - very different. She was expecting a baby. What would she have done if Willie had been put in jail?'

So they hadn't known that Marvin had a thin skull, that the slightest blow could have killed him. All those years of worry, of covering up.

'What happens now?' Lydia asked.

'It's up to the police and I know that Dwayne wants to take his father back to Canada to bury him. How long that will take I've no idea.'

'Will I be arrested?' Iris looked fearful.

But though I had no words to reassure her, I hoped that now it was all out in the open, the episode could be closed.

'Anyway,' said Lydia, 'there are other people who should be arrested for far worse crimes than this.'

'What do you mean?'

'That Rufus and his father before him. The trouble they caused. Several people were left bankrupt because of the father, small businesses on the island went to the wall and yet here the son's back, bold as brass.'

This was what Tara had said. Then there was that article in *The Buteman*. 'So why didn't you say something?'

241

'I did,' said Lydia. 'As soon as I knew I called Ewan Flisch, told him to watch out. Like father, like son. I wouldn't have trusted Rufus one bit.'

So that was where Ewan had obtained his information. That was why he was so worried when I first met him.

I left them sitting together in Lydia's room, holding hands for comfort. 'I'll let myself out,' I said.

I drove back to Kilchattan Bay, thinking about it all. Iris was right: it had all been so different in those days. How could we apply the standards of the present to the past?

Now there was just one question left. Who had murdered Ewan Flisch? I had to go to the police, tell them what Lydia had said.

I was so preoccupied with all these thoughts I didn't hear anything till it was too late. As I fumbled in my bag for my key, wondering if I should embark on a final clean of the cottage tonight or leave it till the morning, someone stepped out of the shadows and laid his hand on my arm. It was Rufus.

FORTY-EIGHT

'So you're leaving the island at last, I hear?'

I shook myself free, trying not to show my fear. 'Yes, I'm going the day after tomorrow,' I said, making an effort to keep my voice strong and determined. Unfortunately it came out more as a high-pitched squeak. 'My husband is coming over to collect me.'

He stood over me. 'What information have you finally managed to get, to prise out of the locals?'

I could get a better view of his face as he turned round, reflected in the streetlight. He looked angry, his face twisted in rage.

What was this all about? Did he want me to give him a précis of all the work Tara and I had done on the island? Before I could reply he said, 'Why couldn't you have contented yourself with writing a book of stories about the shows at the Pavilion? Why did you have to go digging up all that stuff about the past?'

As I had no idea what he was talking about, I found it very difficult to make a sensible comment. 'Excuse me,' I said frostily. 'I've some work still to do.' I found my key and pushed it into the lock.

'That's exactly what I want to talk to you about.' He reached over, opened the door and pushed me roughly inside.

He propelled me into the living room. 'Sit down,' he said, forcing me into a chair. 'Now where is that information stored on your computer?' Up close I caught the sour smell of sweat and stale tobacco.

'What are you talking about?' I had at last found my voice. If he wanted to delete everything I had written, that was a silly idea. Apart from anything else, Tara had a copy of everything and of course, after a

243

disastrous episode in the past, I'd learned to make sure I backed everything up.

'I'm talking about what you know about my father.' He stood over me and bent his head down so that he was almost level with me.

So that was it. He had been stalking me, worried about what I might discover. He'd been the person who had broken into the cottage. Leaving the lamp on hadn't been a slip of my mind. Rufus had been here. I suspected he had left the lamp on, not by accident but as a deliberate way of warning me. I shivered. How much more did he know about what I had found out?

He knew I'd been talking to Lydia. Did he know about the skeleton? I thought about Lisanne at the library. Had she told him what I'd been doing? Even as I considered this, what Lydia had said suddenly made sense. Of course! That was the answer. It wasn't only about Rufus and his father and their shady companies: Willie Flisch had had help in disposing of Marvin's body, burying it in the Pavilion. I'd been too stupid to pick this information up.

Did Rufus think I was going to include all this in my book? What did he plan to do? I had to think quickly, come up with some excuse.

'I don't know what you're talking about,' I said, trying to steady my voice, not let him see how scared I was. 'Lydia only told me about her time at the Pavilion, how she was involved in working with some of the big acts of the day. It was all gossip and anecdotes.'

He glared at me, as though not sure whether he should believe me. 'What did you make of what she said?'

I shrugged, trying to keep my voice light. I even tried a laugh, but it came out in a strangulated way. 'Some of what she said was very funny and we'll be able to use a lot of it in the book.'

244

'Did she mention my father? About his friendship with Willie Flisch?'

'No, that didn't come up. We talked about the old days when Lydia worked at the Pavilion,' I said, crossing my fingers he believed me.

He was silent. I could only guess he was weighing up how to get the information out of me without giving too much away. If he told me, I'd have any suspicions confirmed. And if I had no suspicions what was the point in alerting me?

He seemed to relax visibly. 'My family firm has done a lot of work on this island. I don't want any stories about my father, about him running off with money, to be included in your book. Or tales about anything else he might have done. It's all rumour and lies.'

'Even if I did have such information, do you think I'd risk a law suit? We've been ultra careful about everything here, let me tell you,' I stammered.

He looked at his boots. 'The family firm means everything to me. And it only takes the slightest bit of gossip, even if completely untrue, for the reputation to be lost.'

But it was true, I thought, as I stood up, trying to make light of what had happened. True of Rufus also, if Tara was right. My main concern now, my only concern, was to get him out of the house. 'I can let you see a draft of what we've done,' I said, making towards the computer, hoping he wouldn't call my bluff.

He held up his hand. 'That won't be necessary. I should go now.'

Everything depended on whether I could keep my nerve. 'Are you sure you don't want to see it?' I switched the computer on.

He leaned close, his face no more than an inch from mine. 'Not necessary. I'll find out soon enough if

you're stupid enough to include what you shouldn't.'
There was no mistaking what he meant.

As he turned away I kicked my bag under the table.
If he rummaged about in there he'd soon find my
recorder and it wouldn't take him long to make sense of
what Lydia had said.

The noise disturbed him and he turned back. 'What
was that?' he looked round the room. 'That noise?'

Damn! I thought I'd been quiet. 'No idea. You
know what these old houses are like, full of creaks and
groans.'

That seemed to satisfy him and he went towards the
front door, muttering to himself.

A wave of relief swept over me and I thought I'd
have to fall back into the chair, but I had to see him out,
make sure he would go.

At the door he hesitated. 'If there is anything that
comes up about our family, if you write anything in that
book of yours, I'm sure to find out.'

'I'll be off the island very soon,' I said. 'And back
in Glasgow I'll be writing a light-hearted book on
stories about the Pavilion. Your family won't even
come into it.'

He ignored this and went off, making in the
direction of the Kingarth Hotel. I slammed the door
shut and, trembling from head to foot. All I could do
was flop into the chair.

I retrieved my bag from under the table where I'd
kicked it and took out the recorder.

I'd give Rufus a few minutes to get away and then I
could switch it on and listen again to what Lydia had
said. How could I have been so stupid? How could I
not have picked this up earlier?

Was Rufus really only concerned about the
reputation of his family and their firm? Was it all to do

with his father and the missing money, all that had happened all those years ago?

Or was his father's friendship with Willie Flisch behind this concern? Lydia had said, 'Like father, like son.' Was Rufus cheating over the Pavilion contract? After all, it appeared he had cheated before, had ruined Tara's father among others.

I should contact the police straight away. But what could I say to them? I had no proof of anything at all. All I could do was warn Gerry.

FORTY-NINE

I looked at the note again. Why would Gerry write to me instead of phoning me? I'd tried to contact him several times the day before, but the line always seemed to be engaged and when I went over to deliver the draft manuscript as promised he was nowhere to be seen.

I'd had to content myself with leaving the copy propped up on his desk in the portacabin together with a sealed envelope giving details about my suspicions about Rufus. I tried to keep it as vague as possible, but there was no time to be lost. I'd be able to tell him more once we met.

Perhaps he preferred to communicate this way in case he was overheard? I turned the envelope over, this way and that. There was no name on it, no address and certainly no stamp. Hand delivered then. That was even more of a mystery. And the note inside on a torn sheet of lined paper was brief.

'I need to see you first thing tomorrow morning about the draft manuscript. I have really important information for you, but for you alone.'

This was very strange. I tried to think back, to remember how Gerry had been last time I'd seen him, a few days ago. Pre-occupied certainly, but that was only to be expected, given that he had so much on his mind, including the fact that the wrong order for the flooring in the upper hall had been sent and the supplier was blaming everyone but himself. He had seemed delighted at the prospect of having a preview of the manuscript. 'I'll read it as soon as you deliver it,' he said, 'providing I get a few minutes' peace.'

I put the note on the table, sat down and stared at it. No matter what, it wasn't possible to ignore this invitation. Gerry must have found something important and wanted to ask me about it. Yes, that was it. He had some ideas, but before he consulted anyone else he wanted to have my opinion. It was rather flattering he considered my views so important, but then with all the research I'd been doing on the Pavilion, I might have uncovered the final bit of the puzzle. Perhaps he'd spotted something in the manuscript that meant nothing to me, but he recognised?

Simon was still asleep when I crept out of the cottage early the next morning. He was due to take Dwayne and Susie to the airport in the afternoon, but this wouldn't take long. Now I was curious to hear the end of this story, find out if my suspicions were correct or just that ...suspicions.

I went round to the back of the building to the portacabin, but it was locked up. I rattled the door to no avail then gazed round, thinking Gerry might be on his way over from the main building. Or perhaps he meant to meet me there?

The Pavilion was eerily quiet. It was too early for the workmen who would be feasting on bacon rolls in the local cafe to keep their strength up for the day ahead.

Strangely the main door yielded easily to my touch and as I entered the building my mobile beeped to alert me to an incoming text. Absentmindedly I checked it as I looked around for Gerry. 'Come up to the top balcony,' said the message.

That was very strange, very strange indeed. Was that part of the building not out of bounds? There was a still lot of scaffolding about and I picked my way carefully up the stairs.

'Are you there, Gerry?' I called but there was no sign of anyone. After all, this might be some kind of practical joke for all I knew. But as usual, curiosity got

the better of me and I went up the last remaining stairs
to push open the door leading out onto the top balcony.

Ah, there was someone there, over by the far corner.
It wasn't Gerry - it was Rufus.

FIFTY

For a moment I was too startled to speak. 'Where's Gerry?' I asked, looking round though there was nowhere to hide out here.

Rufus ignored the question. 'Glad to see you made it,' he said.

'So you sent the note, pretending to be Gerry?'

He shrugged. 'If you'd known I'd sent it would you have come?'

That was a moot point. He was probably right.

'Well, now you're here we can have a little chat. About how you're not going to publish all this stuff about the Pavilion's history. I thought you'd understood what I was saying to you last time we met.'

'How did you know what was in it?'

He laughed. 'I also have friends.'

'The only person I gave that manuscript to was Gerry.'

'Whatever. But you're not going to publish it.'

Now I was astonished. 'Why on earth would I choose to do that after all the time I've spent on it?' Gerry must have warned Rufus, but why would he do that?

Rufus was still speaking. 'Because,' he said in a chillingly calm voice, 'you're not going to be around and they won't publish it if something has happened to you.'

For a moment the full impact of his words was lost on me. 'What do you mean? I'm going off the island, certainly, but only so that I can write it all up.'

'Uh, uh. I think it's more serious than that. I'm afraid I can't allow it. The truth might come out, someone just might catch on to something in the book and it would be all over, I'd be finished. And my father's reputation would be ruined, after what he did to help a friend.'

Suddenly everything became clear. 'It was you, wasn't it? You were the one responsible for Ewan's death? He found out about you.'

'It wasn't what you think,' he said, angrily. 'He wanted to stop the contract. Said we were thieves. What rubbish. Everyone has to make a bit of profit on the side, especially these days.'

'Ah, and there was that business about your father … the story that he made off with money?'

'If the Pavilion renovation hadn't got the go ahead, none of the story would ever have got out. It would have stayed hidden where it belongs. Once people read what you said about my father, they would have been suspicious of me....' His voice trailed away.

'But surely it wasn't really anything to do with you? That was all to do with your father.' I tried to recall exactly what I'd said about the early days of the building work, but there was certainly nothing libellous.

'That's the whole point you stupid woman! Don't you understand how bad that would have been for us? Someone would have begun to make enquiries, discovered what was going on.' He gave a hollow laugh. 'Like father, like son, isn't that what they say?' Exactly what Lydia had said.

So Rufus had been stealing from the project, falsifying accounts. And he must have had an accomplice. Who else knew what was in our history of the Pavilion? Only Gerry. Of course.

'Why didn't you just admit the truth, why didn't you tell someone?' This did explain why Rufus had been stalking me. He thought I knew all about the death of Marvin, knew what had happened to Ewan Flisch. Trouble was I did know, but not when he thought I did.

252

If he hadn't alerted me, I might never have guessed the full story, never have made the connection between Rufus and Ewan's death.

'Don't be ridiculous. How could I let this rest? If it had ever got out that my father knew who was responsible for Marvin's death, had helped hide the body, at the very least he'd have been charged with aiding a crime.'

'But all that was in the past, it's all over.' I didn't add that it's impossible to charge a dead man.

'Not for me it isn't. And I certainly don't want you blabbing off about it to all and sundry, putting it in your book. Much better you meet with an accident here, on the balcony of the Pavilion. You've been so nosey, no one will suspect a thing. And once you're gone, there will be no book. Enough talking.'

He moved toward me and grabbed me by the arms. I tripped on the pieces of scaffolding lying around the ground here, started to struggle, tried to push him away from me, but he was much stronger and slowly but surely I could feel myself being edged towards the rim of the balcony wall. I grabbed on to the low ledge with both hands, feeling the roughness beneath my fingers, feeling them scratch and tear on the uneven surface.

This was it, then. Why had I become involved in something that didn't concern me? There had been no need. It was nothing to do with me.

Suddenly I was lifted off the ground, could feel my hands slipping off my hold on the ledge, no matter how hard I tried to tighten my grip. Rufus' face was close up beside mine. I could feel his hot breath on my face as I tried to swivel myself round, tried to spot anything I might use to keep my balance, but there was nothing and my grip on the ledge was slowly loosening. 'Let go, let go,' he shouted, his face suffused with rage as he pushed me higher, tried to prise my hands free.

Suddenly there was a movement behind him, a slight shadow of someone sliding out on to the balcony. It must be Simon. He had guessed where I'd gone and had come to rescue me. I tried to keep my eyes fixed on Rufus. If he realised Simon was here, there would be no chance for me to escape. But no sooner had that thought flashed through my mind than it was followed by another - would Simon be strong enough to tackle Rufus, even if I was able to help him?

I concentrated all my efforts on staring at Rufus, terrified he would notice we were no longer alone. My throat was so constricted by his grasp I couldn't speak, even if I'd wanted to. Please let him hurry up, I prayed.

There was loud yell as Rufus was grabbed from behind. 'Gotcha!' said a voice. But it wasn't Simon pulling Rufus away, it was Dwayne.

He reached over and grabbed Rufus more tightly, forcing him to release me. I slid out from under them and scurried to the far end of the balcony, my heart pounding fit to burst, slowly sliding down the wall on to the ground.

'I think you owe an explanation, Rufus,' Dwayne growled. Rufus was strong, but Dwayne was stronger, much stronger.

Rufus scowled, wriggling ineffectively to free himself from Dwayne's grasp. 'That stupid woman! Why did she have to get involved in all this? Why couldn't she have stuck to what she was supposed to - writing a pleasant history about the Pavilion, recording the anecdotes from all the people who remembered the good old days.' He said this with a sneer, struggling again to release himself from Dwayne's grasp, but Dwayne had no intention of letting him go and moved to increase his hold.

'Because she wanted to see justice done. That's why. Do you think that once she knew what had happened, she could have ignored it?'

Rufus made no reply. He seemed to have given up the fight and now stood quietly as though awaiting his fate.

Dwayne turned to speak to me. 'I think you should call the police,' he said.

That split second of Dwayne slightly releasing his grasp was enough for Rufus to take his opportunity and he slipped out of Dwayne's reach.

'Not so fast,' said Dwayne, making to grab him again. But Rufus was now possessed of a maniacal strength and he pulled and pushed Dwayne, moving him towards the edge of the balcony.

I'd been cowering in the corner all during this exchange, but something now made me move forward. It was very unlikely I could do anything to help the situation, but I didn't think before acting.

'Get off, 'I said, grabbing hold of Rufus by the arm.

H struggled, tried to shake me off, moved to the other side of Dwayne and as Dwayne lunged at him yet again, he tripped on the pieces of scaffolding lying at the edge.

Dwayne and I both tried to grab him, but it was too late. There was a scream as he hurtled off the balcony, flew through the air and landed with a thud on the ground below.

We rushed to the edge, but it was too far down to see properly what had happened. Some of the workmen, hearing the commotion, came rushing out through the main doors. We saw them bend over Rufus, then look up at us. One of them shook his head. It was too late. Rufus would never now face justice.

FIFTY-ONE

'Gee, I guess all this means we're related.' Dwayne was gazing at Tara as though he found it hard to believe.

Tara grinned. 'We've a lot of catching up to do.'

We were all crammed into the living room of the cottage at Kilchattan Bay and by the looks of things we'd be here for a few days more, while the investigations continued.

Susie muttered something under her breath. I could only guess it was to do with the continuing postponement of their return to America.

The police had lots of questions for us and I had plenty of my own. But not as many as Simon. Relieved as he was about my narrow escape, he chided me about my involvement yet again in something that wasn't my concern.

'Do you go looking for trouble, Alison?' he said.

'Of course not. What an idea.' I tried to change the conversation. 'It shouldn't be too long before you can go back to the U.S.,' I said.

Susie was willing to take Simon's part in this discussion. 'I still don't understand how it all came about,' she said, 'not to mention the way you became mixed up in it all.'

'I didn't intend it should all work out like this,' I replied. 'I suppose I should have realised that if you try to uncover the past, you find a lot of events some people would rather keep hidden.'

'So Rufus Beale was defrauding the Pavilion?'

'Mmm. He wouldn't have seen it like that. It was what his father had done: set up companies, made money and then let them fail, leaving a trail of unpaid creditors. It was just business to him.'

256

Susie shuddered as Dwayne said, 'He should have known he couldn't get away with that.'

'Poor Ewan Flisch.' Tara turned to me. 'He was put in a terrible position.

'Yes. When Lydia hinted what might be going on, he didn't know what he should do. I guess he was about to expose Rufus, but Rufus got to him first.'

'Gerry was in on it all?'

'That was why Gerry was furious when Ewan got the job: he saw all the plans he and Rufus had made coming to nothing. I'd no idea. I certainly wouldn't have warned Gerry if I'd realised.'

Well,' said Simon, 'You should be grateful you've a good friend like Susie. If she hadn't been so worried about you, hadn't asked Dwayne to follow you, goodness knows what would have happened.'

That didn't bear thinking about.

Tara stood up. 'I'll have to go. I promised Meg I'd be back by teatime and she does fret about me.'

'Just a minute.' I wasn't going to let her escape so easily. 'Now it's time for some truth about you, Tara. Why did you apply for this job?'

She laughed. 'You and I are two of a kind, Alison: naturally curious. I'd heard stories in the family about my grandfather, about my mother, but there was no one willing, or able, to tell me the truth. When the post of researcher came up, I had to have it, no matter what.'

I could sympathise with that. And she had been excellent.

'Wait, what about Marvin? What happened there?' Simon reminded us of the final link.

'From what we know he did have a thin skull, so whether Willie Flisch killed him in a fit of temper, or whether it was an accident, we'll never know. But Rufus Beale senior did help hide the body, of that I'm sure.'

'He'll be taken back home,' said Dwayne. 'It's the least I can do.'

Suddenly I realised how exhausted I was. Simon leaned over and took my hand. 'I think that's all we can do for the present,' he said.

Tara left with Susie and Dwayne, though Dwayne's demeanour showed he was still trying to come to terms with the odd appearance of this relative of his.

'I'll be glad when we're home,' I said, putting my head back.

'Cup of tea?' said Simon.

'Tea? I think I'd rather have a large glass of wine.'

EPILOGUE

'Ladies and Gentlemen, take your partners for the first dance.'

A thousand stars glimmered through the newly exposed glass roof of the large hall of the Rothesay Pavilion as the crowds of dancers made their way on to the floor to the strains of, 'It's good to be back.'

Simon took my arm and led me from my seat to join the others. 'He'll need to lose some weight,' he whispered as we watched Jacky, the compere, unbutton his tuxedo.

I laughed as we whirled round the dance floor, almost bumping into Susie and Dwayne.

'Gee,' said Dwayne, 'this is some place.'

Susie smiled. It had been a great week. We'd celebrated their wedding at Rothesay castle in glorious sunshine and they were spending a few more days on the island before heading back to California.

'I'm so happy, Alison,' Susie whispered.

'I'm happy for you, 'I said, but I'd miss her very much when she and Dwayne left to begin their new life together. My final words were lost as they danced off into the throng.

At the far end of the hall I could see Tara with a young man, their heads bent close together. He looked all too conventional for her in his light suit and tie, but that was the thing about love: it was unpredictable.

Simon held me tightly. 'That was a close thing, Alison. I thought you weren't going to get involved again in anything dangerous?'

I drew back in astonishment. 'Of course I didn't intend to,' I said. 'I was only here to write up this history of the Pavilion.'

'Very well it's been received too,' he smiled.

I thought back to earlier in the day, to the launch of the book, 'Fond Memories of the Rothesay Pavilion.' It had been such a good event and the book had been much praised. Tara and I glowed in the fulsome compliments we'd received from all quarters.

'Yes, it was good,' I agreed. This publicity would do my reputation as a writer no harm at all.

The dance came to an end, the last notes dying away as we made our way back to our seats.

'An amazing place,' said Dwayne, gazing round.

He was right. The original Art Deco fixtures had been lovingly restored, the building given a makeover that would make it one of the best attractions in the country.

The commission to write the history of the Pavilion hadn't turned out quite as expected. But all that was over now and this sparkling building on the seafront at Rothesay would be a new beginning for everyone. Including me.

ACKNOWLEDGEMENTS

Grateful thanks to the following:

James McMillan of the Rothesay Pavilion for a guided tour that let me see nooks and crannies I didn't know existed, Judith Duffy for editing assistance, Bill Daly for proof reading of the manuscript and for helpful suggestions, the editor at NGP for invaluable advice, Paul Duffy for technical assistance and for helping me avoid some serious mistakes, Mandy Sinclair for the cover design and last, but by no means least, Peter for his never failing support and for checking the nautical terminology. Any errors are my own.

MYRA DUFFY

LAST FERRY TO BUTE

An Alison Cameron Mystery

Read an extract here

Published by New Generation Publishing

PROLOGUE

All day the mist had drifted in across the waters of the Firth of Clyde and little by little the mainland disappeared into swirling fog.

The last ferry from Weymss Bay loomed through the darkness, foghorn sounding in the eerie stillness, heading towards the island of Bute and a safe berth for the night in the main town of Rothesay. Cars crowded nose to tail on the car deck, hemmed in by heavy lorries transporting vital goods to the island.

Andy, the deckhand, shivered in spite of his thick oilskins. Not long now and he could head for home. Perhaps he'd call in at the Golfer's Bar, have a couple of pints and watch the end of the Manchester United game on SKY.

As the ferry swung into port, he watched his mate Sammie scramble up the ladder to the upper deck to join the extra lookouts, deftly unwinding the thick ropes and tossing them to the waiting crew on shore. The winches would keep the boat safe and secure until morning. Andy pressed the button on the control panel and the great ramp of the ferry juddered down. A signal to Sammie that they were berthed and one by one the cars and the lorries left the deck and bumped their way off on to dry land.

At the stern of the ferry the last car sat immobile. Andy cursed under his breath. If this was a breakdown it would hold them all up: the last thing he wanted on a night like this. He ran up and knocked on the car window, trying to see through the tinted windows. 'Problems?' he mouthed to the driver.

There was no response. He peered in, screwing up his eyes for a better view of the inside. The woman driver sat motionless, staring straight ahead.

This was the last journey the owner of this dark blue saloon car would ever make.

ONE

It all began with a phone call.

'Hello, Susie. How are you?' I glanced at my watch. Almost eleven o' clock. My friend Susie has been working in Los Angeles for more than two years, but still wrestles with the time difference and there was a pile of marking sitting reproachfully on the dining room table: my own fault for not making an earlier start.

'Susie? It's not Susie. Were you expecting a call from Susie? If so I can phone back later if there's a problem. It would be no bother. Or if you are going to be chatting for a long time I could phone in the morning though I expect it would have to be early because...'

'Hello, mum. No, it's okay. I thought it might be Susie at this time of night.'

'It's not late, is it? Were you off to bed? It's only....'

'No, no, it's fine. I'm always pleased to hear from you.' I paused, a sudden fear striking me. 'There isn't any difficulty about your holiday, is there?'

'No, no, I'm all set for tomorrow. I wanted to speak to you before I leave.'

My fiercely independent mother lives in a small flat in a sheltered housing complex, where she makes a good attempt to run everyone's lives. Fortunately it keeps her too busy to run mine: at least most of the time. My only sister, Caroline, had the sense to marry and emigrate to Canada many years ago. This leaves her well out of reach for most of the year, but not entirely safe: my mother was about to descend on her for several months. 'No sense in going all that way for a couple of weeks,' she had said. I wasn't sure Caroline would agree. 'And it will be a chance to see Alastair.' I didn't bother to explain Canada is a very big country and the university where my son teaches is nowhere near my sister.

'I wouldn't trouble you, Alison, except that I seem to remember you said something about going to Bute? With some of your old friends?'

'Yes, that's right. We're having a reunion of my college year next April.'

'Ah,' she said with a long sigh. 'So you won't be going over for a while yet?'

'Not exactly.' I hesitated before saying any more, judging it best to find out what my mother wanted me to do before committing myself.

But the persistence which gave her the iron will to organise the sheltered housing complex was also evident in her dealings with me. 'What does that mean? Are you going over to the island or not?'

I couldn't bring myself to lie. 'I'm going over in a few days as it happens. Betsie's asked me to check out some of the hotels and the Pavilion, where we start the weekend.'

A pause. 'And what's wrong with Betsie? Why can't she do it? I thought you told me it was her idea. Really, Alison, I think you have quite enough to do without organising a big event like this. I scarcely see you for a start.'

No need to say this was because she was far too busy with whist drives, bus outings, film shows, tea dances and making the warden's life difficult to have time to fit me in, but all I said was, 'Yes, Betsie has already organised the reunion but she lives in France when she's not travelling round the rest of Europe because of her antiques business. When she contacted me about her plans for this reunion I volunteered to help with any last minute details.'

'You have plenty to do what with Deborah being home and...'

'Mother, is there something special you wanted to talk to me about or is this a general call before you go off to Canada?'

'No need to be cross, Alison.'

'I'm not cross, mother.'

'You only call me mother when you're annoyed about something.'

I took a deep breath and tried to bring her back to the main reason for her phone call. 'Did you want something from Bute?'

'No, no,' she said impatiently. 'Nothing like that, but I do want you to find something out.'

This was more interesting. 'What exactly?'

'It's all to do with Jessie. You remember Jessie McAdam, my old friend. She went to live on Bute a few years ago, went to that wee house in Port Bannatyne where her mother had once lived. I think it was a holiday home.'

'Yes, I remember,' I cut in, watching the hands of the clock move round to the half hour.

'Well, last year she fell and broke her hip and wasn't fit to look after herself. So she moved into the Hereuse Nursing home - you know that very expensive place out past Craigmore, overlooking the little bay? She has a lovely room right at the front. The view is spectacular I believe and so much better than the outlook here...'

I could feel the beginnings of a headache. Why on earth was my mother phoning me at this time of night to tell me this long story about Jessie?

'Mum, what do you want me to do?' I said patiently.

She seemed to recollect the reason for her call. 'It's the residents, you see. Jessie thinks items belonging to them are going missing. And what's worse, Jessie says they keep dying.'

What I was tempted to say was, 'Of course they keep dying, they're elderly.' Instead I tried to be tactful. 'We all must die sometime, mum.' I waited for her response, hoping my mother wasn't going to be depressed by this news from Jessie. I should have known her better.

'Not like this,' she snapped. 'Jessie thinks all these deaths in such a short time are suspicious and when you go over to Bute I want you to go along to the Hereuse Nursing home and find out what's going on.'

My mother often surprises me but this request startled me. What on earth had Jessie been saying to her? This was hardly the time of night to be discussing Jessie's imaginings. What's more, if I didn't make a start soon, I'd have to spend most of the night marking essays.

Making an attempt to end this strange conversation, I said, 'I'm sure there's nothing to be concerned about. Jessie isn't used to living with so many elderly people.'

This response didn't satisfy her. 'She's not a woman given to exaggeration, Alison. She's very level headed and if I weren't off to see Caroline I'd go myself. I can't leave it till I come back: I'm far too worried about Jessie for that. I thought if you were going to be on the island anyway, but if it's all going to be too much trouble...'

I interrupted her. Sometimes it's easier to agree and even if she wasn't going off on holiday, it wasn't a good idea to have her rushing into this nursing home, accusing them of harming the residents.

So I took a deep breath and said, 'Fine, I'll go along, but don't expect too much from what I find out. Those who've died were probably ill or had serious health problems. That does happen in a nursing home.' I didn't want to raise her expectations and said, 'Anyway, apart from that difficulty with her hip operation, I thought you said she was in good health?'

'No, Alison, you don't understand. It's much more serious than that. Jessie thinks she'll be next to die …and she thinks she's going to be murdered.'